"RAISE SHIELDS— WEAPONS ON STANDBY. . ."

"No response from the Nuarans, sir," Worf said.

"They are still closing, Captain," Data said, scanning his console.

Once more, Picard thought. "*Enterprise* to Nuaran vessels. I repeat, we are on a peaceful mission, and we request communication with you."

Again, there was no response, and Picard drew in a breath of frustration.

"Lieutenant Worf, go to yellow alert—arm phasers and lock on targets." Picard leaned forward in his chair. "Range, Mr. Data?"

"Thirty thousand kilometers . . . twenty. . . "

On the viewscreen, the five Nuaran spacecraft had grown from flitting pinpoints to sleek harbingers of death.

"Optimum range, sir," Worf said.

"I'm aware of that, Lieutenant," Picard said evenly. "Hold your fire."

The Nuaran ships continued to close, rushing like mad birds of prey, till they were almost directly on top of the *Enterprise* . . .

Look for STAR TREK Fiction from Pocket Books

#6

STAR TREK ®
THE NEXT GENERATION

POWER HUNGRY

HOWARD
WEINSTEIN

POCKET BOOKS

New York   London   Toronto   Sydney   Tokyo

An *Original* Publication of POCKET BOOKS

POCKET BOOKS, a division of Simon & Schuster Inc.
1230 Avenue of the Americas, New York, NY 10020

This book is published by Pocket Books, a division of
Simon & Schuster Inc., under exclusive license from
Paramount Pictures Corporation.

ISBN: 0-671-67714-4

First Pocket Books printing May 1989

10 9 8 7 6 5 4 3 2 1

POCKET and colophon are trademarks of
Simon & Schuster Inc.

Printed in the U.S.A.

To Susan . . .
for sharing the voyage

Author's Notes

It's January as I write this. An old year gone, a fresh one just starting. A new President is taking up residence in the White House. A decade is nearly done. Hell, a whole *century* is winding down. What a time to be alive—a wondrous, terrifying time.

We're so close to making great dreams come true. And just as close to destroying the only place we humans can call home. Surrounded by omens, we're witnessing a duel between hope and hopelessness. And it's too early to guess which combatant will win.

It's the nature of science fiction to be ahead of its time, to peer through the mists of uncertainty, to offer a glimpse of a possible future. For decades, SF writers have told cautionary tales of civilizations fallen victim to self-inflicted calamities. In the past few years— and in 1988 in particular—we on earth have seen inarguable evidence that many of their auguries are coming to pass. Is it too late for us to change our ways?

There are some encouraging signs, however. Awareness of danger is half the battle. Finally, belatedly, there's a dawning realization that we've landed ourselves in a heap of trouble.

The first 1989 issue of *Time* magazine is sitting near me as I write these notes. Each year *Time* devotes a major portion of its first issue to a profile of the Man of the Year—the person or group who, during the previous year, most affected the world for good or ill. This time, *Time* broke precedent and designated Endangered Earth as Planet of the Year. The cover story cataloged the multitude of ecological crises that dominated the news in 1988—beach and water pollution, destruction of rain forests, overpopulation, world hunger, the greenhouse effect, garbage disposal, nuclear waste, and more. *Time*'s conclusion: our planetary condition is critical, but not yet terminal. There are feasible solutions—if we have the will to put them into effect.

In the years I've been involved with *Star Trek*, as both fan and writer, I've seen plenty of evidence that *Trek* fans are not only good-hearted dreamers but doers as well. At many of the conventions I've attended, weekend activities have included collections for local food banks, blood-donation drives, charity auctions, and fund-raising raffles.

Can such individual efforts save the world? Of course not. Do they make it better? You bet. The problems of planet Earth may seem unsolvable when viewed as one gigantic, hopelessly tangled mess. But we can clear away a chunk here and there, and maybe we can grapple with problems reduced to a more manageable scale. Maybe the trick, then, is to put *everybody* to work on solving *something*.

Take hunger, for instance. Folksinger activist Harry

Chapin tackled world hunger before most other celebrities. No, Harry did not conquer world hunger before his tragic death at thirty-eight in a 1981 auto accident. But he did set an example by doing two hundred concerts a year, half of them for charity. And he set a process in motion by involving people who later played key roles in such events as Live Aid and Hands across America. Those big events may be past, but lots of good folks, famous or not, are still working hard in communities all over, still fighting to get food to hungry people.

Harry Chapin's work did not go unnoticed. In December 1987 I was one of several thousand people who attended a tribute to Harry at Carnegie Hall. A long list of musical stars—including Bruce Springsteen, Paul Simon, Pete Seeger, Kenny Rogers, Harry Belafonte, and Peter, Paul and Mary—came to sing Chapin's songs and celebrate a life well lived. In honor of her husband, Sandy Chapin accepted the nation's highest civilian award, the Congressional Gold Medal, which has been given to fewer than 120 people in American history—a select group that includes George Washington, Charles Lindbergh, Winston Churchill, Robert Kennedy, and Bob Hope.

Just recently, Harry Chapin's unfinished final album was released. It is called *The Last Protest Singer*. The timeliness of some of the tunes is an eerie echo of Harry's passionate vision and a reminder that we haven't come far enough in the eight years since his death, I suppose. In one song, "Sounds like America to Me," Harry sings:

When a child is hurting, silence can be wrong
I know when old folks are helpless, I can't just pass
    along.
And I know when someone's hungry, I can't just sing
    this song.

And when I hear somebody crying,
I can't just wonder who that it could be.
Well, I hear somebody crying now
And it sure sounds like America to me.*

Not only America, Harry.
Are we listening?
I hope so. And I hope you all enjoy this new novel.
Thanks.

Howard Weinstein
January 1989

P.S. I'd like to thank Gene Roddenberry for creating a Next Generation about which to write. I've enjoyed getting to know this new crew as much as I did the original.

I'd also like to thank Dave Stern and Kevin Ryan at Pocket Books, Dave McDonnell, Jonathan Frakes, Sharon Jarvis, Joan Winston, Joel and Nancy Davis, Peter Davis, Bob and Debbie Greenberger, Cindi Casby, Lynne Perry, Marc Okrand, my family, and Mail Order Annie for various forms of assistance, inspiration, and abuse. I *could* have done it without you, folks . . . but it's better *with* you.

POWER HUNGRY

Prologue

STRING AND BRASS HARMONIES danced and soared, filling Will Riker's cabin with the intricate contrapuntal melody of Pachelbel's timeless *Canon in D*. The First Officer of the starship *Enterprise* reclined in his armchair, eyes closed, savoring the final notes, the crystalline trill of a solo trumpet.

When that last pure and perfect note had faded, Riker opened his eyes and propped elbows on knees, looking for reactions from his companions, Captain Jean-Luc Picard and ship's counselor Deanna Troi, both seated facing him. "Deanna?"

"Absolutely beautiful." Troi's large dark eyes glistened with pleasure. "I've never heard that piece before."

"It's very old," Picard said, "Seventeenth-century earth, I believe."

1

"That's right," Riker said. "I've always been partial to baroque."

"I had a hunch," Riker said, grinning through his beard.

Picard's eyes narrowed. "Imagine—we're listening to music composed seven hundred years ago. . . . What a pity the creators of great art can't know their work lives on long after they've gone to dust."

The tall first officer leaned back again, hands clasped behind his head. "I wish I'd had the time to learn more about music, maybe try my hand at composing."

"It's never too late to learn something new," Deanna said. "It would be refreshing for you to develop some new activities for your spare time."

"That's true—but then I'd need to develop some new spare time," Riker said ruefully. He smiled. "My commanding officer keeps me pretty busy."

The electronic tone of the cabin intercom sounded and was followed by the calm voice of Lieutenant Commander Data. "Bridge to Captain Picard."

"This is Picard. What is it, Mr. Data?"

"We have received a priority code communication from Starfleet Command, sir."

The captain and first officer exchanged concerned glances. "Pipe it down here."

"Yes, sir."

The comm screen over Riker's desk lit, displaying the Starfleet insignia. "Request voice print identification," said the computer's soft feminine voice.

Picard leaned forward and crossed his arms. "Picard, Jean-Luc, captain, U.S.S. *Enterprise.*"

"Voice print verified." The insignia's stylized starfield was replaced by a severe-looking woman in a wine-colored Starfleet uniform. She peered out from under dark bangs that were long enough to cover her eyebrows, and she spoke with a slight drawl. "Captain Picard, I'm Captain Kimberly Schaller, Starfleet Command. We've intercepted some Ferengi communications—looks as if they've developed quite an interest in the sector you're headed for."

"The Thiopan system?" Picard's jaw tightened. "What sort of interest?"

"We believe they would like to make it part of their alliance. Thiopa is centrally located between our border and the Ferengi fringe systems. They've traded with other nonaligned planets out there, but haven't been able to establish a heavy presence before. How familiar are you with Thiopa's current situation?"

"I know the standard mission profile," Picard said. "Which I take it is about to be substantially complicated?"

Schaller managed a small smile. "I'd say that's an understatement, Captain Picard. We'll feed all the latest information to your computers. I strongly suggest you and your senior staff review it before you get to Thiopa."

"We shall. Should we expect a Ferengi presence in the area?"

"'Expect' may be too strong a word—what we intercepted wasn't that specific. Let's just say you should be cautious. I know you're on a mercy mission, so I'm sure you would prefer to avoid a military confrontation with a Ferengi task force."

Picard frowned. "The Ferengi are usually quite reticent to engage in direct combat. Does your information indicate a change of heart?"

"I can't say for sure. But they do know the *Enter-*

3

prise is traveling alone with five automated cargo carriers. In their eyes, that might make you an enticing target."

"Understood. We'll be careful."

"Very good, Captain Picard. If we get any other relevant information, we'll transmit it to you as fast as possible. Schaller out."

Picard faced his officers. "Your musical composing career will have to wait, Number One. We'd better get up to the bridge."

Chapter One

Captain's Log—Stardate 42422.5.

The *Enterprise* is two hours away from the Thiopan star system on what has become a dual-purpose mission. We are responding to an urgent request from Thiopa's planetary government for Federation assistance in dealing with a critical drought and resultant food shortage. The Thiopans have only recently disengaged from a long-standing association with the despotic Nuaran Imperium. And now Starfleet has informed us that the Ferengi Alliance has designs on this sector. It is hoped our convoy of food and other desperately needed supplies will not only alleviate Thiopa's crisis but will also give the Federation a chance to establish formal ties with the planet before the Ferengi can take advantage of the chaotic situation.

THE *ENTERPRISE* CRUISED SERENELY through open space with five stubby cargo ships trailing her in delta formation like ducklings tagging along behind their mother. The freighters were linked directly to the starship's main computer; any changes in course or speed made by the *Enterprise* were automatically copied by the entire convoy. The only hindrance to the starship caused by the presence of the cargo drones was a reduction in speed; they were simply incapable of anything faster than warp three.

Jean-Luc Picard sat alone in the captain's ready room just off the main bridge, enjoying the view of space offered by this chamber, a view unimpeded by the enhancements of viewscreen technology. Stars glowed in a rainbow of colors, veils of dust reflected and refracted the starlight shining through them, tendrils of gaseous material drifted and roiled like tinted smoke.

Picard found the sights of outer space endlessly fascinating, soothing and stimulating all at once—a paradox that never failed to please him. He enjoyed those sights here more than anywhere else. The ready room had become his favorite place on the ship, a sanctum for private pondering, yet only steps away from the main bridge.

But the very existence of this little refuge from the hurly-burly of command had come as something of a surprise. . . .

Darting like a skimmer-bug on a pond, the shuttle pod in which Picard was a passenger turned smartly and approached the maze of girders orbiting high over the ruddy surface of Mars. With a bit of free time on his hands, Jean-Luc Picard had hopped a supply transport on its way from earth to the Utopia Planetia Fleet Yards. It was a purely unofficial visit, but curiosity about the first of the new Galaxy class starships being built here was reason enough to come and take a look.

Cradled inside its construction bay, the U.S.S. Enterprise, *NCC-1701-D, was still the object of intensive activity, with work crews swarming over her. She was now nearly complete, and Picard's solemn features softened into a smile of satisfaction as he gazed at her.*

"She is beautiful, Captain Picard?" Lieutenant Snephets, Picard's escort, was an Oktonian female with four pale pink eyes. Like all Oktonians, she phrased statements as questions.

Picard replied with a nod and just a tinge of awe. "She is indeed, Lieutenant." She was, without a doubt, the most beautiful spacecraft he'd ever seen. He smiled inwardly at the affection he already felt for this vessel he would soon command. He suspected she'd be an easy ship to love.

Picard had spent the bulk of his career—for that matter, most of his adult life—as an explorer. For twenty-two years he'd commanded the deep-space trailblazer Stargazer. *She'd been a good ship, taken Picard and his crew through some dicey situations, but no one who'd lived aboard her would ever have described her as top of the line.*

"Captain, a pleasure it has been working on Enterprise?*"*

Picard knew Lieutenant Snephets wasn't asking a question, but her tone of voice compelled him to answer out of politeness. "I'm sure it has. She's a most impressive vessel."

Snephets skillfully docked the shuttle with the access port on the starship's expansive flank. "You are greatly honored, sir, being her first commander?"

"Yes, Lieutenant, I am."

The pod door slid open and a burly bearded man in a gold uniform greeted Picard in the corridor. "Engineer Argyle, sir. Welcome aboard. The bridge has been completed, if you'd like to see it."

"I would indeed, Mr. Argyle."

"This way, Captain." He led Picard to a turbolift and they stepped in. "Bridge," said Argyle as the doors shut. For a long, embarrassing moment, nothing happened. The engineer swallowed, repeated the order, and the lift finally started moving.

"Not quite shipshape yet, Mr. Argyle," Picard said, with a hint of understanding.

"She will be, sir."

They arrived at the bridge and stepped out. Picard stopped suddenly, gaping. The lighting, the space, the obvious attention to details . . . The Enterprise *wasn't going to be just another ship, he realized. It was going to be like home.*

"Would you like to see the conference lounge and your ready room, sir?"

"Both right here on the bridge level?" Picard almost gaped again. "Isn't that wasted space?"

Argyle couldn't help beaming. "Not on the Enterprise, *sir."*

An easy ship to love. Until he'd actually toured her from stem to stern, nothing could have prepared Picard for the sheer size and volume of the *Enterprise.* Quite simply, she represented a quantum leap in design and construction, beyond any other vessel in the fleet. And his first year in command had made him wonder how he'd managed to survive two decades in the comparatively cramped confines of the old *Stargazer*. It hadn't taken long for him to come to appreciate every inch of "wasted space" built into the Galaxy class design—most of all, his personal retreat, his ready room.

Picard again skimmed the summary of Captain Schaller's report on his desktop computer screen. Would the Ferengi really have the stomach for a confrontation? Fueled as they were by the thirst for profit, the Ferengi had demonstrated time and again that they preferred to avoid armed conflict whenever possible. But Picard's own experiences with the Ferengi Alliance told him that vigilance would certainly be in order. More than likely, the Ferengi would be skulking about on the periphery, maintaining a low profile, cautiously keeping their hand in play and keeping an eye on what the Federation was doing. And there was no reason why they shouldn't, since Thiopa was in free space.

The intercom tone sounded, followed by Riker's voice. "Captain Picard . . ."

"What is it, Number One?"

"Sensors picking up some activity at extreme range. I thought you'd want to know."

"I'll be right there."

The captain strode onto the bridge, glancing at his regular staff at their posts—Riker and Troi seated on either side of his command chair in the center well; Lieutenant Worf, the Klingon security chief, at his tactical panel on the horseshoe-shaped upper deck; Data and young Wesley Crusher at the forward Operations and Control stations.

As he started to sit, Picard noticed a less familiar face attending the Mission Operations monitors directly behind Worf. She was young, with auburn hair and a sprinkling of freckles spilling across her nose. Lieutenant White, he remembered, sliding into his contoured seat. He inclined his chin toward the viewscreen. "What's out there, Number One?"

"I can't tell for certain, sir. Three or four small ships at the limit of our sensor range."

"Any discernible heading?"

"Not since we picked them up. We've been transmitting standard hailing messages—no response."

"Captain," Data broke in, "two ships are now moving evasively but in our general direction."

"Mr. Worf," said Picard, "still no response to our hails?"

"Negative, sir. Recommend defensive posture—shields up, weapons on standby."

"Agreed. Make it so. Mr. Data, tactical display on main viewer."

A grid replaced the starfield on the bridge screen. The *Enterprise* and her five cargo carriers appeared on the left side of the grid. Two fast-moving blips were approaching from the right.

The pair of spacecraft closing on the big starship were slender projectiles, dark, fierce, and anonymous in their simplicity, without muscular bulges or bristling weapons. Their elemental design hinted at singleness of purpose. They were killers.

Without slowing, they split apart and veered around the *Enterprise,* one to either side, then suddenly cut and crossed, unleashing a pair of torpedoes at one of the trailing cargo ships. The burning blue streaks found their mark and the freight drone exploded in a puff of shimmering shards.

Picard gripped his armrests as he watched the destruction on the viewscreen. "Damn. Position of intruders?"

Data scanned his console. "Retreating at . . . warp eleven." His eyebrows rose in surprise at the speed—faster than the *Enterprise* could manage.

The aft turbolift snapped open and Geordi LaForge burst onto the bridge.

"Mr. LaForge," said Picard, "I thought you were off duty."

"The chief engineer's never off duty, Captain," LaForge replied, activating the bridge engineering console.

Picard and Riker exchanged a meaningful look. Geordi's unexpected appearance at a critical moment was another indication that his promotion to chief engineer was more than deserved.

"Mr. LaForge," Picard said, "I do not want to lose another freight drone. Can we extend our shields to protect them?"

LaForge's compact form tensed as he checked his readouts. "In this formation, it'll be tough, Captain. We can do it, but not without a serious drain on overall available power."

"Then tighten the convoy. Make sure Mr. Worf has enough power for phasers." Picard faced forward again. "Mr. Data, have you identified the intruders?"

"Yes, sir. They are Nuaran interceptors."

"Captain," Worf said, "Nuarans are among the most effective warriors in the galaxy."

"And the slimiest," Geordi added. "Even the

Ferengi won't deal with them. What are they doing out here?"

Riker stroked his beard. "Maybe the Thiopans can tell us."

"Maybe we can find out ourselves." Picard swiveled halfway around in his chair. "Mr. Worf, hailing frequencies."

"Open, sir."

"Attention, Nuaran spacecraft—this is the U.S.S. *Enterprise.* We are on a non-hostile mission. We request contact to discuss your unwarranted destruction of a Federation cargo vessel." Picard's voice was calm, almost soft.

He waited almost a full minute without getting a response before speaking again.

"Repeat, Nuaran spacecraft—this is the U.S.S. *Enterprise.* We are on a non-hostile mission—but if you interfere, we *will* take defensive action."

He knew perfectly well the Nuaran ships were within reception range. Most likely they thought very little of his warning. After all, he had allowed them to pick off a cargo carrier without firing a return shot. But he would not do so again. "Mr. Worf, your assessment. Do two Nuaran interceptors pose a danger to this ship?"

"Not likely, sir. Not as long as we've got full shields."

Data glanced back over his shoulder. "What about three? That is the number now on an intercept course."

Picard's jaw muscles tightened. "I think we've given them sufficient time to reply to our messages. Number One?"

Riker nodded. "Concur, Captain."

"Mr. Worf, fire across their flight path, close enough to make it clear we'll tolerate no further interference."

"Understood," the Klingon security chief said. "Tracking lock engaged."

The Nuaran ships hurtled toward the *Enterprise,* twisting and twirling in an intricate set of evasive course changes. Again they fired torpedoes—and this time Worf reacted with a precise phaser burst. The intruders tumbled away, desperately trying to avoid being hit. All three recovered and fled out of phaser range.

"I think we made our point," Picard said. "Mr. Crusher, resume heading for Thiopa. Data, keep sensors on maximum range. If the Nuarans pay us another visit, I want to know about it."

"Dr. Pulaski to Captain Picard." The voice of Picard's chief medical officer came over the speaker.

"Yes, Doctor. What is it?"

"I have a very impatient ambassador cooling his heels in my outer office."

Picard and Riker looked at each other. "We were supposed to meet with him fifteen minutes ago," Riker murmured.

"Why is he in your office, Doctor?" asked Picard.

"He couldn't get through to you on the bridge, so he buttonholed the nearest officer he could find—who happened to be me."

"Give my apologies to Mr. Undrun and escort him to the bridge conference lounge, please."

There was a pause at Pulaski's end, and Picard could almost see *that look,* that patented Katherine Pulaski expression of displeasure when something went against her grain.

"What is it you're not telling me, Doctor?" Picard asked.

"You haven't met Ambassador Undrun yet, I take it." It was a statement, not a query.

"No, I haven't. Is there something I should know about him?"

"How shall I put this? He has what my grandmother used to refer to as a vexatious personality."

"Thank you for the warning. Report with him to the bridge conference lounge, Doctor."

"We're on our way."

Picard, Riker, and Counselor Troi stood and moved to the adjoining lounge, with its long table and high-backed chairs. "Number One," Picard said as they sat, "you've dealt with Ambassador Undrun since he came aboard. Is he that much of an irritant?"

"I agree with Dr. Pulaski's grandmother. 'Vexatious' is a suitable word. Consider yourself lucky you've been spared up till now, sir."

When the door opened, the pair who entered looked almost comical—Kate Pulaski, long-legged, regal, striding two paces ahead of Federation Aid and Assistance Representative Frid Undrun, child-sized and anything *but* regal. Undrun was bundled in baggy knit clothing more suitable for a winter's day than a climate-controlled starship. He wore a hat (several sizes too large for him) pulled down around his ears and a pair of ill-fitting thermal trousers. He had a face like a clenched fist, framed by tufts of gold hair. Appearances aside, when he spoke, his voice boomed with unexpected power.

"Mr. Riker, this starship of yours is *still* unacceptably cold."

With a visible effort at self-control, Riker kept his

voice quiet. "I'm sorry you're uncomfortable, Mr. Undrun. The best we can do is adjust the environmental controls in your cabin. The rest of the ship must be maintained at levels appropriate for our working crew."

Undrun snorted and turned to Picard. "Captain, is this true?"

"I'm afraid so, Mr. Undrun. I'm sure you can understand the necessity of providing climate conditions that will permit the *Enterprise* crew to operate at peak efficiency. I realize your home world is quite warm—"

"Warm?" said Undrun disdainfully. "You would find Noxor Three much more than warm, Captain. Now, what was so urgent that you kept me waiting for fifteen minutes?"

"Please, sit down, Mr. Undrun," Picard said calmly. "We were attacked by Nuaran ships. I'm afraid one of the cargo drones was destroyed."

Undrun's rump had barely touched the seat cushion when he bounced to his feet again. "Destroyed? My emergency relief supplies were *destroyed?"*

Picard winced. He suddenly had deeper understanding of the word "vexatious." "Mr. Undrun—" he began.

"Do you realize the worth of what's been lost? I knew something like this would happen when they gave me only one ship, too few personnel, insufficient supplies, *obviously* too little protection . . ."

Riker's eyes flashed. "The *Enterprise* and her crew can do the job."

"Can they, now?" Undrun parried caustically. "I can't do mine if I'm handicapped by the incompetence of others. The key to this mission is not simply giving the Thiopans handouts of food. We must help them become self-sufficient again."

Picard shook his head. "Mr. Undrun, you know as well as I that the Prime Directive limits what we may do for the Thiopans. They've made it quite clear that all they currently want is humanitarian aid to relieve the immediate and most critical conditions of famine. Your supervisors at the Aid and Assistance Ministry have made it equally clear to me that we are not empowered to coerce the Thiopans into accepting any help for which they do not voluntarily ask. I shall make the offer of additional assistance during our meeting with Sovereign Protector Stross."

"Your assignment, Mr. Undrun," Riker added tersely, "is to get these supplies delivered."

"What's left of them," the ambassador said. "I know my job, Mr. Riker. I trust you people know yours." Undrun pivoted and left in a huff.

The officers present traded pained expressions. "See what I mean?" said Riker.

"I do indeed, Number One. Remember, patience is a virtue," Picard answered, not without sympathy.

"In the case of Mr. Undrun," said Kate Pulaski, "a sorely tested virtue."

Chapter Two

THE *ENTERPRISE*'S TEN-FORWARD LOUNGE was nearly empty, with just a handful of off-duty personnel scattered singly or in small conversational knots at tables around the softly lit room. Frid Undrun edged inside with a diffident step, not certain he really wanted to be here. But the lounge was large enough and empty enough to convince him he could go unnoticed. The few other occupants were clustered near the huge observation windows looking out on the stark darkness of space. Undrun sat as far away as he could, with his back toward both windows and people. He sighed deeply, and his shoulders went slack beneath his rumpled jacket.

"Can I get you something, Mr. Undrun?"

Undrun stiffened and turned to glare at the intruder. He saw a dark-skinned woman in a flowing maroon robe and a hat bigger than the one he was wearing. For a moment he felt compelled to smile at her. But he maintained his formal pose. "What makes you think I need something?"

The woman shrugged. "You looked kind of tense." She smiled again. "I'm Guinan. I guess you could say I'm the host here." She produced a small tray from behind her back and proferred a glass filled with a smoky burgundy drink. "I thought you might enjoy a taste of Kinjinn wine."

"No, thank you."

"It's got a lovely flavor. Even better than the original, I'm quite sure."

Undrun cocked his head. "What do you mean?"

"It's simulated, made from synthehol."

"The only good thing the Ferengi ever gave the galaxy," Undrun snorted.

"So you can enjoy the taste without any ill effects."

"Well . . ." After a moment's consideration, Undrun took the glass and sipped gingerly at it, like a child coerced into downing some dread medicine. He swallowed and his eyes widened. "Hmmm. Not bad."

"Kinjinn wins again. Now, can I get you to enjoy our magnificent view? It's one of the best things about Ten-Forward."

"I would rather not, thank you just the same," Undrun said tightly. He sipped the wine again, and his pinched face relaxed a degree or two. He leaned forward, dropping his guard just a bit. "Spaceflight has always made me a touch queasy. It's bearable as long as I can't see what's going on outside."

"I understand. Then you just stay right here. You know, I've found that if I don't look out of those windows, I forget I'm on a ship at all."

18

"Yes, yes." Undrun nodded. "I've found the same thing. It's as if we're not even moving. Please . . . sit down, Guinan. I *can* call you Guinan, can't I?"

"That *is* my name."

"And you can call me Ambassador."

"Is that your name?"

"No, but I like to hear the title."

"Very well—Ambassador it is."

Undrun drained his glass. "May I have some more of this Kinjinn wine?"

Guinan reached for the decanter on her tray, refilled his goblet, then poured one for herself.

"Thank you," he said. "This ship is quite amazing. It must take quite a gift to be in charge of it, in charge of all the people."

"You mean like Captain Picard and Commander Riker?"

"Exactly. I could never do a job like theirs. I—I'm afraid I don't deal with people very well."

Guinan fixed him with a warm gaze. "You must be better with people than you think if you've become an ambassador."

Undrun shook his head sadly. "I'm much better with plans and plants. My home world, Noxor Three, used to be subject to wide swings in rainfall and food supply. We finally had to devote a lot of effort and expense to learning how to manage our agriculture and ecology. That's where I got my interest in this line of work. I want to teach other worlds how to do what we did." He paused and sighed again. "I just wish I didn't actually have to talk to the people I want to help."

Guinan made an open-handed gesture toward his

empty glass. "I'm glad you're enjoying the wine. Can I get you another?"

"Oh, my—I didn't even realize I'd finished it." He drew his arms close to his chest. "I really didn't intend to stay here this long or—or to talk to anyone. I—I'm sorry. I hope I didn't bore you."

"Not at all. You just did what everyone does in Ten-Fore. You relaxed."

"I—I've relaxed quite enough for now, I think. I really should get back to work. Thank you for—for listening." Undrun slid out of the booth and carefully moved away from Guinan, as if hoping there was a direct correlation between increasing distance and reestablishing propriety.

"Feel free to come back anytime, Mr. Ambassador," she called out.

Undrun ducked his head in faint embarrassment and left the room without another word.

Picard clasped his hands together on the conference table and leaned forward. "Exactly what do we know about the Nuarans, Data?"

The android blinked slightly as he accessed the requested information. "The Nuaran Imperium is a military dictatorship with absolute control over four star systems, which include a total of seven inhabited planets. Little is known about the history or development of Nuaran society. The first known contact occurred sixty-seven solar years ago when they attempted to conquer Beta Li'odo, which, unknown to the Nuarans, had just signed a treaty with the Federation. The Starfleet cruiser U.S.S. *Polaris,* which had just departed from Beta Li'odo, answered the Li'odan distress call and engaged the invading fleet in a short but decisive battle, during which the *Polaris* disabled one Nuaran ship."

"Judging by the fighters that attacked us, the Nuarans haven't been resting on their laurels," said Riker.

"I agree," Picard said. "In sufficient numbers, they could be a threat, even to a starship. Mr. Data, what's their relationship with Thiopa?"

"Most interesting, Captain. The Nuarans had evidently visited and traded with Thiopa before Thiopa's present leader, Ruer Stross, assumed power. Then, once Stross became leader, the relationship became increasingly active. The Nuarans found Thiopa valuable for both its natural riches and its location. The Thiopans agreed to let them find and exploit a variety of resources—minerals, plants, fossil products—and the Nuarans began utilizing the planet as a port facility."

"What did the Thiopans get in return?" Counselor Troi asked.

"Technology," said Data. "When Stross took control, Thiopa had barely begun industrialization. In less than forty years they progressed from steam engines to nuclear fission and fusion and to intrasystem spaceflight."

Captain Picard's forehead creased in thought. "Rapid progress indeed. The same path of development took two centuries on Earth."

"True," Riker said, "but we did it without outside help."

Data's head tilted inquisitively. "Was Earth offered extraterrestrial assistance?"

"Not that we're aware of," said Riker with a half-grin. "It might have taken us longer to get where we got, and we might have taken some wrong turns along the way, but at least we made it on our own terms without giving the planet away to predatory aliens."

"Would Earth have declined such help had it been available?" Data asked.

"Probably not," Picard replied. "It takes a powerful will to say 'No, thank you' when someone comes along and offers you a shortcut to the future. Human history contains plenty of examples of weakness winning out just when strength was required."

The blank look on Data's face made it obvious he was awaiting additional input before declaring his confusion resolved. "So you are saying it would be preferable to reject such help?"

"How shall I put this? In the best of all possible universes, devoid of all negative motivations, a helping hand would always be welcome. Unfortunately, not all superior beings have the purest of motives. In return for their help they may exact a price, and that price is often too high."

"And sometimes," said Troi, "even when the motives are pure, the temptation to play God is irresistible."

"Ahhh," Data said. "This is why the Federation adopted the noninterference directive?"

"That's right," Picard said. "The framers of that directive had the wisdom to apply the old adage about the road to hell being paved with good intentions."

"Data, what other records do we have of Nuaran activities in this sector?" Riker asked.

"They have established labor colonies on several uninhabited planets and planetoids. Thiopan slaves were used in those outposts."

Troi's eyes widened. *"Slaves?"*

"Yes. Thiopan political prisoners were disposed of by trading them to the Nuarans like any other commodity. This evidently occurred later in the relationship, when the resources Nuara valued began to grow scarce on Thiopa."

Troi looked stunned. "After only forty years these abundant Thiopan resources were already running out?"

"Yes, Counselor."

Riker shook his head in disbelief. "The Thiopans allowed the Nuarans to plunder their world, they engaged in something as barbaric as slave trade—and the Federation is still willing to consider forming an alliance with these people?"

"Doesn't sound promising, I agree," Picard admitted. "That's part of why we're here—to get some idea whether these things are part of Thiopa's past growing pains or part of a continuing pattern of behavior that may be deemed questionable by Federation standards."

"The Thiopans did ask for our help," Deanna Troi pointed out, "knowing full well what principles the Federation stands for. And they've severed their relationship with the Nuarans. Maybe they're asking for a second chance."

"Yes. For now let's try to see this situation from the Thiopans' point of view," Picard said. "They saw themselves in a galaxy full of more advanced civilizations. I'm not sure they can be blamed for their willingness to be dragged into the twenty-fourth century, no matter what the cost."

Riker's even features darkened. "Some costs are too high, no matter what the return."

"That judgment is not ours to make, Number One,"

said Picard. "Counselor Troi, psychological profile of the Nuarans, please."

"By our standards, very alien both psychologically and intellectually. Totally motivated by a desire for self-advancement—"

"Sounds like the Ferengi," Riker said.

"Only up to a point," Troi countered. "The Ferengi are very cautious, but the Nuarans are willing to take great risks in the expectation of great gains."

"The risk of attacking a starship, for example?" said Picard.

Troi nodded. "They don't operate according to the rules we use to govern social and political interactions. Traders and diplomats who've had contact with them report that Nuarans either follow no recognizable rules at all or feel no compunction about changing the existing rules to suit their needs. It's possible that they don't care about the consequences of their actions. It's also possible that their thought processes simply don't encompass the concept of consequences."

"All of which means that, on top of the Ferengi threat, we're going to have to be on constant alert while in the vicinity of Thiopa. We don't know why the Thiopans broke off relations with the Nuarans, but it's already clear the Nuarans aren't about to accept being dismissed without getting in a few last words." Picard pushed his chair back from the table and rose to his feet. "Thank you for your thoughts. You may return to your posts."

"Captain," said Troi, "I would like a word with you and Commander Riker."

Data exited to the bridge, and Troi faced Picard and

24

Riker. "It's about Ambassador Undrun. I sense a deep insecurity in him."

Picard frowned. "What sort of insecurity?"

"As if he feels he's a fraud and that others might discover this. His insecurity may lead him to try to overcompensate, to cover up what he sees as his own failings by doing things that may not be what we expect from him."

"Great," said Riker. "He's not only insufferable—he's unpredictable, too?"

Picard pursed his lips. "Are you suggesting some sort of preferential treatment for our troublesome Mr. Undrun?"

"I am reasonably sure we won't have any major problems with him as long as we don't corner him or overwhelm him with accusations of incompetence. His job-performance record is good."

"Which means if we handle him carefully," Picard concluded, "we can expect Undrun to get his job done at Thiopa."

"Yes, sir. I just thought you should both be aware of a possible problem area."

"Thank you, Counselor," Picard said.

They left the conference lounge and took their seats on the bridge. The *Enterprise* was nearing Thiopa now, and the planet had grown large on the main viewscreen. It wasn't a pretty sight. A sickly brown haze formed an atmospheric envelope around Thiopa, and the main continent was scarred by ragged gashes in its mountain ranges, where mineral deposits had been carelessly mined. Great swaths of forest had been cut away. And through intermittent gaps in Thiopa's shroud of fouled air, the eye had no trouble confirming what the ship's sensors recorded: water-borne pollution blemished Thiopan seas like spreading tumors.

"Is that as bad as it looks?" Picard asked.

"Yes, sir," Data said. "While we were in conference, Wesley ran some comparisons with sensor readings of Thiopa from twenty years ago."

"Your report, Ensign Crusher?"

"Yes, sir. The atmosphere now contains fifteen percent less oxygen, twenty percent more carbon dioxide, and seventy-five percent more industrial pollutants, including twenty-five known carcinogens and at least a dozen other toxic wastes. The water tells pretty much the same story, and the mean temperature of the planet is up by almost two degrees Centigrade."

"If Thiopa were a human patient, Captain," Data added, "its condition would be critical."

Captain Picard folded his arms across his chest. "How much of Thiopa's ecological disaster has been caused by nature and how much by the Thiopans' own hand," he wondered. "Good work, Ensign. Continue on standard orbital approach—assume orbit when ready."

"Yes, sir." Out of the corner of his eye, Picard saw Wesley smile to himself, clearly pleased by his captain's words of praise. Data, too, gave Wesley an encouraging nod.

Picard half turned toward his first officer. "Your assessment, Number One?"

"Thiopa doesn't look like a place I'd want to hang my hat for very long."

"Agreed. Your judgment about the cost of progress being too high may apply here after all."

"Maybe, sir. But right now, I'm more curious than anything else. What force could drive a planet so far toward suicide before its inhabitants could cry out for help?"

Picard leaned back, his expression reflective. "We'll soon find out."

Chapter Three

"*LORD STROSS*, you must stand still!"

Ruer Stross, sovereign protector and all-powerful ruler of Thiopa, stewed silently, regarding his own image in a full-length mirror as his valet flitted around him.

"Supo, *will* you hurry up—"

"Hold your arms up. I've *got* to see that these sleeves fit just right, or—"

"Or what? Will my arms fall off?"

Supo froze. His clenched fists landed firmly on his hips, or where his hips would have been had they been discernible. But his ample belly obscured such anatomical landmarks. Supo was shaped something like an upright sack—head perched on narrow shoulders; girth steadily increasing down his body as if flesh had surrendered to gravity; stubby legs and dainty feet, which stood on their toes most of the time.

Most Thiopans had elegantly sculpted triangular faces with high cheekbones blending into a long chin, large upturned eyes without lashes or brows, and three or four sensory whiskers on either side of the face where many other humanoid races had ears. But "elegant" was not a word that would come to mind when describing Ruer Stross's domineering valet. He had a huge beak of a nose, bulging eyes, and whiskers that always seemed to be drooping—except when they were twitching in exasperation. As they were now.

"No, your arms won't fall off, but you could very well be the laughingstock of your own anniversary feast, and then everyone would blame me. They'd say, 'Poor old Supo—blind as a burrowskratt, eh? Can't even dress his master, eh?' And wouldn't you just love that, making *me* the most disgraced servant on the planet, in the galaxy, in the universe?"

"All right, all right," Stross said, smiling placatingly. "Didn't mean to growl. I just hate spending this much time getting dressed."

"I know," Supo said, already back at work, fitting, pulling, snipping, polishing.

"Don't think I'd be doing this at all but that Ootherai's insisting."

"I know," the valet said again. Supo's fingers, the only parts of him that were graceful, fluttered around his master as he made certain that the billowy tunic, with its shiny snaps and rows of medals, was draped perfectly over Stross's barrel-chested body.

Stross puffed out regular breaths through his nose, as if venting steam from an overstoked boiler. His hair and whiskers had long since gone white with age. But his eyes, with the large pearly irises characteristic of Thiopans, were still clear and vibrant.

Supo stepped back with a flourish. "Done! Perfect!"

"Good," Stross said with a sigh. "Can I take it off now?"

"No! You'll wrinkle it or pop the snaps or lose the medals. *I'll* take it off you." The valet delicately released each fastening and slipped the jacket off Stross's shoulders in one smooth motion, then immediately hung it on a dressing form. Stross, meanwhile, shrugged into a pullover robe that came down to his knees. It was a drab tan, wrinkled and spotted with food stains, but he settled into it like a man released from bondage. He tied a coarse length of rope around his waist and pushed the loose sleeves of the robe up to his elbows. One stayed up, the other sagged. He didn't care.

"I'm hungry," Stross announced.

Supo whirled so quickly he almost toppled the clothing dummy. "No! No snacks before tonight. You'll inflate like a gas bird and this uniform will never fit. You eat too much, master. And the only exercise you get is lifting food to your mouth!"

Protector Stross snorted. "You win, you little tyrant. And that's only because I'm tired of hearing you scream at me. After this feast tonight, I'll eat whatever I damn well want."

"And I'll alter all your clothing so you won't have to run around naked," Supo shot back as he strutted toward the door. It slid open and he left without a look back. "And I found that brueggen cake you hid in the nightstand, so don't even look for it," he called from the corridor.

Stross reached out toward the table next to the bed and yanked the drawer out. *Empty—I'll bet that little rodent ate it himself.*

"Did you lose something, my lord?" Different voice, this one a smoky purr.

Stross looked up to see a tall woman shadowed in the foyer of his bedchamber. "Yeah. Food. Come on in."

She stepped into the pool of light spilling from an asymmetrical lamp stand whose severe design of black metal and gray glass echoed the stark austerity of the rest of Stross's furnishings. Ayli herself was anything but austere.

Honey-colored hair cascaded over her shoulders and framed a face with all the cool beauty of a flawless gem. Her eyes were darker than those of most Thiopans, imparting to even her most casual glance an air of mystery. Her whiskers were starting to turn gray, but that aside, she seemed as youthful as she had on the day she first became Stross's shadowreader over twenty years earlier. Her satiny dress whispered as she walked to an oval table flanked by a pair of straight-backed chairs.

"Is Supo still treating you with his usual lack of respect?" she asked lightly, settling into a chair with prim dignity.

Stross joined her at the table. "Why should that change? Sometimes I think I should've given *him* to the Nuarans."

Ayli regarded her leader with a tolerant smile. "And who would look after you? Without Supo to see to your outer shell and me to see to your life-current—"

"You're as arrogant as he is," Stross said, laughing. "Don't forget Ootherai."

Ayli grimaced. "I hate him," she said without passion.

"I know you do. And although he won't say it—because he's so much cagier than you are—I know he hates you, too."

"And you like it that way," Ayli said. "It's your assurance that your two most trusted advisers won't plot against you behind your back."

"There's something to be said for that. I need a shadowreader and I need a policy minister, and I couldn't do better than you and Ootherai. Now, Ayli, I've got a lot to do today, so let's get to it."

Ayli lifted the leather case she'd carried in with her and set it gently on the table. When she released the top latch, the hard sides fell away to reveal a collection of tubes and box shapes, all made of finely machined black metal. With a practiced deftness, Ayli unfolded the tubes on their silver hinges and had her apparatus assembled in a couple of minutes. The device was composed of an eyepiece connected to a kaleidoscopic set of prisms and mirrors enclosed within the cylinders. The main vision tube was girded by four rings, and she used those to adjust the focus as she peered into the device.

Stross, waiting patiently, could see flashes of light and color dancing across her face as the complex optical mechanisms inside the apparatus captured light beams, dismantled them, and reassembled them in a way that only a handful of mystics like Ayli could use to determine the course of future events.

Shadowreaders had been present throughout Thiopa's history. In ancient times their omens literally changed the course of life on the planet as they advised some leaders to shun wars, others to launch them. As science gained a foothold on Thiopa, before Stross was born, people who wanted to embrace the new ways turned away from the old, and shadowreaders fell on hard times. No respectable government leader would admit to consulting the flickerings of light and dark—though a good many did so in secret.

In the outlying realms, including Thesra where Ruer Stross grew up, a few raggedy shadowreaders still scratched out a meager living by reading omens and foretelling the future for common folk whose lives had yet to be enriched by the new ways of science. Stross never forgot how much respect his parents had for their local shadowreader, a toothless old man named Onar. And Ruer never forgot it was Onar who'd warned them of the earthquake that swallowed up most of Thesra when he was only ten. Ruer's parents and the others who believed Onar's prediction had escaped barely a day before the quake. But most of the townsfolk thought Onar was just an old fool. They stayed. And they died.

By the time Stross led the military revolt that overthrew Protector Cutcheon, Thiopa was well on the way to becoming a modern world. For a boy who'd been born into a village without running water or power, science and technology were like magic. Ruer Stross didn't understand them, but he worshiped them. To him, they were no different, no better or worse, than the form of magic Onar the shadowreader used to save him and his family from the destruction of Thesra. As far as Stross was concerned, both kinds of magic channeled the natural forces of the universe.

If they worked, that was good enough for him. He had plenty of scientists and engineers and technologists, but shadowreaders were hard to find in the new world.

He'd had his agents scour the planet for someone who really had the gift of light and dark. Too many shadowreaders were frauds. A few were genuine, but most of them didn't seem to be very good. It took him twenty years of searching, trying, dismissing, before he found the bewitching young woman named Ayli.

She straightened and looked at him grimly. "There are many dangers ahead for you, Ruer. Are you sure you want to hear about them?"

"That's what I pay you for. Let's have it."

Her dark eyes clouded with concern. "The omens don't carry any answers this time—just questions."

"Well, just knowing the questions has to help. Don't you think?"

"I don't know. I've never seen the shadows so dark before."

He slapped his palms on the table, making her jump. "Enough warnings about the warnings, Ayli. Tell me what you read there."

Ayli took a deep breath, then spoke. "For the first time I cannot see you reaching your goal."

"Fusion?"

She nodded. "Your dream is to see all Thiopans joined together in one unified culture and society before you die. But you know your life-current won't run for that much longer."

"True. I want Fusion to be the gift I leave behind. The Thiopans' differences have kept them from uniting—it doesn't take a genius to see that. When we get everybody speaking the same language, believing in the same things—that's when we will be strong

34

enough to take on the universe and win. You believe that, don't you?"

"Yes, my lord. I do. But not everyone does."

"I know that. Where is the greatest danger to this mission of mine?"

"In the sand—the Endrayan Realm."

"You mean the Sa'drit Void," he growled. "The damn Sojourners. Damn them to hell, every last one of them."

"Some people would say the Void isn't much better than hell."

Stross suddenly rose from the table and began to pace the hardwood floor. "They live like savages out there—no power plants, no water system, no heating or cooling, no food processing facilities—"

"But they have weapons, they have communications, they have the rail line we abandoned. They have the will and the capability to come out of that desert and hurt you, Ruer."

"I know. What I don't know is *why*. When we got rid of Cutcheon and his band of idiots, Thiopa was barely living in the present. Whole realms were still living as I did when I was a child, without enough food, drinking water that made people sick. In forty years I took this world from the past to the future. Why do these crazy Sojourners want to destroy all that?"

Ayli remained calm. "Because they believe your rush toward the future may have destroyed that very future. They blame you for the drought and the crop failures. They blame you for the brown air and the poisoned water."

"Progress always requires sacrifices. Why can't people understand that? Do they really want to live in the past again? In a world where people grow old and broken before their time, where babies die . . ." Stross shook his head. "If they're going to blame me for the bad things, why won't they give me credit for the good?"

"That's the way people are, Ruer. They always want what they don't have. And they'll turn on their leaders the moment things go wrong."

"Can't they see over the horizon, as we can?" Stross asked, hands outstretched plaintively.

"Not when they're scared—as some of them are now. So scared that somebody like Lessandra can lead them around by the nose and turn them into a mob of monsters," Ayli said.

"They haven't won yet, these Sojourner bastards."

"Maybe not, Ruer. But don't forget the darkest shadow: the Sojourners are committed to their mission—to take this planet back to the old ways— just as you are committed to *your* mission—to unite Thiopa under Fusion." She paused. "And, my lord, they believe in their leader as much as we believe in you."

A third voice, cultured and sly, spoke from the doorway. "And if we eliminate their leader?"

Policy Minister Hydrin Ootherai entered. He was much younger than Stross, and taller and thinner, with a shaved head and a pointed beard. Ootherai wore a smartly tailored suit appointed with black braid and brass. Where Stross scorned the use of physical adornment for the sake of effect, his policy minister embraced the concept.

"If you kill Lessandra," Ayli replied, speaking directly to Stross, pointedly ignoring Ootherai, "someone else will take her place. The Sojourners have come this far—they're not about to bend."

"Then perhaps they'll shatter," Ootherai said.

"As they did when you hunted down Evain and arrested him? That was twenty years ago, and since then the Sojourners have only become stronger."

"Evain was a philosopher, not a fighter," said Ootherai. "When Lessandra took his place, we were presented with a new foe, one who was tougher, more radical, more willing to employ strategies of violence."

"And how do you know you won't get someone even more radical if you do away with Lessandra?"

"You have such a simple view of things, my dear."

"You can't see anything that's not right in front of you, Ootherai. You discount Evain's contribution to what we're fighting today. *He's* the one who updated the old Sojourner Testaments. His writings provided the foundation for what Lessandra's doing now. She's just added the idea of a holy war to win the world back from us before it's too late."

"You give far too much credit to some muddle-headed itinerant—"

"Enough!" Stross exploded, hammering his fist on the table. "You're arguing about what has already happened. I need to know what *will* happen. As for getting rid of Lessandra, we don't need to create any more martyrs. I need specifics, Ayli."

The shadowreader cleared her throat. "You face perils in dealing with the Federation starship that's coming here. If you're to gain the most benefit from the relief supplies the *Enterprise* is bringing, without risking major losses, you must keep control of events.

37

You must not let the Sojourners reach the starship crew with any of their propaganda and lies."

"Control," Ootherai said. "That's what I always recommend."

Ayli went on, ignoring the policy minister. "I see the Sojourners striking where they can have the most impact—at the moment of your greatest triumph."

Stross frowned. "The anniversary feast?"

"The shadow-light relationship tells me it is a certainty."

Ootherai rolled his eyes. "One does not need to be a shadowreader to predict that, my lord," he said. "For this event I have designed the most stringent security measures we've ever had. You will have an unblemished celebration tonight, I can assure you."

"Just as you assured him there was no way Bareesh and this realm could be attacked by terrorists?" Ayli asked quietly.

"I never said we didn't make errors. We do, however, learn from our errors and strive to make our efforts more effective. I've never heard such standards of accountability applied to a shadowreader. Our agents discovered a massive propaganda campaign and nipped it in the bud, before these"—the policy minister reached into his coat pocket and removed a wrinkled sheet of paper—"could be spread around Bareesh City, not to mention the whole realm. Under torture, the terrorists admitted to being Sojourner sympathizers."

Stross blinked in disbelief when he saw the propaganda leaflet. "Sympathizers . . . our citizens helping the Sojourners?"

"Yes," Ootherai replied quickly, "but we don't believe there are very many of them. It's a small movement, and we're expending a great deal of effort toward arresting them and convincing potential traitors that the rewards of treason are not pleasant. We'll have them eliminated in no time."

"That's not what my readings say," Ayli said.

"Your *readings?* You sound like a scientist who knows—"

"Shadowreading is something *you* can't understand."

Stross cut the bickering short by snatching the leaflet from Ootherai's hand and studied it closely. It showed a photo of Stross, the sovereign protector, at a rally, dressed in his ceremonial tunic, waving his hands—but his face had been replaced by a death's-head. The caption ridiculed him as "Uncle Death."

"The children call me uncle because they know I love them," Stross sputtered, so distressed he could barely speak. "I've made their lives better . . . and that's why they love me."

"Everyone knows that, my lord," Ootherai said, trying to soothe his leader.

"These monsters take that love and pervert it into this?" Stross gritted his teeth angrily. "If they want death, I'll give them death. I'm the sovereign protector and I'll live up to that title."

"They're sand spiders," said Ootherai. "We'll crush them."

"Ruer," Ayli said urgently, trying to reach him through his rage, "you can't let the Sojourners distract you from your goal: Fusion for Thiopa. If you get sidetracked into a war and forget what you're trying to do for this world, your enemies will win—even if they lose."

Stross shook his head. "What can I do?"

"Draw a shroud over them so their poison cannot escape. Above all, you must keep the Federation and its emissaries from hearing their demon's version of the truth."

Stross remained silent for a long moment. He wanted nothing more than to crush the Sojourners for mocking him, but he heard the sense in what his shadowreader was telling him.

"All right," he said finally, "we'll do as you suggest, Ayli." He turned to his policy minister. "Tighten your security precautions for the anniversary feast, Ootherai, and make sure there's not a Sojourner or one of these"—he crumpled the propaganda leaflet in his hand—"within a hundred miles of here when the *Enterprise* arrives."

"Yes, Lord," Ootherai said.

"I'll be in my workshop. If anyone bothers me, it had better be important." Stross rose and shuffled out of the chamber through a side door.

The policy minister watched him go, and shook his head. "I cannot understand why a leader, whose government policy is built on the development of technology, can give credence to the ritualistic pronouncements of a woman who professes to foresee the future in the flickerings of light through prisms and mirrors."

"Again you fail to see what is right in front of you, Ootherai," Ayli said. "Ruer Stross listens to me because I am right."

Chapter Four

WESLEY TAPPED a final command into his console. "Standard orbit established, Captain."

"Thank you, Mr. Crusher. Mr. Data, sensor readings?"

"Close-proximity scans confirm Wesley's earlier findings, sir." The android turned halfway toward Picard and Riker, who were seated behind him. "Since the causes of Thiopa's environmental difficulties will be vital to our evaluation, I will need additional historical data on Thiopa."

"What sort of data?" Picard wanted to know.

"Weather and water temperature records, readings on levels of atmospheric and oceanic pollutants, rates and methods of industrial development. I would like to conduct my research via direct contact with Thiopan scientists and information banks, with your permission, Captain."

"By all means. If they'll talk, we're certainly free to listen. Keep me informed. Mr. Worf, contact the planetary government."

"Channel open," said Worf.

"This is Captain Jean-Luc Picard of the U.S.S. *Enterprise,* requesting contact with Sovereign Protector Stross."

A reply came quickly. *"Enterprise,* this is the Thiopan Space Communications Network. Please stand by while we transfer you."

"Enterprise standing by."

After a couple of seconds the image of a bald man with a beard replaced the planet on the bridge viewscreen. "Captain Picard, I am Policy Minister Ootherai. Sovereign Protector Stross asked me to welcome you to our world."

"Is your sovereign protector available?"

"At the moment, he isn't. But I am authorized to speak for him and on behalf of our government, Captain. We extend our warmest greetings and our appreciation for the emergency supplies you've brought to help us in our time of need. Lord Stross is busy preparing for tonight's anniversary feast here in our capital city of Bareesh."

"Anniversary *feast?"* Picard wasn't sure he'd heard that last word correctly.

"Yes. The fortieth anniversary of Lord Stross's elevation to the protectorate. He has been our leader longer than anyone else in Thiopan history. We would be most honored to have you and your senior officers as our guests at the feast. Do you need some time to consider the invitation, Captain Picard?"

Picard smiled cautiously. "No, not at all, sir. We shall be happy to attend."

Ootherai clapped his hands. "Wonderful! The feast will commence in about two hours. Beam down to the government center coordinates you've already been given. I'll be there to greet you myself."

"Thank you, Minister Ootherai. Now, as to the primary purpose of our mission—have your storage facilities been prepared to accept our cargo of relief supplies?"

"Yes, they have. If you care to transport down and examine them . . ."

"Actually, I'll be sending my first officer, Commander William Riker, down for that purpose. We have the coordinates."

"Excellent, Captain. I shall inform Facility Supervisor Chardrai. And I and the Sovereign Protector will look forward to meeting you and your party at the reception. Until then, Captain Picard . . ."

"Your hospitality is appreciated. Picard out." The planet reappeared on the viewer, rolling on its axis ten thousand kilometers beneath the *Enterprise*.

Riker's eyes narrowed skeptically. "A feast? They're in the middle of a famine and they're having an anniversary *feast?*"

Picard looked at him. "Perhaps it won't actually be a feast, Number One. If food is as scarce down there as we've been led to believe, the menu may be a meager one."

"The celebration could be a morale-booster," Counselor Troi suggested. "When circumstances are especially trying, people can benefit from an appropriately scaled celebration to lift their spirits and help them look forward to better times."

"Like those jazz concerts you've been trying to

organize," Picard said to his first officer. "Morale boosters for times when the captain behaves in a particularly tyrannical fashion."

Riker grinned. "Which reminds me, Worf . . . Geordi's sold me on the idea of you auditioning for me. He says you're pretty good on that Klingon instrument you play."

"A *chuS'ugh,* Commander."

"First chance we get."

Picard leaned close to Riker. "Worf in a jazz band?" he murmured. "Why do I have a hard time picturing this?"

"He may discover a whole new career," Riker shrugged. He could tell Picard would need additional convincing.

"Counselor, Commander Data," Picard said, "I would like both of you to accompany me to this reception on Thiopa."

"I'm not sure I like the idea of you beaming down, Captain," said Riker.

"Protocol, Number One. Besides, how hazardous could it be? And you have other responsibilities on Thiopa."

"For which I have to bring Undrun with me," Riker sighed.

"I'm afraid so," said Picard. "I have faith in your good judgment and restraint in handling him."

Riker stood and shook his head. "So while I'm taxing my self-restraint, you, Deanna, and Data will get wined and dined like diplomats. I get to tour a warehouse . . . Doesn't seem fair somehow." He was already several strides up the ramp toward the turbolift.

"It's not likely to be a sumptuous affair," Picard said. "We'll probably eat stew from wooden bowls."

That conjecture prompted a fragment of a grin. "I hope so."

"Number One—"

Riker paused at the open lift doors. "Sir?"

"Be careful down there. And don't let the irksome Mr. Undrun distract you from making the most useful observations you can. The Federation is relying on us, and I'm relying on you."

Riker nodded. "Understood, Captain."

Riker waited next to the transporter console, trying to control his growing impatience as Undrun carefully arranged his hat and fur collar to leave as little bare skin as possible. "Ambassador Undrun, it's not cold in Bareesh."

"Cold is relative, Mr. Riker."

"Whenever you're ready, sir . . ."

After a little more fluffing of his collar, Undrun finally announced, "I am ready."

"Good. Take this." Riker handed Undrun a filter mask designed to fit snugly over eyes, nose, and mouth.

Undrun held it at arm's length. "And do *what* with it?" he demanded.

"Our sensors report a good deal of air pollution in the area to which we're beaming down. We're not permitted to be transported without adequate protective equipment. If you'd like me to help you—"

"I'm capable of putting on a filter mask, Commander."

Riker backed off a step. "Fine." He put his own mask over his face and stepped up onto the transporter platform. Undrun followed, and when they were both set, Riker gave the order. "Energize."

He and Undrun shimmered back into being on a vast concrete dock on a bank of the Eloki River—or what was left of the river. Though the opposite bank was at least a kilometer away, the river itself was just a weak trickle running diffidently down a muddy midstream channel. The rest of the riverbed was now hard and dusty, baked and blistered by the sun. Barges lay embedded in dry mud like fossilized creatures trapped by a world gone environmentally mad.

Riker immediately realized that it was a good thing they'd worn the masks. All around them, industrial stacks loomed overhead, spewing gaseous and particulate filth into the mustard-colored sky. The sun glowered down through the smog, a vague pale disk diminished by the veil of poison strangling the planet.

Directly behind them, recessed back from a huge square building, was a vestibule, which, when they ducked into it, turned out to be a sort of airlock. The outside doors thumped tightly shut, and a red light began flashing over the inner doors. Hissing pumps sucked out the fumes in the airlock and vented them back outside. The warning light winked off and the inner doors slid aside, permitting entry to a dim corridor built from prefabricated sections. Riker cautiously lifted his mask. The indoor air smelled stale and artificial, but it was breathable. He nodded and Undrun took his own mask off, then carefully replaced his hat.

The corridor led in only one direction. As Riker and Undrun followed it, they glanced through small windows at the cavernous interior of the depot, which extended ten levels above them and five below ground. Some areas were wide open, apparently to allow for storage of massive industrial beams and girders. But most of the structure's space was divided into cantilevered platforms, divisible as needed, depending on what was to be kept there. A variety of containers and crates, some molded of plastic or metal, others made of old-fashioned wood, lay scattered about the warehouse's interior.

The corridor led them to a glass-walled office warren, where a lone Thiopan sat at a desk and a guard stood just inside the door. The two men wore similar utilitarian uniforms, one-piece and gray, with pockets and simple markings. The guard wore a squared-off helmet and cradled a rifle, which Riker guessed to be some sort of beam weapon. On his hip was a holstered pistol, and a functional knife was nestled in a shoulder scabbard.

The man at the desk looked up as Riker and Undrun entered, but the guard made no move to stop them. "You must be from the starship. I'm Chardrai, supervisor of this here palace."

"I'm Commander Riker. This is Ambassador Undrun of the United Federation of Planets Aid and Assistance Ministry."

Chardrai nodded a gruff greeting. He was short and stocky with heavy jowls and grizzled hair and whiskers. "Can I get you a drink to clear your mouth of the taste of that soup we call air?"

"We're fine; we wore masks. Is it always like that out there?"

Chardrai reached into a cabinet behind his desk and popped the top off a bottle. He poured light green liquid into three cracked and grimy mugs. "Today it's a little worse than usual. Weather's been inverted for the past three weeks—traps all the fumes inside. But then, that happens about every other month." He shoved the mugs across the desktop. "Sorry about the crockery. But the drink's refreshing. Guaranteed."

Riker wiped the rim with his fingers and took a sip. Whatever the stuff was, it tasted mercifully cool and tangy.

Undrun merely stared at the cup with a curled lip. "Totally unsanitary," he muttered.

"Maybe so," Chardrai said. "But not compared to what's outside." He ended with a chuckle that sounded more fatalistic than humorous.

Undrun placed the mug back on the desk. "No, thank you, Supervisor."

"Suit yourself." Chardrai lifted Undrun's mug in one large hand and poured the contents back into the bottle. Then he sipped his own. "Good stuff, though."

"I'm sure." Undrun surveyed the room they were in—rusting corrugated walls, chipped concrete, service pipes crusted with corrosion at their joints, duct tubes disconnected and hanging from the ceiling. "Is the rest of the facility in as poor condition as this office?"

"Hey, now," Chardrai growled, "this isn't no hotel. It's a warehouse."

Undrun aimed a chilly look at him. "We have pure, disease-free foodstuffs, seeds, plants, and medicines to transport down here, Mr. Chardrai. I will not have them stored in a vermin-infested bacteria incubator."

The supervisor roused himself from his chair. "Now you wait a—"

"Excuse me," Riker said, clamping a hand on Undrun's shoulder and steering him toward a far corner. "We're not exactly getting off on the right foot here, Ambassador Undrun."

"Oh, and I suppose that's my fault?"

"You didn't even give the man a chance to—"

"To tell me that this"—he fluttered a hand around the office—"is not indicative of the way they run this so-called storage depot? I have a responsibility to—"

"To deliver your cargo and let the Thiopans do with it what they choose. And if they choose to let rats eat it, we've got no say in the matter."

"I'm sorry, Commander Riker, but that's not how I operate."

"You'll operate according to the standards Captain Picard and I establish. And going out of your way to offend these people is not—"

"You can't censor me. I have a mandate to conduct this mission in any way I see fit." Undrun shook loose and spun away from Riker, who towered at least two and a half feet over him. "And if you lay a hand on me ever again, I'll see to it that—"

Chardrai slammed Undrun's rejected cup down on his desk, sending ceramic shrapnel across the room and stopping the argument cold. "You haven't even seen the facilities. I'll show you around, and then we'll talk about whether this place is clean enough for your cargo containers."

"It's not only cargo containers," Undrun snapped. "I want to see where my A-and-A personnel will be housed when they beam down."

Chardrai's eyes darted from Riker to Undrun, and his voice rose in alarm. "Hold on there. Nobody told me anything about people coming down here. If you think you're going to send down some kind of police squad to meddle in—"

Undrun waved his arms angrily. "Nobody is meddling in anything. We're here at your government's request to save Thiopa from starvation and drought. But I can't do anything for you people under these conditions."

"I've got no authorization to let anybody—"

A muffled explosion shook the entire building. Office windows cracked and chunks of ceiling insulation and ductwork fell in on them, as a fine dust coated the room.

The guard turned reflexively toward the door, pointing his weapon at a lethal angle. Supervisor Chardrai grabbed his communications headset, a simple wireless device, and jammed the receiver plug into his ear. "What the hell is going on?"

An agitated voice shouted back over a desk-mounted speaker. "Explosion on the river side! Took out most of a wall. Everything's on fire!"

"This is Chardrai," he yelled into the mike arm. "All fire-control equipment to the river wall—now!"

The supervisor and his guard raced out of the office, Riker and Undrun following. As they ran back through the corridor, Riker felt acrid smoke searing his nostrils and throat. Rounding a corner, they were staggered by the heat of a raging blaze licking at the twisted wreckage of the warehouse wall. Whatever caused the fire had erupted inside and blown the metal wall outward. Men in protective coats and hard hats were already fighting the fire with foam and water. But the heat forced everyone else to retreat.

Riker couldn't stop coughing as he staggered back to the relative haven of Chardrai's no-longer-sealed office. He did his best to cover his mouth and nose, but he had to breathe, and every short gasp felt as if someone had sprayed acid into his lungs. Chardrai and the guard stumbled in after him—and then he realized that Undrun hadn't made it.

Keeping low to avoid the smoke, Riker searched until he found Undrun crumpled on the metal-grate floor. He scooped the ambassador up in a fireman's carry and made his way back to the office as quickly as he could. Inside, he dumped the ambassador on the floor and fell to his knees, his chest heaving. He tried to talk, but that only brought on a racking cough. He bent over, trying to recover.

Three guards wearing filter masks bustled past him carrying something, which they threw into a chair. Riker wiped his burning eyes and saw that it was a raw-boned Thiopan wearing frayed work-crew coveralls. One sleeve was torn and his face was battered and bleeding.

"Who is this?" Chardrai demanded.

"The terrorist responsible for the bombing," said one of the outside guards. "We caught him trying to escape."

"A Sojourner," Chardrai said, his voice taut with fury.

The captive made no reply. Chardrai encouraged him with a backhand blow across the face. The man's head snapped back, then lolled on one shoulder. "How did you get in? How many others helped you?"

"They usually work in threes," said the chief guard. "We think the other two got away."

Chardrai grasped the prisoner's hair and yanked his head back. "You're a traitor—and you're a dead man."

The prisoner's bloody lips widened into a grotesque grin. "You're a man of few words, Supervisor Chardrai."

"How do you know my name?"

"We know a lot of things. You people haven't figured out yet that we're smarter than you?"

Chardrai struck him again, opening a gash over his right eye. "If you're so smart, how come you got caught?"

"I'm expendable. My seven friends got away."

"Seven?" Chardrai roared at the guards. "You said two!"

"He's lying," said the flustered guard. "He's a Sojourner. They're born lying."

Supervisor Chardrai let go of the prisoner's head, but the Sojourner kept it upright, apparently out of spite as much as anything else, Riker thought.

"It's not treason," said the prisoner, pausing to spit blood, "to fight against a tyrant who's sworn to destroy my people, a tyrant whose insane policies are going to destroy Thiopan civilization. You can kill me—"

"I will," Chardrai snarled. "You can count on that."

"—but you can't kill what we stand for. The people hear us—and they will fight with us. Only by returning to the old ways can we save our world from Stross."

"I've heard enough pollution out of you." Chardrai backhanded the man again, stunning him. "Kill him," he told the guards.

The chief guard looked concerned. "We've got orders to interrogate all Sojourner captives."

"I just did. This man won't tell us anything."

"What should we do with the body?"

"I don't care." Chardrai paused and seemed to reconsider. "No, wait—leave his body where his friends will find it."

Riker stood unsteadily. "I don't like anything I've seen here, Supervisor. I'm concerned about bringing those supplies down here."

"The main part of this place wasn't damaged, Commander. We can still fit those supplies in. Guaranteed."

"I'll have to talk to Captain Picard about that." *And a great many other things,* Riker added silently. He stepped over to Undrun's unconscious form and tapped his communicator. "Riker to *Enterprise*—two to beam up. And have a medical team standing by."

It hadn't taken long for Picard to review the files on Thiopa. There wasn't that much information there. A fairly primitive world with the good fortune—or bad, depending on one's point of view—to be located in a sector in which several small and large powers had taken an interest. Picard mulled over the bare facts as he got ready to beam down for the Thiopan anniversary feast. The Nuarans had played Mephistopheles and found Sovereign Protector Ruer Stross to be a more than willing Faust. And Thiopa had clearly benefited from the resultant pact. Life was, no doubt, more comfortable for most people, thanks to the obvious benefits of modern technology. But just as obviously, there had been a debit side to this soul-selling business, as there usually was.

Correction—as there *always* was.

Picard's ruminations were interrupted by the intercom tone followed by Dr. Kate Pulaski's voice over his cabin speaker. "Captain Picard, please report to sickbay."

"What is it, Doctor?"

"Your first officer and Mr. Undrun have beamed back in less than pristine condition."

"Are they all right?"

"They will be."

Picard was already halfway to the door. "On my way."

He hurried into sickbay to find Will Riker sitting on the edge of a bed. His face and uniform were smudged with soot and dust, but at least he was upright. Undrun wasn't. He was on the next bed, unconscious.

"What's wrong with them, Doctor?"

"Smoke inhalation. Undrun is in worse shape. He's under sedation."

Just then, Riker coughed. Pulaski pressed a small inhaler to his mouth, and he tried to squirm away.

"Breathe," she ordered in a tone suggesting she would not take no for an answer. Riker meekly complied, then set the inhaler aside and gave Captain Picard a compressed version of their eventful visit to Thiopa.

Picard's face betrayed his distress.

"You don't look pleased, sir," Riker concluded.

"I didn't send you down there to have buildings blown up around you."

"Captain, I'm not thrilled about your going down there," Riker said.

"Well, you're certainly in no condition to go in my place."

"Sure I am," said Riker, slipping off the bed.

"No, you're not," Pulaski said, shoving him back.

54

"But I agree with him, Captain. It doesn't sound as if Thiopa's the safest place to have dinner."

"No, perhaps not. But they invited me and I've accepted. In addition to the diplomatic importance of the feast, I need more information about what is happening down there. Meeting Stross and Ootherai could add key pieces to this puzzle."

"I still don't like it," Riker insisted.

"Objection noted, Number One. I'll be careful."

Chapter Five

CAPTAIN PICARD, Counselor Troi, and Commander Data beamed down to a broad plaza surrounded by the cluster of buildings that made up Thiopa's government center. The half-dozen buildings appeared to have been built at roughly the same time. All were constructed of gleaming white stone, glass, and steel and designed with sweeping curves and hard angles. Their austerity stood in jarring contrast to the older, less dramatic structures on streets outside the plaza.

"Interesting architecture," Picard observed. The sun was setting, casting long shadows. Picard's nose twitched as he inhaled a careful sample of the thick air. "I see what Riker meant about the air quality. Let's go inside."

The *Enterprise* trio headed for the building that was illuminated by the most colorful floodlights, the only one in the square that was drawing people in. The

Thiopan groups and couples didn't look like victims of famine, Picard noted. They were all exceptionally well dressed and seemed far from emaciated. Inside the glass-front lobby, chandeliers of abstract crystalline shapes hung from arches towering up to an asymmetrically sloped ceiling. At the center of the lobby, a crowd milled around a showcase containing a scale model of a city with the current government center at its heart. But the old brick and dark-block buildings presently surrounding the real plaza were not part of the model. They had all been replaced by high-rise structures that complemented the government compound.

Data circled the model like a curious child. "Most interesting, Captain."

"And extremely ambitious," said Picard, brows arched, "considering all the problems this society is supposedly facing."

"Captain Picard!" Policy Minister Ootherai was making his way toward them through the lobby, dropping a word here and there to well-heeled Thiopans as he passed. He finally reached the starship officers.

"These are members of my senior staff," Picard said, "Counselor Deanna Troi and Lieutenant Commander Data."

"A pleasure to meet you and to welcome you to Thiopan soil. I see you're admiring the model for our new capital complex."

Picard smiled thinly. "Most impressive. When is it to be built?"

"We're planning to start demolishing the old quarter of the city when the weather turns cooler, in about two months. We don't really have a winter anymore, it seems, so we're looking forward to rapid progress on Stross Plaza."

"Named after your leader?" said Troi.

"Yes, an appropriate monument to the sovereign protector, which he'll get to see and enjoy while he's still alive. Posthumous honors leave much to be desired, I've always believed. Let honors be for the living—and certainly Ruer Stross deserves to be honored on a grand scale. He's quite anxious to meet you. Come this way—and then I'll escort you to your seats in the feast hall."

"Stop fussing!" Protector Stross slapped Supo's hands away from the collar the little valet was struggling to straighten. Supo flew back several steps and Stross wrenched the collar straight himself. He looked in the mirrored wall of the anteroom and nodded. "There. It's fine. Everything's fine."

Supo hung his heavy-nosed head. "No, it's not fine, but—"

"But it will have to do," Stross said with finality. He faced his mirrored image again. All his medals were straight, collar upright, braid in place, billowy sleeves unrolled, glittering sash tied evenly about his belly.

He had recovered from the earlier shock of learning that some of his citizens were actually aiding the Sojourners—an hour or two in his private workshop, building, had done the trick—and felt prepared to face his audience tonight . . . even the visitors from the Federation.

As if on cue, the anteroom door swung open and Ootherai entered with the starship officers. He announced each one by name.

Captain Picard then extended his hand in respectful

58

greeting. "It's an honor to meet you, sir. I thank you for receiving us."

"The honor is mine, Captain. You're the ones bringing the relief supplies. *We* thank *you* and the Federation. There are lots of lives at stake, sir."

"The Federation believes in helping those in need."

"Well, we'll do our best to repay this good-neighbor generosity. Supo, go out there and see if you can find Dr. Keat." The valet ducked his head and scurried out a side door. "I want you to meet her. She's one of our success stories—one of our best hopes for the future. We sent her off-planet to study when she was a little girl—and now she's come back to rescue our science program just when it's blown up in our faces."

"Uh, Lord Stross," Ootherai said tightly, "is this the time for—"

"Quiet, Ootherai. These people came to help us. I want them to know they're not pitching treasure down a sewer pit."

Data cocked his head. "Sewer pit, sir? A refuse disposal site—"

"Just an expression. You're a literal fellow, aren't you, Mr. Data?" Stross chuckled. "What I mean is, we want you to know we're working hard to help solve our own problems, Captain. Fact is, we've got a big announcement to make tonight—oh, here she is now." Supo had returned with a willowy young woman dressed in a high-necked gown that was somehow demure and alluring all at once. Her skin was almost bronze-colored, much darker than that of the other Thiopans they'd seen. Huge pale eyes, golden hair and whiskers, and the dusky complexion combined to lend her an exotic look that Picard found striking. His smile warmed and he clasped her hand.

"Dr. Kael Keat," said Stross, "meet Captain Jean-Luc Picard, Counselor Deanna Troi, and Lieutenant Commander Data of the Federation starship *Enterprise.*"

"Dr. Keat, your reputation precedes you," Picard said.

"Though only by a minute or two," Stross laughed.

"Your sovereign protector thinks very highly of you. He credits you with having saved Thiopa's scientific community from catastrophe."

Dr. Keat's lashless eyelids flickered. "Lord Stross is prone to exaggeration at times. But we are doing some exciting work—which only builds on what was done before I took over as head of Thiopa's Science Council. Our aim is to find a way to survive and to adapt to the effects of the natural disasters we're suffering through now."

"Sounds like admirable work, Dr. Keat."

Data stepped forward. "I am very much interested in learning more about your climatic changes and your strategies for adjusting to them. Could we discuss your work at greater length?"

"I don't see why not," Keat replied. "We could meet at the Science Council labs tomorrow. Will you be available then, Commander Data?"

"With Captain Picard's permission . . ."

"By all means," Picard said.

"Sorry I can't chat with you all a bit longer," Stross said, "but Ootherai here has a number of other people I'm supposed to talk to before this feast gets going."

"We understand," said Picard. "A head of state does have certain responsibilities."

"I'd like to talk more," Stross added. "Ootherai can

set up an appointment for tomorrow, if you'd like, Captain. He can answer any questions that might come up tonight. Otherwise, just enjoy yourselves." Supo opened the side door for him and Stross left the room.

Ootherai motioned back toward the lobby. "The feast hall should be ready. If you'll allow me to accompany you to your seats . . ."

"May I tag along?" asked Dr. Keat.

"Please do," Data answered eagerly. "I am very curious about your analyses of the causes of Thiopa's ecological difficulties. One can discern only so much from a brief period of orbital observation. Without the proper historical perspective, contemporary examination is of limited value. The relationships between atmospheric components and their relative levels of modification could prove most enlightening, taking into consideration, of course, the overlapping cause-and-effect curve of—"

"Mr. Data," Picard interrupted, "you're babbling again."

Data's yellow eyes widened. "So I am, sir. Sorry."

"Quite all right, but this is a social occasion."

"I am not entirely proficient in social occasions," Data said, emphasizing the last two words as if referring to a course he was in danger of failing.

"Why not, Commander?" Kael Keat wanted to know.

"It was evidently not part of my programming."

Keat did a double-take. "Programming? You're an android?"

Picard and Troi exchanged a knowing glance. No matter how long they served with Data, his shipmates

61

never tired of seeing other beings surprised to discover that they'd been conversing with a machine rather than with a naively charming human with unusually sallow skin. "Not just an android," Picard said with pride. "One of my most capable officers."

"Well, I'm not sure who's more anxious to talk to whom, Mr. Data," Dr. Keat said. "I've never met anyone like you before. Perhaps I can help you sharpen those social skills this evening." She took Data by the arm and began leading him out of the room.

Smiling, Picard and Troi followed.

"What did he call it, again?" Riker asked Geordi LaForge as they strode along an *Enterprise* corridor.

"A *chuS'ugh*—and don't ask me if I'm pronouncing it right. Klingonese always sounds like somebody either gargling or getting strangled."

"I'll tell him you said so." Riker chuckled.

"He already knows."

"What does"—Riker hesitated, then came up with his best approximation of the instrument name—*"chuS'ugh* translate as?"

"'Heavy noise.'"

Riker's expression turned skeptical. "And you've heard him play it?"

"Yes, sir."

"What does it sound like?"

"That's a tough one, Commander. Not like anything I ever heard before."

"Then it's not likely anybody's written any great jazz arrangements for it," said Riker with a wry smile.

"So you'll improvise. Isn't that what jazz is all about?"

Another all too familiar voice broke in from behind them. "There you are, Riker. Stop!"

Riker turned and let a shoulder slouch as Frid Undrun shuffled up to them. "What is it, Mr. Ambassador? I'm off duty."

Undrun halted and teetered back on his heels. "Oh, well . . . I'm *never* off duty. We needa discush what happened down there . . . We needa make some d'cisions," he asserted, losing a few syllables along the way.

Riker eyed the ambassador skeptically. "We can't make any decisions until Captain Picard returns from the planet and you sleep off the rest of that sedative."

"What sed'tive?"

"Did Dr. Pulaski release you from sickbay?"

Undrun's chin jutted defiantly. "I releashed myself. Don't need anybody to tell me—"

"You're going right back to sickbay." Riker tried to steer the bleary-eyed envoy into an about-face, but Undrun eluded his grip. "You either cooperate—"

Undrun backpedaled. Cooperation was not his first choice. Riker strode forward and in one smooth motion picked Undrun up and slung him over his shoulder. "You didn't see this, Geordi."

LaForge trailed behind. "See what? I'm blind, remember?"

"Riker," Undrun shrieked, "I warned you if you ever tushed me again—"

Fortunately, sickbay wasn't far, and it wasn't long before Riker was depositing his cargo in front of a startled Dr. Pulaski. "I think you lost something, Kate."

"Where did he come from?"

"If you're referring to the larger philosophical context, I haven't got a clue. I'd batten my hatches if I were you."

"Consider them battened."

Riker and Geordi resumed their musical mission, arriving at Worf's cabin in time to hear a basso profundo bleat. Something like a forty-foot sheep jabbed with an electric prod. Riker looked horrified. "You sure about this, LaForge?"

"He's just tuning up. Don't worry. I told you, I've never heard anything like this instrument."

Another *blaaaaaat,* slightly higher in pitch.

"Tuning up?"

"Don't you want this combo to sound original?"

"Sure, but I still want it to sound like jazz." Riker's brow wrinkled doubtfully. "Okay, let's get this over with."

Geordi answered with a wide grin. "That's the spirit."

"When in Rome . . ." Picard shrugged. He and his companions got to their feet but didn't join in the ovation with which the Thiopan celebrants greeted their sovereign protector on his grand entrance into the feast hall.

"Feast" appeared to be the right word for the celebration after all. By Data's estimate, there were 2,836 people in the massive hall. Judging by their enthusiastic reaction to Stross's appearance, they were all partisans of the beleaguered government. The applause went on and on as spotlights and laser beams danced across the long dais where Ruer Stross waved clenched fists over his head and savored the adulation.

"Quite a spectacle," Picard said to Troi, bending close to her ear to make himself heard over the cheering. "I think this level of revelry far exceeds the morale-building threshold you suggested. They're well past the point of ostentation."

Troi nodded. "Do you think they lied to the Federation about this famine?"

"I don't know. If so, did they really think they'd get away with it?"

Data leaned closer to them. "Their ecological problems are quite apparent, sir, and more than severe enough to contribute to an extreme food shortage."

"This celebration hardly reflects the restraint one would expect from the leaders of a world whose inhabitants are threatened with starvation. Just look at all those groaning boards of food waiting to be served."

"This wouldn't be the first time that leaders have exhibited bad judgment," Troi pointed out.

Picard snorted. "Let them eat cake?"

"Cake?" said Data, scanning the hall. "I do not see any baked goods."

"It's an expression from earth history, late seventeen hundreds, the French Revolution."

"Ah, yes," Data said. "Your ancestral land, sir. Marie Antoinette, queen of France and wife of King Louis the Sixteenth, was popularly believed to have said 'Let them eat cake' in response to a critical shortage of bread. That attribution was never confirmed, however."

"That's not the point, Data," Troi said patiently. "The French nobility lived extravagantly while the rest of the people endured poverty. Cruel indifference on the part of leaders has contributed to many revolutions throughout history."

"Do you think that's what we're facing here?" Picard asked her.

"It's a possibility, sir," Troy said, "but it would be very difficult to isolate an admission like that from anyone in this group, especially now, when they're so excited about this anniversary celebration."

"All the more reason for us to meet tomorrow with Stross and Ootherai."

The ovation finally subsided and the diners took their seats again. An army of waiters began circulating with rolling carts and fine silver trays, all heavily laden with food. The *Enterprise* officers were seated at a small private table in a front corner of the vast hall. A waiter served them almost immediately, setting before them bowls overflowing with fruit.

"Generous," Troi noted. "If the Thiopans really are starving, I feel a little guilty about gorging myself."

"We've got four shiploads of food up in orbit, Deanna," said Picard. "If we do our job, those hungry mouths will be fed . . . for a while at least."

"It's tuned," Worf intoned. He cradled his *chuS'ugh* in the crook of one arm. The instrument, which was made of dark, dull-finished wood, had a pear-shaped soundbox about two feet high. Its wide base rested on Worf's thigh. At the tapered upper tip was a small air grate. A short bridge with four thick strings of coiled steel was set at an odd angle against the instrument's midsection. In his other hand, the Klingon gripped a stubby bow.

To Riker, who had visited many different worlds

and sampled numerous alien cultures, this was without doubt the strangest musical instrument he'd ever seen. He extended a tentative finger toward the strings. "May I?"

Worf nodded. Riker plucked the thinnest string—the thickest was nearly as big around as his little finger. A tone came out of the soundhole low on the instrument's belly—pleasantly mellow, to his surprise—but that was overwhelmed a second later by a brassy dissonance howling from the grate at the top.

Riker's hand jerked back by reflex, as if he'd been burned. "What the hell was that?"

Worf almost smiled. "Harmony."

"All right, Worf." Riker leaned against the wall, arms crossed. "As they used to say in the old days, 'lay some sounds on me.'"

The Klingon gave Geordi a hesitant glance. "He means play," Geordi assured him.

With an incongruous flourish, Worf stretched his bowing arm, positioned the bow across the strings, and began sawing at them while pressing the strings with his other hand. Riker winced at the noise that came out—harsh, clashing, ponderous, and low enough to make the floor shake.

"Pick up the tempo," Geordi shouted.

After about two minutes, which were among the longest in Riker's life, Worf stopped. "That's—uh—distinctive, Worf. How long have you been playing?"

"Since childhood—this very same instrument. I grew up among humans, as you know, but my parents wanted me to learn about my own culture, too. They paid a lot of money for this *chuS'ugh*, then realized

67

there was no one who could teach me to play it. They finally found a computer lesson program. Not as good as a live teacher—"

"He's too modest," said Geordi seriously, "but he turned out to be a natural. So—what d'you think?"

They both looked at Riker, who wanted nothing more than to make his escape. Hoping his feelings didn't show in his eyes, he furiously tried to formulate an answer that wouldn't offend the very large Klingon warrior who'd just bared the artistic corner of his soul, at Geordi's urging. The first officer's mouth opened, but no words came out. *Think fast, Riker . . .*

"Well, it's not what I expected," he said at last. "I don't know what I expected. I've never heard Klingon music before."

"Isn't there a saying, 'Close enough for jazz'?" Geordi prodded.

"Yes—yes, there is. I'm just not sure this *is* close enough for jazz. I'm not underestimating your talent, Worf. God knows, I couldn't play that thing. What kind of piece was that anyway?"

"A Klingon classic." Worf's face remained impassive, but his eyes revealed a mixture of disappointment, pride, and hurt. "You didn't like it."

"To be honest, I'm not sure what to make of it."

They both turned to Geordi, who tried to save the situation. "Hey, it'll grow on you, Commander."

Riker backed toward the doors, which obligingly slid open. "I'll get back to you."

"Maybe it just needs some accompaniment," Geordi called after him.

"Maybe," Riker called back. Then the door closed.

"Don't worry, Worf. *I* like your music. I'll talk to Commander Riker later. Meanwhile, maybe we should work on your stage presence—y'know, a little chatter between songs," Geordi said brightly.

"Humans wouldn't know good music if it knocked them over," Worf grumbled. "They'd rather listen to feeble imitations of mewling infants." He gently laid the instrument back in its molded case.

The bowls of fruit were just the first of five courses served at the anniversary banquet. By the time dessert arrived—multi-layered platters of pastries—Picard felt more than a bit stuffed. As he surveyed the huge hall, the image of fatted calves ready for slaughter darted into his mind. The evening meal left no doubt that Thiopan cuisine was excellent, but hadn't yet provided a shred of illumination as to what was really going on here on this planet. The important announcement that Stross had hinted at had yet to be made; maybe that would contain at least a nugget or two of information Picard could use to start piecing this puzzle together.

He sampled a tasty spiral crust with a perfect chiffon filling. So far, in the half-day since the *Enterprise* had approached Thiopan space, they'd been fired on by Nuarans, had a brush with Thiopan terrorists, taken their first disconcerting measure of the extent of ecological damage on the planet, and weathered repeated petulance on the part of the Federation envoy, Frid Undrun.

After finishing the pastry, Picard licked his fingertips and noticed Troi staring at him. "Something on your mind, Counselor?" His tone was more brittle than he had intended. Not that it mattered; it was rather hard to hide moody undercurrents from an empath sitting eighteen inches away.

"You seem tense, Captain."

His stoic features rippled in resignation. "It's been a Murphy's Law kind of day. I fully expect it to end with a Ferengi waiter scuttling out here to serve us poisoned coffee."

Up on the dais, Protector Stross had begun to speak. "I'm not going to bore you with a long speech," he said to a twitter of appreciative laughter. "I do have an announcement, though. Something big. Or I wouldn't tear you away from those desserts."

"He has a natural charm," Troi whispered. "It is understandable that Thiopans would have accepted his rule for so long."

"You all know," Stross went on, "that we've had some problems lately. Our planet is hot, it's dry, some people are going hungry. But we'll soon change all that. And I want to introduce the scientist who's making that change possible—the head of our Science Council, Dr. Kael Keat."

The young woman swung gracefully out of her chair and joined her leader at the lectern as the audience clapped politely. Picard wondered at the lack of enthusiasm. Was it possible that these people didn't know who Keat was, or had the excitement been lulled out of them by a night of overeating?

"Thank you," said Keat. "All the bounty we've enjoyed tonight must be made available to every Thiopan, not just the ones lucky enough to come to this feast. Soon we'll have a way to make that dream come true. Never again will we be at the mercy of shifting winds, unpredictable rain, scorching heat, and deadly cold. Never again will we be made to feel like our primitive ancestors, cowering before forces we can't understand. The Science Council is ready to unveil a project that will make us stronger than nature—a weather control shield that will solve our environmental problems for all eternity." Because of her low-key delivery, it took several moments for her meaning to sink in. Then the crowd began to murmur and the murmur grew into a rumble of sustained applause that soon spread across the hall like a wave.

"In ten years' time," Kael Keat said, her voice still tranquil, "we'll make Thiopa a temperate paradise." The applause broke out again, longer and louder now.

After a minute, Stross signaled for attention.

"That's our goal, my friends," he said. "But first, we have to unite this world and all her people—one mind, one goal, one faith." The crowd had fallen silent. Stross spoke with simple intensity. "Harmony. That's what we need. No more squabbling over old ways or new ways. Let's just take the best way. Once we have achieved Fusion, we'll be strong enough to take on the one enemy that really *can* kill us all— nature. With your help, I know we can do whatever needs doing. Thank you, my friends." The ruler of Thiopa ended his speech with his head bowed in humility.

And the members of the audience jumped to their feet as if programmed to do so. By comparison, the welcoming ovation they'd given to Stross at the start of the evening had been restrained. Now the great hall exploded with a fervor that was equal parts religion and lust. These people were True Believers, Picard realized as he and his officers stood at their table without joining in.

Data's head swiveled in birdlike movements as he watched in wonderment. "The degree of arousal is most interesting."

"It is all a matter of knowing the right things to say to the right people," said Troi. "That is part of what makes a good leader."

"Or a dangerous leader," Picard added.

Troi nodded, suddenly apprehensive. "Captain, I *do* sense danger."

"What kind of danger?"

Before she could explain, one of the Thiopan waiters scrambled past their table and flipped it over, splattering food on people and walls. Picard grabbed Troi as they fell back across their toppled chairs. Startled guests fell silent as suddenly as if a plug had been pulled when the lone server leaped on top of another table and unfurled a banner.

"You're eating well while babies starve in the Endrayan Realm—because this corrupt government *wants* them to starve! Their only crime is that their parents refuse to sell their heritage in return for food that's rightfully theirs! They refuse to surrender to the genocide you call Fusion! There's plenty of food for all Thiopans, but Stross won't let those babies have it. Why?" He whirled to stare right at Stross. "Why, Sovereign Protector? The Sojourners will never accept Fusion. Join us and save Thiopa! Join Stross and our world dies! Please—"

His speech ended in the piercing whine of a blaster beam. Picard jerked his head toward the source of the terrible sound and saw three guards firing, their blue bolts knocking the man off his makeshift podium. By the time he hit the floor, he was dead, his chest smoking where the beams burned through his clothing.

* * *

72

Will Riker pulled off his boots and flopped back on his bed, undecided about whether to read or listen to music. He felt too tired to read—

"Commander Riker, this is Lieutenant White on the bridge."

Riker rolled toward the intercom screen next to his bed.

"This is Riker." White's freckled face appeared on the viewer. "What is it, Lieutenant?"

"Sorry to disturb you, sir. Captain Picard and the away team are beaming back up. He wants you to meet them in the bridge conference lounge."

"On my way. Riker out."

By the time he reached the bridge, Picard and the others were already waiting for him. He strode into the lounge and stopped short when he saw food and drink stains dotting their uniforms. "Those Thiopans must throw wild parties."

Picard paced in front of the wall of windows on the outside bulkhead. Thiopa shone brightly below, the light from its sun bouncing off the thick layer of clouds and pollution shrouding the planet. "Sit down, Number One."

"You sure you three don't want to change first?"

"It looks worse than it is. I want to do this as quickly as possible, then get some sleep." With no more preface than that, Picard launched into a terse report of the anniversary celebration. Then he sat down at the end of the table.

Riker's mouth quirked in disbelief. "The security people shot this protester just for shouting and waving a banner?"

"A rather extreme punishment," Picard agreed,

steepling his fingers. "Did you sense anything, Counselor?"

She sighed before replying, obviously trying to sort out the emotions she'd absorbed during the brief but violent incident. "Terror, determination—and great anger."

"From whom?"

"From everyone around us."

"I understand," Picard said, his expression grim. "The Sojourners are clearly a longtime thorn in the government's side."

"Yet," Data pointed out, "in spite of the importance of the storage facility and the anniversary feast, the Sojourners managed to breach security in both instances. Security that was most likely more stringent than usual."

"Both those breaches proved highly embarrassing to the government," Picard said. "The Sojourners gained little else. But they were evidently determined to let us know of their existence, and their determination."

"Still," Troi said, "all we know about their cause are slogans spoken by an apparent terrorist and a protester before they were executed. Unless we can find out more, we have no way of knowing if their grievances against the government are valid."

"They're valid to the Sojourners," Picard said. "They're willing to die for their cause—whatever it may be."

"Do these incidents otherwise affect our basic mission to Thiopa?" Data wondered.

Picard spread his hands in uncertainty. "A good question, Data. We're not permitted to interfere in this world's internal quarrels. But if Thiopa proves unstable, the Federation may have to look elsewhere in this sector for an ally against the Ferengi."

"But we don't have to make that decision, Captain," Riker said, "just a recommendation."

"Exactly—but we may have to make a decision on whether to complete our mercy mission or abort it."

Troi's large eyes grew concerned. "Captain, if there are people starving on Thiopa—"

"They may not be starving merely because of ecological catastrophe," Picard suggested. "Their plight may be caused as much—or more—by political decisions made by the government in Bareesh. If that's the case, then who's to say that our emergency relief supplies will ever get to the people who truly need them?"

Riker planted his elbows on the conference table. "The Thiopans must really need that food, and not just to feed those Sojourners and their sympathizers out in this Endrayan Realm. Things must be worse than that feast made them appear or they wouldn't have sent such an urgent S.O.S. to the Federation. Agreed?" He glanced around for signs of dissent, got none, and continued. "Let's proceed under the assumption that we've got something they want and they've got something we want."

"Information about just what's going on down there," said Troi.

"Right. So let's go through the motions of making our delivery, but we'll drag our feet, make them think we just might take our container ships and go home."

"A reasonable first approach, Number One," said Picard. "Apply a little gentle pressure. Which I can also apply when I meet with Sovereign Protector Stross tomorrow."

"I am scheduled to meet with Dr. Keat tomorrow as well," Data added. "So our approach is three-pronged."

Picard leaned back in his chair, his eyes revealing his weariness. "Tomorrow had better provide us with some answers. I want to start tying up loose ends—the quicker the better. Data, what about this weather control project? Is it possible?"

"In principle. Weather is a product of atmospheric density and constituents, land mass arrangement, air and water temperature, wind speed and direction, amount and intensity of sunlight reaching the planet, cosmic radiation, angle of planetary axis, precession of equinoxes, and effects produced by flora and fauna, including—"

Picard waved his hand impatiently. "I don't need a catalog of factors."

"Of course. As I started to say, weather control is theoretically possible, up to a point. In terraforming a planet, technicians and designers can actually create weather in an environment where none exists. But that takes years, or decades, depending on the original state of the planet. However, even the most advanced technology in the Federation is not capable of controlling or manipulating the weather around an entire planet simultaneously."

"What *can* be done?"

"Pockets of artificially controlled weather can be created by interrupting, redirecting, or augmenting key natural wind currents, modifying the temperature of large bodies of water, adding or deducting atmospheric moisture—"

"All these strategies sound as if they'd require immense amounts of energy," Picard said.

"That is true, Captain."

"It also sounds like a house of cards," said Riker. Data tilted his head quizzically, so Riker explained. "Complex interrelationships of factors—change one, and it affects all the others, which in turn add their own effects."

Data grasped the meaning. "That is correct, sir. And even advanced computer modeling is inadequate for predicting exact results, since there are too many variables that cannot be controlled or even charted."

"Bottom line," said Picard. "Can the Thiopans successfully accomplish what Stross and Dr. Keat say they're going to do?"

"Based on our limited observations of Thiopa's level of technology, and the Thiopans' lack of success in managing their environment, I would tentatively conclude that such a project is beyond their capabilities."

"Tentatively?" Picard said.

"Yes, sir. It is possible that they possess knowledge of which we are not aware. Possible—but unlikely."

"When you meet with Dr. Keat tomorrow, try to find out enough to make that analysis more definite. All right, then, if there's nothing else . . ."

Riker lifted a hand. "There is one thing."

"Which is . . .?"

"Undrun. Do we tell him what we're planning?"

Picard nodded. "He is the Federation's liaison with the Thiopan government so far as the relief supplies are concerned. He has a right to be informed as to why we're not delivering them just yet. Computer, where is Ambassador Undrun?"

"Sickbay."

"Picard to sickbay."

Kate Pulaski answered, her voice tired and hoarse. "Sickbay here. What is it, Captain?"

"Rough day for you, too, Doctor?"

"Only since Mr. Undrun checked in."

"Is he awake and lucid?"

"He is."

"Ambassador Undrun, this is Captain Picard."

Undrun's voice came over the intercom. "I want you to force the Thiopan government to provide a more suitable place to store the Federation's emergency supplies."

Out of the corner of his eye, Picard saw Riker shake his head wearily. "We are not permitted to force them to do anything of the sort. I'll send you a transcript of the conference I just had with Commanders Riker and Data and Counselor Troi. If you review it, you'll be completely briefed on the decision we've just made to delay delivery of the relief cargo to the Thiopans."

"I want that food delivered as soon as possible," Undrun blustered.

"Mr. Ambassador, you're the one who just said that the Thiopans haven't provided an appropriate storage facility. That is what you and Commander Riker will see to first thing tomorrow. The delay is merely procedural."

That caught Undrun off guard and he stammered for a moment. "I—I—That food has to get through to starving people. Is that clear?"

"Quite clear, sir."

Undrun lowered his voice suspiciously. "I may be drugged, but I'm not stupid, Captain Picard. If you interfere with the completion of my relief mission in any way, I'll lodge a formal protest with Starfleet. I can make you very sorry—"

"I already am," Picard muttered under his breath.

"What was that? I didn't hear you."

"I started to say I am in agreement with you about the importance of this mission. Good night, sir."

Picard's jaw muscles twitched. Somehow, when it came to Ambassador Frid Undrun, the single simple word "vexatious" no longer seemed adequate.

Chapter Six

IN THE SA'DRIT VOID, on the high side of noon, the sun held dominion. It filled the sky and parched the land. It whitewashed everything within sight of its unblinking glare. Only now, as it rode toward the barren horizon, did merciful shadows begin to steal across baked rock and dust, like creatures creeping from daytime hiding places.

One of those shadows, cast by the crags atop a savage ridge of time-torn stone, fell across a subordinate ledge. That ledge, in turn, hung over a narrow pass between flat-topped peaks. From that vantage point, two lookouts lying on their bellies watched the lifeless plain stretching vastly below them.

There were living things out there, and they were getting closer. At first they'd looked like mites wriggling in the distant shimmer of the sun's fire. After a time, they had resolved into animals with men riding on them. The lookouts were both women, one young, one older, with wrinkles framing her eyes and whiskers already turned gray. The younger peered through binoculars, touching a servo button to focus the zoom lens.

"How many, Mori?" asked the older sentry in a hoarse voice.

Mori didn't answer right away. She watched the odd gait of the animals—there were two—as their slender legs plodded in slow sequence, heads swaying to an altogether separate rhythm. These were full-grown ealixes, taller than a man, rotund bodies covered with the fine pinkish hair that didn't fill in until the gentle beasts were well into their second year. The light coat protected their hide from the sun but allowed air to circulate and help keep them cool.

"Two animals, two riders—carrying a body."

The older one muttered a sharp curse. "Another dead fighter for Lessandra's collection," she hissed. "Can you make out their faces?"

Mori squinted into her viewer. The riders were dressed in standard desert garb—loose robes of pale cloth, gathered at the waist with a bright sash, woven leggings and sandals. The robes had a scarflike collar, the ends of which dangled open during the scorching days, ready to be bundled around the neck to retain body heat when temperatures plunged after dark. Floppy hoods were also stitched onto the garments, and the approaching travelers had pulled theirs up to protect their heads from the sun. Their faces were hidden in shadow. "No." Mori rolled onto one elbow to look at her companion. "Glin, do you really think Lessandra's wrong about all this?"

Glin's scowl softened as she scrutinized her young

partner. Where Glin's face was weathered and lined by time and bitter experience, Mori's was as fresh and smooth as a newly bloomed flower. She was a grown woman now, though she had recently cropped her hair short and ragged in an effort to look older—an unsuccessful effort. But the hardscrabble life that lay before her would rob Mori of her innocence soon enough.

"Yes," Glin finally said. "I think Lessandra's wrong. It's gone too far. She's pushing Stross as if she thinks we're the ones with the power."

"We *do* have power," Mori protested.

"Enough to hurt them—but not enough to win. If it comes to a war, the numbers say we have to lose. A lot of us think Stross would rather do other things than pick up the pieces after we set off bombs. He'd rather not send hoverjets out here to try to catch us in the open."

"Which we almost never are." Mori looked away, annoyed at Glin's implication.

"That's my point, little one. Your father taught us what Sojourners knew in the old times."

Mori turned back, her head tipped like a student afraid to answer a question. "That the Hidden Hand leads us on the better path?"

"Exactly. All the dead we've buried make it obvious that the better path is negotiation."

"Lessandra says the government will never negotiate."

"Then we've got nothing to lose. We will make the offer. If they come to the table to talk, we don't have to accept any terms we don't like. We're free to resume our fight. Same if they refuse to talk at all. But if we can talk *and* agree, then we'll gain what we want most—the right to live peacefully in our own lands and by our own rules."

"But Lessandra says the government is ruining the whole world and that we are not immune to their toxins. If they poison their air and water, they poison our air and water, too. She says we have to make the rest of the world return to the old ways. It's not enough for us to go back to them."

Glin's eyes narrowed. "I know what she thinks. What do *you* think?"

"I—I'm not sure."

"Lessandra says things that differ from what your father wrote and preached all those years. He didn't believe in forcing other people to follow our ways unless they wanted to."

"But he's been gone for twenty years—almost my whole life," Mori blurted. "How do we know that what he believed back then is right for what we face today?"

"Because what he believed came from the old times. He rediscovered the Testaments and made them fit our world. Lessandra can reinterpret Evain all she wants, but that doesn't make her right."

"If my father was as persuasive as everybody says he was, he could have settled all this."

"Mori, he's dead."

"We don't know that, not for sure." The young woman's voice quavered.

"Mori—"

"We don't know!" Mori scrambled to her feet. "Just because the government said he died in prison doesn't mean it's true. All those stories—"

"Are just stories. Nobody knows if those other prisoners really saw your father alive. Now go tell

Lessandra we saw fighters returning. Tell her one of them is dead."

Sandals scuffing in the dirt, Mori hurried off with her head bowed in dejection. The Sojourners never believed anything the government said, so why were they so willing to believe that her father had died in captivity two years after he was captured? They had charged him with treason, found him guilty, sentenced him to life in prison—but they never said they would execute him. Elders, like Glin, had told Mori that the government wanted to keep Evain alive as a symbol of swift but fair justice and as a warning to other Sojourners of the government's determination to keep order. If Evain had been executed, as many people demanded, martyrdom would have imbued his legacy with a power he could never have attained in life.

Still, only two years after his conviction, the government announced that Evain had taken sick and died, in spite of the best medical care available. On his deathbed, he had recanted all his Sojourner beliefs, they'd said, and endorsed Stross's vision of Fusion—a united Thiopa marching boldly toward the future under the banner of progress through technology. They built a tomb for him in Heroes' Park, in the heart of the capital, and schoolchildren were taught from then on how the government's most implacable enemy had seen the light in his last mortal moments, thanks to the kinder and gentler wisdom of Sovereign Protector Ruer Stross . . . *Uncle Stross.*

Mori was only five when it happened. Evain's death left her an orphan with no close relatives. She was raised by the community that had followed her father.

But she'd never felt neglected; all her father's closest friends had taken an active role in her upbringing. She had never wanted for love or attention—quite the opposite. At least a half-dozen good people thought of her as their own child. But she had always felt closest to Lessandra, Glin, and Durren, who might be one of the fighters now on his way back to the Sojourners' sacred mountain stronghold. If he was the one who had died—She stomped on that morbid thought before it could take root. Durren was too wily to get caught.

Mori made her way up the rocky trail, following the narrow steps chipped into the stone two thousand years earlier by the first Sojourners. She hadn't been born out here in the wilderness but in a city, like most Thiopans. Mannowai City was the capital of the Endrayan Realm, not as grand as Bareesh but quite comfortable and modern, and the center of the renaissance of Sojourner teachings led by her father. Mori had vague recollections of having visited this ancestral land as a toddler, on a pilgrimage with her father and others, but she couldn't be certain if her memories were of the trip itself or of hearing others tell about it in the years since.

It wasn't until a couple of years after her father's death that the core of the Sojourners, numbering three or four hundred, had left the cities and towns of the western Endrayan—which were within easy striking distance of government police forays from the adjacent Bareeshan Realm—and returned to the holy place from whence Sojourner beliefs had originally sprung.

So Mori had essentially grown up here. She'd

forgotten most of her childhood knowledge about navigating city streets and had acquired the skills needed to survive in the unforgiving Sa'drit Void. It seemed now as if she'd always known how to find food and water, how to conserve what little could be found, how to coexist with the Mother World and her Hidden Hand, never forgetting the fundamental principle of the Sojourners' belief: that the land did not belong to the people—the people belonged to the land.

Conditions here were not as primitive now as they had been in the old times. The new Sojourners had modern weapons, tools, and techniques to help them. Evain, and later Lessandra and the other leaders of the group, understood the practical need to utilize every advantage they could in their war with the government.

Mori hurried along the path that wound around the rim of Sanctuary Canyon. Here, forces she could barely fathom had wielded the very powers of creation to sculpt a landscape she would always regard as miraculous. The canyon itself was a broad chasm, a semicircle of layered rock that widened as it rose. But it did not open to the sky, for at the widest point, the canyon blended into thousand-foot-high walls that leaned in as if frozen in precarious midcollapse. In the bowl of the central hollow, the furies of wind and water, fire and ice, had cut through giant blocks of sandstone, reshaping them into fragile arches. On one side, floodwaters had crafted a gallery of swirling chambers and tunnels that overlapped with astonishing complexity.

But most miraculous of all was the cradle of everything the Sojourners had been and might become—

the Stone City. All those primal forces had carved a long, low diagonal cleft in the belly of Mount Abrai. There, perched in this niche above Sanctuary Canyon, Mori's ancestors had built their most sacred place. At this time of day, the rays of the setting sun streamed over the cliffs that guarded the front of the wide gorge, splashing the facades of the Stone City with golden light. The buildings were as old as the Sojourners, constructed of meticulously honed sandstone bricks. They ranged in size from hovels to a four-level structure with arched ramparts.

Mori found Lessandra hunched over the furrows of her garden in a pool of afternoon sunlight. Although the Stone City was in shadow most of the day, hardy species of plant life needing minimal light managed to sprout, including vines bearing the sweet blue silberry. But this year's vines were shriveled and barren. A hint of a breeze riffled Lessandra's white hair as she pressed seeds into the ground and patted handfuls of gritty soil over them.

"Nothing grew this year, Lessandra," Mori said. "The underground springs have dried up. What's the point of planting more seeds?"

Lessandra picked up her walking stick, dug it into the ground, and used it to stand up. Her right leg was missing below the knee, the hem of her legging pinned up to cover the stump. She propped the stick's padded knob under her arm. She wasn't young, and she looked older. One lashless eyelid drooped, and a fine network of creases incised her leathery skin. She fixed Mori with a one-eyed gaze. "Because it's our way. It's a renewal of hope that our Mother will forgive us for what's been done to her land. She'll see we're trying to make it better. And she'll send us the water we need. Sacrifice and resurrection. Why are you questioning the Testament?"

Mori replied with a sullen shrug. "It just seems so useless."

The old woman rested her weight on the crutch. "You know better than that," she scolded.

"We spotted someone coming."

"Who?"

"Couldn't tell. Too far away. Looked like two alive, one dead."

"Don't know who." Lessandra sighed. "Well, we'll know soon enough. Spread the word—tell everyone to gather here once the travelers are inside the canyon. I'll do the service then. I'll be inside meanwhile." She muttered an invocation over the newly planted seeds, then hobbled to the open door of the two-story building adjacent to her garden.

The two surviving fighters rode their ealixes through the pass below the lookout point atop the broken back of the Abraian range. They followed the meandering arroyo that led into Sanctuary Canyon, but that was as far as the beasts could go. Surefooted as they were in open terrain, they were simply too bulky to clamber up steep slopes, so they were turned loose by their riders to join the small herd of perhaps two dozen animals grazing on the brambles and prickle brush that grew along a desiccated stream bed. The tired trickle of water springing from a subterranean source was just enough to keep the ealixes alive.

Using a rough-weave blanket from the dead man's pack, the riders fashioned a sling in which to carry the corpse up the switchback trail snaking to the top of the canyon bowl. By the time they reached the encampment, all three hundred residents were gathered in the natural amphitheater behind Lessandra's abode. Gouged out of the stone by prehistoric water flows, the theater had been enhanced by Sojourner masons, long since dead, who had cut curved benches into the mountainside. Mori and Glin waited near Lessandra as the pair of riders gently laid their burden on the ground, then pushed back their own hoods. It was Mori's first chance to see who had lived and who had died. The dead man was Bradsil. There was a scorched spot on his chest where he'd been shot, and his face was puffed and caked with blood. He had been beaten before they executed him.

Mori was sorry that Bradsil had been killed, especially since he and his wife were expecting a baby. But she hadn't known him well. And she was relieved to see that her father's friend Durren had come back in one piece. Durren had been one of Mori's surrogate parents, probably her favorite. She greeted him with a hug, then looked up into his weathered face, with the long scar down his left cheek. She had always been curious about how he got it, but she was afraid to ask. His whiskers sagged, matching the weariness in his heavy-lidded eyes.

The other survivor was a fighter not much older than Mori, and his eyes still displayed fire through the veil of his fatigue. "They murdered him," the younger man said fiercely.

Lessandra limped forward. There was no sound at all from the rest of the gathering. "Did you find him, Mikken?"

The young fighter cradled his rifle like a beloved child and nodded. "They murdered Bradsil and then threw his body where they knew we'd find him."

Glin stepped forward. "How many more, Lessandra?"

"As many as it takes," said Lessandra with a flinty glare.

"As many as it takes to satisfy your hunger for vengeance against Ruer Stross? That's not enough of a reason anymore."

"Who chose you to decide where the Hidden Hand points us?"

"No one—yet. But many of us question whether *you* can see where it points anymore."

A reed-thin man with a gray beard came up alongside Glin. "We proved we're willing to fight," he said, "and our raids have gotten more daring. They know nothing is safe from us. It's time to see if we've scared them into talking peace on our terms."

"Jaminaw," Lessandra said disdainfully, "you're a fool. Durren, did you accomplish your mission?"

He nodded. "The bomb went off as planned. Someone from the starship was there when it did, according to our agents inside."

"How much damage did it cause?"

"Enough."

Lessandra turned back to her critics. "Then Bradsil didn't die for nothing. They accomplished what they set out to do."

"But what will *that* accomplish?" Glin demanded.

Lessandra dismissed the retort with an imperious wave of her free hand. "This isn't the time or place for an argument. We have a service to perform." She limped over to face the others. "In time of death and sorrow, it is our custom, as it has been since the old times, to tell of the garden. Our Mother World created a garden, and she herself was the garden, one and the same. She allowed us to live there, and she allowed those early people to flourish. But soon the people forgot their Mother's words and ways, and they turned to new ways, bad ways. The Mother World had no choice but to punish the people, and she sent them from the garden. We Sojourners know that only when all our people live by the Mother's word again will we be allowed to return to the garden where life first bloomed. When that happens, it will bloom again, and we shall be home, living in peace and plenty for all time."

Lessandra scanned the faces of the people sitting on the stone benches, then cleared her throat. When she continued, her tone was strident. "The government of this world violates everything we believe in. They are raping our Mother World. As long as they do so, we can never compromise." She raised her hand and traced a circle in the air, then continued in a singsong: "Lord of life, Lord of death, two halves of the same. You are the master of all. You permit our sojourn in your garden-womb. Unless there is death, there cannot be life. Grant us peaceful renewal. Harvest our souls."

She bowed her head for a few moments of quiet, then looked up and waved to a pregnant woman seated in the second row of benches. "Kuri, come here."

Bradsil's widow, Mori thought, and watched as Kuri approached Lessandra. For the first time she realized

Kuri couldn't be more than a year or two older than she was, and she wondered if she could be as stoic if her husband was killed.

"We confirm the circle of life," Kuri whispered, her eyes dry and unseeing, as she repeated Lessandra's gesture. "The circle and the cycle are all in life and time. There is no beginning and no ending, just the circle."

Lessandra patted Kuri's bulging abdomen. "You and your child are symbols of the circle, as are we all. Within that circle, we all share your loss."

Kuri nodded numbly, then turned back the way she had come.

At a signal from Lessandra, two burly young men picked up the blanket-wrapped body of Bradsil. "Take our brother and commit him to the Cave of Remembrance," she intoned.

Mori glanced at Glin and sensed her barely suppressed anger. When Kuri and the bearers were out of earshot, Glin exploded.

"That cave is overflowing with your dead bodies, Lessandra! When will you come to your senses and stop this bloodshed?"

"When they give us back our world," the other woman replied.

Mori couldn't listen any longer.

Bad enough that there was bloodshed between the Sojourners and Stross, but for the Sojourners to fight among themselves . . .

She ran until she reached the ledge. From there she watched the ealix herd grazing calmly down in the crook of the canyon. She started when she felt a strong hand enclose her shoulder, but relaxed when she realized it was Durren. "What's wrong?"

She shrugged, blinking back tears. "I guess I'm just confused."

"About what?"

"Whom to believe, what to believe . . ."

"You believe what your father taught."

"I'm not sure I even remember what my father taught. I certainly don't remember my father." She took a composing breath. "He taught me to think. You taught me to act—to ride and shoot, to survive out there." She nodded toward the dusk-shrouded desert. "It's easier to believe in actions. Especially when everybody's thoughts collide."

Durren smiled down at her. "To tell you the truth, I always had a hard time understanding everything what your father said myself."

She gave him a quizzical stare. "You did? But you were almost like brothers."

"Even brothers don't always understand each other. To Evain, everything was so complicated."

"You loved him, didn't you?"

"Yes, I did. He was a good man. He believed in the right things, and he put his life on the line for them."

"Would I have loved him if I'd known him?"

Durren nodded. "I'm sure of it."

They were quiet for a few moments, watching the tranquil ealixes down below. "Durren, did you—"

He winced briefly. "Oh, Mori, don't ask me that."

"I *have* to," she said, her expression hardening. "Did you find out anything about my father?"

"Little one, that's not why we went to Bareesh."

"But you know what that escaped prisoner said when we saw him at Crossroads. He swore he talked to Evain in the prison hospital less than a year ago."

"I know what he said."

"And you said you'd see what you could find out—"

Durren's temper flared. "We were on a mission. We lost a good fighter. We're lucky the two of us got away alive. Mori, we can't drop everything to find out about rumors—"

She cut him off. "Do *you* really think he's dead?"

"I don't know."

"Do you think there's any chance at all he might not be?"

He took a deep breath before answering. "A chance."

"That's all I wanted to know." She smiled. "I'll see you later, Durren."

"Durren." Lessandra beckoned him over to where she was talking with Glin and Jaminaw. "This is our time; I'm sure of it. It's in the Testaments, just as Evain preached before they caught him. This starship that has arrived—it's the Hidden Hand working for us."

He shook his head. "I don't understand."

"Durren, do you think we can kidnap the captain of the *Enterprise?*"

Glin's eyes opened wide. "Have you lost your mind?"

"No," said Lessandra, "I'm using my mind, which is something you should try doing more often. Durren, what about it?"

He thought a moment. "Our agents say the captain stays on his ship. It was his executive officer, a man named Riker, who beamed down with some Federation representative."

"Good enough. This executive officer, Riker, will do as a hostage."

Glin's disbelief grew. "And what if this captain—what's his name?"

"Picard," said Durren.

"What if this Captain Picard won't bargain with us?"

Lessandra's face remained impassive. "Then Executive Officer Riker may very well become a casualty of war."

Chapter Seven

WESLEY CRUSHER sat cross-legged on his bed. "I *do* miss you, Mom, but it's not as bad as I thought."

Beverly Crusher, on Wesley's cabin viewer, feigned deep distress. "Words to warm a mother's heart."

"You know what I mean," Wes laughed. "I hardly have time to think about it."

"Are you eating?"

Wes rolled his eyes at the indignity of this maternal interrogation. "Of course. How's your job going?"

"Well, I've discovered that being chief of Starfleet Medicine has its good points and its bad points. Too much administration, not enough medicine."

Wesley glanced at the time on his computer screen. "Mom, I have to go."

"Bridge duty?"

"No, I have to give a report to Captain Picard."

Beverly's eyebrows arched beneath her red hair. "I'm impressed."

"No big deal." Wesley shrugged. "It was just a little research project Data gave me."

"Has he learned to tell a joke yet?"

"Not exactly," Wesley said. "But he keeps trying. Maybe by the next time we see you . . ."

"Oh, Wes," she sighed, "I wish that could be soon, but I just don't know when I'm going to be able to escape this bureaucratic black hole."

"I understand, Mom. Well, I better get going."

"Bye, honey. I love you."

"I love you, too, Mom. Bye."

Dr. Crusher's wistful smile faded from the viewer, and Wes felt a little blue, the way he always did after they'd spoken by comm channel. These were the moments when he felt most alone. But he'd stayed with the ship by choice, and now he had work to do.

He slid off the bed, straightened his uniform, and headed for the bridge.

Captain Picard peered across his ready-room desk. "I gave this assignment to you, Mr. Data."

"And I gave it to Ensign Crusher, sir. I felt it would be useful for him to gain experience doing research not directly related to his special skills in engineering and propulsion science."

Seated on the corner of Picard's desk, Riker nodded his approval. "A reasonable reassignment, Data. Very well, Mr. Crusher. Report on the Sojourners."

Wesley swallowed, wishing his mouth didn't taste like he'd taken a swig of composite-repair glue. He stood so stiffly he could barely breathe. "Yes, sir."

"At ease, Ensign," Riker said. "My granddad used to tell me, 'Look 'em in the eye and tell 'em what you know.' "

"Yes, sir." Wesley loosened up as he went along. "There wasn't that much information in the Federation files, so I did a little searching. The Sojourners were originally a small religious group that began in the Endrayan Realm—that's the province next to the one where the government is now—about two thousand years ago. They believed in coexisting with nature. I guess you could say that belief was the basis for their whole religion. The realm where they lived wasn't very fertile, but it was possible to farm there with the help of irrigation. And there were lots of mineral and ore deposits, so mining also got started there."

"On a small scale, no doubt?" said Picard.

"Very small, sir, since there wasn't any industrialization at all on Thiopa until about a century ago. But the other Endrayans, the ones who didn't join the Sojourners, started exploiting the land, digging irrigation ditches, diverting streams and rivers, digging mines. To the Sojourners, all those things were violations of the land—they call Thiopa their Mother World."

"An image," Data interjected, "that is common to many primitive humanoid cultures throughout the galaxy."

"Anyway," Wes continued, "the Sojourners left the settled part of Endraya and moved out into a really isolated desert area called the Sa'drit Void. Even today the Void is pretty much unsettled. When they got there, they built a village in a place called Sanctuary Canyon. They have a very strong belief in sacred places, and they decided this would be the most sacred Sojourner place in the whole world."

"What happened after that?" said Picard.

"This small religious village existed for a couple of hundred years, almost like a monastery. Some people left the group, some others came to join it, but the population never varied much from three or four hundred. The Sojourners did a lot of writing and praying, and they sent what they called mentors out to other parts of the world to try to convert people to the Sojourner way, without much success. The movement broke up after two hundred years, and the Sojourners blended back into the developing society in Endraya—"

"Until Ruer Stross led his military coup and took over Thiopa," Data interrupted.

Picard gave him a sidelong glance. "Thank you, Mr. Data—but Ensign Crusher is doing fine."

"Data's right, sir," Wesley went on. "When Stross became sovereign protector and started dealing with the Nuarans, it was as if Thiopan society went into fast forward. A lot of people who weren't Sojourners got scared by what was happening. A teacher named Evain, who lived in Endraya, started studying what the original Sojourners had written down almost two thousand years ago. Those writings are known as the Testaments. Evain started updating all those old books and preaching a modern version of the old religion."

"How large a following did he have?" asked Riker.

"Not very large at first, maybe a few thousand. But they tended to be young, well-educated people. Then, after ten years or so, Thiopa started seeing the negative side of uncontrolled technology—like all the pollution down there now. And more and more people started paying attention to what Evain and the other Sojourners were talking about. They had demonstrations and riots and strikes. The government even had to declare martial law for almost two years. They had troops guarding factories, and they started arresting suspected Sojourners."

"Interesting," Picard said. "Did they arrest this Evain?"

"Not right away. Things got better for a while, then worse again. Especially in Endraya, which was the least prosperous realm on the planet, because of the dry climate out there. About twenty years ago, the Endrayans started running out of water for irrigation, and more and more people there joined the Sojourners, or at least sympathized with them. Stross was afraid the Sojourners threatened his government. So they arrested Evain."

"Did they execute him?"

"No, sir. But he died in prison a few years later, or so they say. At about the same time, the most dedicated Sojourners moved out to the Sa'drit Void, where their religion got started. And that's where they still live. As we've already seen, they're capable of mounting very successful terrorist attacks on the government, even right in Bareesh, the capital."

"Hmmm," Picard mused. "I wonder where these Sojourners are getting their weapons?"

"I wondered about that, too, Captain," Wesley said. "But I couldn't find out anything."

"Thank you, Mr. Crusher—very thorough job of research," Data said.

"Better watch your back, Data." A smile played across Riker's lips.

Data's head swiveled as he took the phrase literally. "That is difficult without a mirror, sir."

Riker and the others stifled their laughter. "Never mind, Data."

"Ahh," said Data after a moment. "A colloquialism."

He and Wes returned to their bridge shift, leaving Picard and Riker to their deliberations. "There's obviously a lot of symbolism involved in this conflict," said the first officer. "Two thousand years of religious passions unleashed . . ."

"Mmmm. Are you a religious man, Number One?"

"You can't grow up in Alaska, as I did, with all that pristine natural beauty around you, and not wonder about how it got there." Riker's voice took on a husky reverence. "Standing on the edge of a glacier, with amazing mountains on one side and a pod of orcas leaping out of an icy ocean on the other—that's a religious experience. But if you mean religious in the formal, organized sense, no, sir."

Picard rested his chin on his hand. "I sang in a church choir when I was a boy."

"I never knew that, sir."

"Yes, well, it was more of a musical experience than a religious one. But we sang in one of those magnificent cathedrals . . . must've been a thousand years old, taken generations to build. Incredible architecture and workmanship, soaring spires and arches."

"I know the kind you mean. I saw some when I toured Europe."

Picard fell silent for a lingering moment, then looked directly at Riker. "But I never felt a holy presence in that place, Number One. Never felt that sensation of wonder and belonging until my first voyage into deep space. That's when it dawned on me that no structure or philosophy devised by man could ever hope to represent or replicate divinity." He shrugged. "At least, that's my opinion."

"Mine, too, Captain. So here we are, mixed up in a fight that seems to be as much religious as it is political."

"Yes. I wish I had a better grasp of the inflammatory capabilities that seem to be inherent in that combination. What's your prognosis for a peaceful settlement on Thiopa?"

"Not good, sir."

The intercom tone was followed by Data's voice. "Captain Picard?"

"Yes, Data?"

"I am beaming down to Thiopa now for my meeting with Dr. Keat. Is there anything specific about which you would like me to attempt to gather information?"

"Yes. Obviously, find out what you can about this proposed weather control project. But we also need to know more about the role of science and scientists in this society—and how all that relates to the conflict between the government and the Sojourners. Give me a full report as soon as you return."

"Yes, sir."

Data stepped onto the transporter pad. "Energize." His form sparkled and faded—then resumed its solid shape in the lobby of the Thiopan Science Council building, one of the glistening government structures in Bareesh. Kael Keat was just coming down a broad curving staircase to welcome him. "Commander Data, I've got transportation waiting outside. There are some things I'd like to show you." In contrast to the elegant attire she'd worn the previous evening, Dr. Keat was dressed in khaki shorts and a breezy open-necked blouse.

The vehicle was low and sleek, with a tinted canopy allowing the passengers an unobstructed view. Data climbed into the passenger seat as Keat slid in beside him. Door panels glided into place as the bubble top closed automatically over them. Keat touched a hand throttle and they accelerated smoothly, with only the faintest thrum of an engine. "This is our newest model. Solar powered, clean and quiet. We got the technology from the Nuarans before our split. This way, we won't waste fossil fuel on transportation."

"Will that make much difference in your air-pollution quotient?"

"Not much. Unfortunately, I haven't been able to convince the powers at the top that we should phase out all fossil-fuel burning. So what we save on transportation I'm afraid we'll just burn for some other kind of energy production."

"Would it be correct to surmise that you and your government are not in accord on environmental policies?"

Keat threw back her head and laughed. "Are you programmed for understatement, Commander?"

Humor, Data thought. *Another chance to master the art.* The android gazed blankly at her for a moment, then grimaced in the best imitation of her laugh he could muster. "No," he said, instantly resuming his normal equability.

She gave him a double-take glance.

"Was a humorous response on my part not appropriate?" he asked.

"Appropriate, yes. Just—just not very well executed. No offense."

"None taken," he said brightly. "There are many complexities of humanoid behavior for which I was not programmed. My shipmates are sometimes too circumspect in administering corrective comments, even when I ask for them. So I appreciate your directness."

"Well, that's good, Data. Because I am nothing if not direct. It's a good if somewhat troublesome quality to have."

"Troublesome? How?"

"Not everyone appreciates it. My tendency to speak plainly probably closed as many doors for me as it's opened—but the ones it did open were the important ones. Besides, it's just the way I am. You seem to lack the programming for certain subtleties, and I don't have the time for them, so I think you and are going to get along quite well."

"That is gratifying to know, Dr. Keat."

They left the government center and took several turns to reach a two-lane road that hugged the slopes above the withered Eloki River. The highway's elevation made it possible to see a considerable distance both up- and downstream. Both riverbanks were solidly developed; the side they were driving on appeared to be largely residential, whereas the far bank was industrial, with factory and processing facilities extending for several kilometers in all directions. The air was murky on both sides, but the visible blanket of poison haze was far heavier on the industrial bank.

"Are androids like you standard equipment on Starfleet starships?"

"On the contrary, I am the only one."

"Really? Where did you come from? Did Starfleet build you?"

"No, Doctor. I came from the Omicron Theta star system, where I was built at an independent science colony. I was found there by the U.S.S. *Tripoli.*"

"Found? You mean, this colony left you there?"

"In a sense. The colony was destroyed, with no survivors. I had been completed and tested, but not really activated. The colonists left me out in the open, near a beacon."

"How long ago?"

"Twenty-seven years."

Keat grunted in fascination. "Do you know who's responsible for designing you?"

"I did not, until an *Enterprise* mission took us to Omicron Theta. It seems a Dr. Noonien Soong—"

"I've read about him."

"That is not surprising, for someone with your scientific training. Dr. Soong was considered the most brilliant cybernetics expert on earth, but he failed in a highly publicized effort to build a positronic brain. He considered this an extreme disgrace and evidently felt his career had been destroyed."

"That's very sad."

"He disappeared soon after the positronic project collapsed, and no one knew what had become of him—until we found his lab on Omicron Theta. He had gone to the colony under an assumed name and resumed his work there. I am the result," Data concluded with total modesty.

"Looks as if he succeeded after all. Too bad he didn't live to rake in the rewards. That often happens to scientists." Her voice hardened. "As a group, we get more blame and less credit than we deserve—a trap I plan to avoid."

Kael Keat swerved sharply off the main road, and the vehicle bounced down a long gravel drive that dipped between crouched hills. She stopped as they reached a five-meter-high chain-link fence topped with lethal-looking coils of barbed wire. Several hundred meters past the barriers stood a bombed-out building hulk, mostly rubble and twisted girders, with few recognizable walls still standing. "That's where *I* was created, Commander Data."

"I do not understand."

"That building is our monument to stupidity—the remains of our Advanced Energy Institute. The work being done there was supposed to save us from our dependency on nonrenewable energy sources, replacing them with a limitless supply of clean, safe energy."

"It did not work."

"No, it didn't. The Science Council has always been responsible for overseeing all technological development on our world. And when I was young, they could do no wrong. By the time I left Thiopa to study for my advanced degrees, we were already facing the consequences of uncontrolled progress. When I was offworld, I saw a whole new approach. I learned that technological advancement didn't have to be won at the expense of global health and sanity. By the time I came home, it was obvious to me and other younger scientists that if we didn't change our ways, progress was going to be fatal to Thiopa. And we said so. In fact, we screamed as loud as we could."

"Apparently, no one listened."

"Not until the Advanced Energy Institute place blew up one morning. The head of the Science Council was a little burrowskratt named Buvo Osrai. He always told Stross what the protector wanted to hear, the truth be damned. Never told him that we had to stop plundering our own world—and had to stop the Nuarans from doing it, too. Osrai and the other ten Science Council members were down there at the AEI when it went. They were all killed, along with a hundred other people; an additional three hundred were badly hurt." Keat poked the hatch release and the canopy opened. They got out of the vehicle, and Data followed Dr. Keat to the forbidding barricade. "There was a huge panic. Stross remembered how I'd been the most adamant warning alarm, and he shoved me into Osrai's job. He told me I could appoint a whole new council, and he swore he wanted the truth from then on."

"What did you do?"

"I shook like a scared baby—and then I grabbed the opportunity of a lifetime. I had the chance to build a whole new science establishment and do it right."

"Were you successful?"

She flashed an enigmatic smile. "It's still too early to tell. We're just now discovering all the sins that were committed by the scientists who died in that building. But I'm the one who finally made Stross understand that we were destroying Thiopa with the technology we learned from the Nuarans, the bloodsuckers of the galaxy. I told Stross he had to cut our ties with those bastards and beg the Federation for help. Which is why your ship's here."

"Is this weather control project one of your ideas?"

"Mm-hmm. I thought it was the right time for something bold and outlandish. Stross liked the sound of it, and that's all we needed to get the funding." They returned to the vehicle and headed back toward Science Council headquarters.

Data continued conversing about the weather control plan. "From what we were able to observe from orbit, the damage to Thiopa's ecology appears quite severe."

"Oh, it looks pretty severe from inside the damage zone, too, believe me, Commander."

"I studied all available reports on similar attempts on other planets."

"Did you? I would love to see those. We don't have access to all the data you'd have in your ship's computers. Do you think your captain would allow that?"

"I shall relay your request. But you may find those files dismaying. No planet has successfully accomplished what you have set out to do."

"Oh, it's complicated—no doubt about that. But we've got some fresh approaches in mind. My attitude is, everything that's *been* done was once considered impossible. But somebody had to be desperate enough to try it first. And you said yourself that we're pretty desperate here on Thiopa."

"Would it be possible for me to examine your detailed proposal and see some of the actual work you have done?"

"Some of it, yes, but a lot of it is classified. I'm sure you can understand that."

"Completely. But I am always interested in innovation."

When they arrived at the Science Council, Dr. Keat took her visitor up to her office, which had not a book, paper, or computer cassette out of place. "I'm quite fastidious," she admitted. "I drive some of the others crazy when I go into their labs and offices and start tidying up and putting away. There's one guy who loves piles, and damned if he doesn't know exactly where everything is. But I can't work that way."

She guided Data to a computer terminal, which she blocked from certain secret memory files. "Present Commander Data with the original weather control proposal."

The system obliged, and Data skimmed material that was dense with equations and diagrams at a speed that startled Dr. Keat. "Can't your system scan any more rapidly?" he asked.

"I'm afraid not."

He swiveled the chair to face her. "You are planning a planetary net of four hundred satellites?"

"That's right. We'll be using a variety of electromagnetic radiation to produce and manipulate magnetic fields as well as raising or lowering atmospheric and oceanic temperatures."

"Yes, I could see that. But in addition to the actual launching and maintenance of so many satellites, your network will require large amounts of energy and will have to be controlled by a complex and infinitely adjustable computer program."

"Quite true, Commander Data. How we've mastered those obstacles . . . well, that's the part I can't reveal to you. Not now, at any rate."

Data's head tilted. "When?"

The enigmatic half-smile curled the corners of Keat's mouth again. "That will depend on how strong an alliance is formed between Thiopa and the Federation. We're more inclined to reveal secrets to close friends."

"*Enterprise* to Commander Data." Captain Picard's voice issued from Data's uniform communicator.

He touched the chest insignia to reply. "Data here, sir."

"Commander Riker is preparing to beam down with Mr. Undrun. I'd like you to return to the ship. In view of recent events, I'd like to minimize the number of senior personnel down there at any one time."

"Yes, sir. Please stand by." He stood and looked at his host. "Thank you for your time, Doctor. I found my visit quite enlightening."

"If you and your captain have any more questions, feel free to ask. I can't answer everything, but I'll answer what I can. Oh, and don't forget to ask the captain if I can see those files on weather-related projects."

Data nodded, then tapped his communicator again. "Transporter room, this is Lieutenant Commander Data. Ready to beam up—energize."

Riker watched as Data's form sparkled and took solid shape in the transporter chamber. The android stepped off the platform. "Did you acquire any useful information?" the first officer asked.

"Quite a bit, Commander," Data replied.

"Good. I'll look forward to hearing about it."

The door hissed open. Undrun entered from the corridor and Data headed for the bridge. The ambassador was bundled up against what he still perceived as arctic temperatures inside the starship. Riker felt the involuntary prickle of his neck hairs—Undrun's presence was all it took to boost his blood pressure.

"What's the delay, Commander Riker?" Undrun demanded.

"Delay? I was waiting for—" Riker caught himself, closed his eyes for a second, and took a deep breath. "Never mind." He motioned the diminutive envoy onto the platform, then took his own place—on the far side of the chamber. Neither looked at the other. "Energize," said Riker.

"If that so-called storage facility isn't cleaned up—" The hum of the transporter swallowed Undrun's voice.

Seconds later Undrun's voice regained substance at the same rate as his reassembled body. "—I simply will not agree to handing these supplies over."

They had materialized inside the depot this time, midway between the building's airlock and Supervisor Chardrai's office. Hands on hips, Riker looked down at Undrun and made an unsuccessful attempt to smooth the aggravated edge in his voice. "Ambassador, at least give the man a chance to show us something other than the inside of his office."

"It's not my fault our first inspection was interrupted by a terrorist bombing," Undrun sniffed.

They walked briskly to the supervisor's office, where Chardrai was waiting for them. The same guard stood at his post just inside the door. Chardrai greeted them curtly. "Gentlemen, if you're ready, I'll give you that tour of the facility now."

"Will we be safe?" Undrun wanted to know.

"The place is as secure as we can make it. If you'll come this way . . ." Chardrai led the visitors back out to the corridor, then through a metal door to a caged-in catwalk suspended high over the depot floor five levels below. The guard trailed a few paces behind. This passage, with heavy grating for its floor and open-mesh sides and ceiling, was connected to a network of similar walkways winding through the warehouse's cavernous interior, with ramps, ladders, and freight elevators linking upper and lower storage platforms and sections. There were few solid walls and floors, lending the place a skeletal look.

"Down there is where we'll keep the seed," Chardrai said, pointing to the floor below. "We'll—"

"Enterprise to Commander Riker." The voice was Captain Picard's, and it came from the communicator on Riker's chest.

"Excuse me, Supervisor," Riker said. He activated his comm channel. "Riker here. Go ahead, sir."

"We're picking up an indeterminate number of Nuaran vessels at the edge of sensor range."

"Intent?"

"Unknown as yet, Number One."

"I'll beam back up, Captain."

"Not necessary."

"But if the ship could come under attack, I should be there."

"Are you saying Mr. Worf and I are incapable of handling a few Nuaran interceptors without you?"

"Not at all, sir. It's just that—"

"Without the element of surprise, it's unlikely the Nuarans pose any danger to the ship, Number One. I just wanted you apprised of the situation in case we do come under attack and we can't beam you up for the moment."

"Captain," Riker said, "their pattern is to strike quickly and flee. Any combat situation is likely to be of brief duration."

"Lieutenant Worf agrees with your assessment, Number One, and we're taking the necessary precautions.

"Make sure you protect those cargo ships!" Undrun said, leaning into Riker's chest to make sure he could be heard.

"We *will*, Mr. Ambassador," Picard said firmly.

Riker was still concerned. "I'd be more comfortable back up there, sir."

"You've got a mission to accomplish, Commander Riker."

"Very well. But keep me posted."

"Affirmative. *Enterprise* out."

Chardrai, who had remained silent during the exchange, arms folded tightly across his chest, now spoke.

"If you're ready, Commander . . ."

"We are quite ready, Supervisor," Riker said. "Lead on."

Chardrai took him and Undrun through a passage bridging two platforms. Below them was a straight fifty-foot drop to the basement floor. Though little activity could be seen from their vantage point, the mechanical noises of motors and chains and pulleys echoed and creaked through the girders and grates that were this building's bones and sinew. Undrun's habitual bluster seemed tamed for the moment by a fear of falling; he kept a steady grip on the catwalk's railing.

"How old a facility is this?" Riker asked.

"About thirty years,' the Thiopan manager said. "The bomb damage is the first time it's ever needed structural repairs. Pretty solid, overall."

"Have those repairs been made yet?" asked Undrun.

Chardrai gave him a disbelieving stare. "It hasn't even been a day."

"The Federation has made a major investment in this shipment of relief supplies. What if other bombings damage other parts of your warehouse? How do I know that investment will be safe?"

"As I said, we do the best we can. If your Federation would help us control the terrorists who are doing the damage—"

"We can't do that," Riker said. "Our laws are very strict when it comes to interfering in the affairs of other worlds."

Chardrai grunted mockingly. "That's what the Nuarans told us."

"Closing at high speed, Captain," Commander Data reported. "Five vessels this time."

Picard sat calmly in his seat. "Hailing frequencies, Mr. Worf."

"Open, Captain."

"*Enterprise* to Nuaran vessels. This is Captain Jean-Luc Picard. We request communication in the interest of avoiding further hostilities."

Worf frowned. "Captain, I suggest that we raise

shields and arm weapons systems, in view of the Nuarans' previous actions."

"Patience, Lieutenant. Raise shields, weapons on standby. I hope we won't need them." Picard repeated his message.

"No response, sir," Worf said.

"They are still closing, Captain," Data said, scanning his console. "Course—evasive."

Once more, Picard thought. *"Enterprise* to Nuaran vessels. I repeat, we are on a peaceful mission, and we request communication with you." Picard drew in a breath of frustration. "Lieutenant Worf, go to yellow alert. Arm phasers and lock on targets."

"Tracking lock engaged on all five vessels, sir. Awaiting your order."

Picard leaned forward in his chair. "Range, Mr. Data?"

"Thirty thousand kilometers . . . twenty . . ."

"Optimum range, sir," Worf said.

"I'm aware of that, Lieutenant," Picard said, unperturbed.

On the big viewscreen, the five Nuaran spacecraft had grown from flitting pinpoints to sleek harbingers of death. Three ships peeled out of their ever-changing formation and swung wide around the *Enterprise,* then dived toward the freighters trailing behind while the other two intruders cartwheeled toward the starship.

"Hold your fire," Picard said calmly. His gaze never wavered from the on-screen image of the enemy ships, closing, closing, swerving and swooping like acrobats.

Worf tensed over the phaser controls, his warrior's muscles coiled for battle.

The ships moved closer, filling the viewscreen, rushing like mad birds of prey, then speeding past the *Enterprise* and off into space without firing a shot. There was an audible release of held breath on the starship bridge.

Geordi shook his head. "Playing chicken with a starship?"

Data flashed a quizzical look over his shoulder. "Imitating barnyard fowl?"

"An old earth game involving foolish dares," Geordi explained.

"As I understand it," Troi said, "there is a serious purpose to this game—to test the nerve and resolve of a potential opponent."

"That's right," Geordi said. "Make the other guy commit himself, and maybe force him into making a fatal mistake."

Data's brows arched. "Intriguing premise. What is the proper response?"

"Making a first move," said Picard, "that could also be the final move. *Enterprise* to away team."

"Riker here, sir. Trouble?"

"Affirmative. Nuaran interceptors have reentered our orbital quadrant. No shots fired yet."

"We're fine where we are, sir. We still have more to see. We'll stand by."

"Very well. Picard out. Mr. Data, any signs of the Nuarans?"

"No, sir. They have gone out of sensor range again."

Worf growled deep in his throat. "They'll be back."

"The Nuarans weren't exactly happy to go when Protector Stross broke those trade ties," Supervisor

Chardrai told Riker and Undrun as they watched five overhead winches perform an intricate ballet, transferring storage containers across the depot's wide central bay. The hydraulic arms were anchored somewhere up in the dark rafters, with silver cables spinning down like spider's silk.

"How did most Thiopans feel about the Nuarans?" Riker asked.

Chardrai shrugged. "They were robbing our planet and leaving garbage behind. Friends don't do that," he said simply. "Let me take you down to where we plan to store the Federation supplies."

Riker and Undrun followed the Thiopan to the end of the walkway, where an elevator cage dangled in a latticework shaft. The guard lagged behind, mumbling into his wristband communication device.

"Jeldavi," Chardrai called, "what's the delay?"

"No delay, Supervisor. Just checking in." The guard joined them in the lift. But before he could clang the safety gate shut, another pair of guards trotted toward them from an intersecting passageway.

"Going down?" the taller of the two called.

"Down," said Jeldavi, holding the gate half open. The other two stepped in and muttered a thank-you. With a jolt, the car began its descent.

Undrun peered down and turned colors when he saw that the grilled floor panels afforded a sightline all the way down the shaft.

Riker noticed, and tried not to enjoy the moment. "Just don't look."

Suddenly the elevator screeched to halt between levels, staggering Riker, Undrun, and Chardrai, but not the trio of guards, each of whom had braced himself with one hand and taken out palm-sized spray bottles with the other. Before Riker could react, the guards squirted a heavy mist in the faces of the other three. The substance had an immediate effect, and Riker, the envoy, and Supervisor Chardrai collapsed in a tangle of limbs.

Jeldavi, the guard from the supervisor's office, restarted the lift and took it down to the basement level, where pink vapor lamps cast eerie shadows through the support struts. He jammed the control lever to cut power, bringing the car to a jouncing halt, then threw open the gate. He turned to the taller of his two companions. "Rudji, get the wagon. Ligg, tie up Riker." Within seconds, the tall guard came scurrying back with a molded cargo box on top of a wheeled platform. They lifted Riker, now bound tightly hand and foot, and dumped him into the container. Rudji was about to slam the lid when Jeldavi lurched forward and reached inside. He snatched the Starfleet insignia from Riker's chest.

"What's that?" asked Ligg.

"It's a communicator. I saw him use it to talk to his ship." Jeldavi hurled the communicator across the warehouse. It bounced and skittered, coming to a rest somewhere in the shadows.

"Okay. Close it."

Rudji and Ligg complied, latching the cargo box on all four corners.

"Go! Now!" Jeldavi's partners started the cart rolling, and he ran behind. They found a darkened corridor and made a right-angle turn, reaching a wall with a sturdy steel hatch. The massive lock had already been jimmied. Jeldavi jumped ahead and swung it open. The other two rolled their captive into a service tunnel leading away from the storage depot. Jeldavi released the lock and closed the heavy hatch behind him. The lock clicked into place, resuming its intended function, leaving no trace of the three Sojourners, or their hostage, as they made their escape.

Lieutenant Worf's prediction about the Nuarans' return soon came true. The same five interceptors hurtled toward the *Enterprise,* while the starship held its position, making no overt moves, either offensive or defensive. This time the Nuarans cut loose with a barrage of torpedoes, all but one of them aimed at the cargo ships. The torpedoes detonated, but the *Enterprise* deflectors held firm against the onslaught.

Once again the Nuaran ships retreated at high speed following their sortie. And once again Picard sent pro forma messages after them, peaceable in substance but cautionary in subtext. Picard was a man who valued subtlety, but not at the price of clarity. There could be no mistaking his meaning: further harassment would not be tolerated.

Once again the Nuaran spacecraft ignored all hails. And they regrouped for another approach.

Picard crossed his arms over his chest. He knew these adversaries obeyed no rules. Their unpredictability added an unsettling element of danger to the situation. More than once they'd demonstrated their willingness to open fire without provocation. They had refused to respond to repeated requests for communication. And it was quite clear they were not going to disappear of their own volition. Jean-Luc Picard was unusually slow to anger, and he preferred not to utilize the great firepower of the *Enterprise*. But enough was enough. He had ships and a crew to protect, and a mission to complete.

"Captain," Data said. "The Nuaran interceptors have just come back within sensor range."

"Here we go again," Geordi said.

"In this competition known as chicken," Data said, "are there strategies to enhance one's chance of winning?"

"Timing," said Picard. "Not just the right move, but the right move at the right time . . . position of Nuaran ships, Mr. Data?" Picard asked.

"Seventy thousand kilometers and closing."

Picard leaned forward, concentration masking his emotions. "Mr. LaForge, increase the distance between the *Enterprise* and the cargo drones by ten percent."

"Sir?"

"Make it appear they're drifting away from our shield protection."

"Aye, sir."

"Mr. Worf," Picard continued, "establish and maintain phaser lock on all five targets. Geordi, prepare to drop shield protection around the cargo drones for exactly one-point-two-five seconds, on my mark. Program to resume full shield coverage after that time. Worf, synchronize your phaser controls with Geordi's shields. Simultaneous with resumption of shield protection, I want phasers to fire at all five targets. Understood?"

Both officers answered in the affirmative and quickly completed programming for implementation.

"Mr. Data," Picard said, "tell me when they're within five thousand kilometers."

"Aye, sir." Within a few heartbeats, it seemed, Data spoke up. "Approaching that margin, sir. In five, four, three, two, one—*now.*"

"Now, Geordi," Picard ordered.

The momentary power drop in shield coverage registered on the Nuarans' sensors. Only one intruder continued toward the *Enterprise.* The other four seized their chance and dived directly toward the unprotected cargo convoy like sharks sensing floundering prey. It took them just over one second to react to this perceived advantage, by which time it was gone. For just an instant, Picard's ploy left them flat-footed—just the instant needed for Worf to fire the phasers.

"Direct hits on four. One appears to be disabled," the Klingon reported.

"Captain," Data said, "the crew of the disabled vessel is being beamed off and—"

Before he could finish his sentence, the drifting Nuaran ship self-destructed, leaving behind an expanding cloud of debris. The four surviving ships limped clear of the combat zone.

"I guess they don't like to hang around after they lose," Geordi LaForge commented. He glanced at his engineering readouts. "No damage to us or the cargo drones, Captain."

"Open a channel to the away team," said Picard.

"Channel open," Worf said.

"Enterprise to Commander Riker."

Picard's brow creased when they heard no reply. *"Enterprise* to Commander Riker." He waited for a moment, then rose from his seat to face the aft bridge stations. "Geordi, check mission operations monitors."

LaForge lunged for the unmanned console a few feet from his engineering panel. His deft fingers skipped across the touch sensors. He swallowed hard, then turned back toward Captain Picard. "His life-functions monitor's been interrupted."

"What are we receiving?"

"Nothing, Captain, except a locator signal. Not even the readings we'd get if he were dead."

"Channel to Undrun," Picard said. Worf's nod told him it was open. "Picard to Ambassador Undrun. Please respond." His tone remained cool and even. Intentionally. Picard had long ago learned the necessity for a ship's commander to retain every scrap of composure, no matter what the crisis. *"Enterprise* to Undrun. Please respond." After a long moment, he looked back to Geordi. "Readings on Undrun?"

"Telemetry's nominal. He's alive."

"Then he must be unconscious. Mr. Worf, take a security team down to wherever Undrun is located." Picard addressed the intercom. "Bridge to Dr. Pulaski."

"Pulaski here, Captain."

"Report to transporter room two, please. Accompany Lieutenant Worf and his away team down to Thiopa. He'll brief you on the situation."

"How serious are the injuries, Captain?"

"We don't know. Prepare for the worst, Doctor."

"I always do."

Chapter Eight

WORF'S MASSIVE HAND closed around the small communicator as he returned to the storage depot elevator where they'd found Undrun and the Thiopan supervisor, both out cold. Kate Pulaski took some body-function readings and made a quick calculation with her tricorder so she could match her stimulant dosage with the non-Terran metabolisms of her patients. She pressed her hypo against their necks and administered precise injections. Seconds later, they both were coming around.

"Just lie still and let the medication take effect," the doctor said firmly.

Worf opened a channel to the ship. "Captain, Commander Riker isn't here. Ambassador Undrun and the warehouse supervisor were both found unconscious, but Dr. Pulaski says they'll recover."

"Recover from what? Can you tell what happened to them, Doctor?"

Pulaski touched her communicator. "They were overcome by some sort of paralyzing gas. It'll make them a little groggy for a while."

"Are they sufficiently recovered to tell us what happened?"

"They will be in a few minutes, Captain."

"What is that supervisor's name?"

The Thiopan shook his head to clear it, then rolled unsteadily to his feet. "That's me—Chardrai," he said, leaning on the mesh elevator wall for support. "And who're you?"

"Captain Picard of the *Enterprise*. Mr. Chardrai, would you permit us to beam you aboard our ship?"

Chardrai's eyes narrowed in suspicion. "For what?"

"Further medical care in our sickbay—and I'd like to hear what happened, face to face. It shouldn't take long."

"Don't see the harm. Sure."

"Thank you. Lieutenant Worf, have you and your men had a chance to look around down there?"

"Yes, sir. No physical evidence that we could find."

"Very well. Gather your team and Dr. Pulaski's patients and beam up when ready."

The captain waited for Pulaski's summons to sickbay, then went down to interview the only witnesses to whatever happened to William Riker. Undrun and Chardrai were seated in Pulaski's office when he arrived, accompanied by Counselor Troi. Her Betazoid empathic skills were always helpful in such situations, giving him a reliable gauge of the veracity of those being questioned.

Undrun's recollections were hazy at best, as if he hadn't been paying much attention. Supervisor Chardrai, however, was able to give a terse account, moment by moment, right up until the guards overpowered them.

"Had you ever seen these guards before?" Picard wanted to know.

"One of them, sure. Jeldavi. He's been my personal guard for months. The other two I didn't know. I run the place, but I don't get chummy with everybody we got working there."

"Have you had other incidents where Sojourners managed to infiltrate your staff?"

"No. But you can be damn sure I'm going to have everybody checked out when I get back."

Picard crossed his arms impatiently. "Apparently you have a major security problem, Mr. Chardrai. Two breaches in two days, and my first officer abducted in the process."

"As you say, Captain, I've got my problems—and now you've got yours. Can I go now?"

"Yes, of course—and we appreciate your cooperation." Picard's words were polite, but his manner distracted. He waved in the general direction of his Klingon security chief, standing by the office door. "Lieutenant Worf, show Mr. Chardrai to the transporter room and see that he's beamed down."

When they were gone, Jean-Luc Picard turned back to Ambassador Undrun, who seemed even smaller than usual as he sat in a fetal curl. "Are you certain you can't add anything to what Supervisor Chardrai told us?"

Undrun peered up and pulled his sweater up closer to his chin. "I told you, Captain Picard, I just don't remember the details—and I think I'm having a reaction to whatever venomous solution your physician shot into me without my permission."

"Unconscious people have a great deal of difficulty giving permission, Mr. Ambassador, and sometimes they die without treatment," Dr. Pulaski said, an edge sharpening her tone.

"Well, all I know is I feel dizzy." With visible effort, the Noxoran straightened. "And this whole mission is a shambles, Captain. I expect you to exercise whatever power you have to get some cooperation from these Thiopans. That relief aid has got to get to the people who need it."

Picard's jaw muscles twitched. "Ambassador Undrun, you seem not to have noticed that my first officer has been kidnapped by an opposition force which has already demonstrated that it means business."

"I've noticed, Captain Picard," Undrun said, his tone rising defensively. "I'm very sorry that Commander Riker was captured, but to blame me—"

"I never said you were to blame," Picard shot back, trying to temper his exasperation. "The Thiopan situation is far more complicated than we were led to believe. The safety of this ship and her crew have been compromised, and your single-minded concentration on delivering this emergency aid—"

In a fit of indignation, Undrun jumped to his full four and a half feet of height. "Pardon me for trying to do my job, sir. I'm going to my quarters to rest from my ordeal." With that, he shot past an astonished Picard and out of sickbay.

The captain's anger deflated and he let his shoulders

slump. "Well, I certainly handled that well." He managed a fraction of an ironic smile.

"Not without considerable provocation," said Dr. Pulaski. "He's a little weasel."

"He doesn't seem to give a damn about what's happened to Will."

"He's more concerned than he lets on, Captain," Troi said. "He seems to blame himself."

Picard and Pulaski both stared at the counselor. "He what?" said Picard. "He blames himself?"

"He certainly hides it well," Pulaski added.

"Self-recrimination seems out of character, based on what we've seen so far of Mr. Undrun," Picard said.

"I did some checking on his Federation personnel profile," Troi said. "He came from a well-to-do family on Noxor and enjoyed all the privileges that come with wealth. But the Noxorans have a strong dedication to public service. The wealthier the family, the greater the pressure to devote one's life to helping others. It's almost a military discipline that's instilled in young Noxorans."

"All right," Pulaski said, "so he joined the Federation Aid and Assistance Ministry."

"And he rose through the ranks very quickly. It's difficult to tell his age because all Noxorans look youthful, but he's quite young to have reached this level of responsibility. The captain's observation of his single-mindedness was very perceptive."

"It's very obvious," Picard interjected.

Deanna smiled. "Bureaucracies aren't famous for encouraging unbridled creativity. The combination of Undrun's strict upbringing, his narrowly directed

focus on succeeding in public service, his total acceptance of bureaucratic restraints, and his insecurity all
contribute to what we see as insensitive, unbending
concentration on a single task."

"He operates by the book," Picard said softly. "I've
known plenty of officers like that. Frankly, at the risk
of appearing insensitive, I must admit that Undrun's
childhood traumas are the least of my concerns.
Finding out who has Will Riker and getting him back
quickly and safely rank somewhat higher. Counselor,
I need you on the bridge."

Hydrin Ootherai swept into the sovereign protector's sparsely furnished office with a plump female
aide in tow, but stopped abruptly when he saw Ayli
seated on the deep-cushioned couch next to Lord
Stross. The shadowreader half reclined against the
pillowed arm, her legs tucked under her with a feline
nonchalance that somehow made her look years
younger. Her tawny hair fell across her face, but a sly
smile betrayed her pleasure at Ootherai's consternation.

"What is *she* doing here?"

"I asked her to come here. I wanted her reaction to
this."

"Afraid of another opinion?" Ayli challenged.

"Certainly not. Tresha?" He snapped his fingers
and his young assistant sprang into action, setting up a
spindly easel and placing several large boards on the
sill. The boards were covered with a cloth shroud.
When her preparations were complete, Ootherai took
up a professorial position in front of the hidden
display, visibly warming to one of his favorite
pastimes—lecturing.

"You live for these little presentations of yours, don't you?" said Ayli, a flicker of amusement glinting in her deep amber eyes.

"Symbols create reality. *You* know all about creating reality, Ayli."

Stross shifted impatiently. "Get to it, Ootherai."

"Of course, my lord. It's immensely important that we present your weather control plan as the means of saving our world."

"It *will* save the world," Stross said firmly. "But will it get the citizens back on our side?"

Ootherai circled. "Without question. It's got all the right elements. We portray the Nuarans as hateful villains. We offer a homegrown solution to a crisis caused by those villains, and we outline a bold program addressing the worries that give all of us sleepless nights. It's the oldest epic in the universe—good guys against bad, us versus them—and *you*, Sovereign Protector Ruer Stross, are its hero."

Stross laced his fingers and rested his hands on his belly, mulling over the concept. "How do we present it?"

"We mount an all-fronts assault. Special coverage in all the media, flooding our message into every Thiopan home. Rallies. Get children involved right from the start—capture the older generation by grabbing the young ones first. Make ours the tune to which every single Thiopan of intelligence will march. Positive reinforcement in every conceivable form. Mount a religious crusade that will overwhelm those pitiful Sojourners and their outdated beliefs. And at the center of the campaign, this . . ."

With a flourish, the policy minister whipped the cloth off his easel, revealing a crisply drawn logo, with the Thiopan globe in the center, a ring of tiny sparkles around it, and a single stylized flower blooming behind and above the planet, all done in vibrant hues that bore no resemblance at all to the sepia haze that hugged the real world outside Stross's windows.

Ayli peered at the design with a hint of a smile. "Don't be stunned, Hydrin—but I like it. It has a sort of magnetic charm."

Stross nodded. "Not bad, Ootherai."

"Just one little question," Ayli said. "Will this weather control project really work? Or are we selling a fantasy?"

"It will work," Stross growled. "I know it will."

Ootherai waved a hand. "That's of no consequence. The important thing is the perception, not the reality. Getting the people to devote their undying support to Lord Stross—that's what matters."

"Surely you're joking," Ayli said with a skeptical squint. "If the weather control project doesn't succeed, this planet could become unlivable. Or has that trivial fact eluded you and your symbolic brain?"

"Digest this trivial fact, Ayli," Ootherai parried, thrusting his finger at her. "If we don't regain control of the political situation on Thiopa—if we don't crush those miserable anarchists under a mountain of revitalized popular support—this government will be long gone by the time the last molecule of air is polluted beyond breathing."

The intercom on the simple plank desk beeped. "Lord Stross, Planetary Communications calling," said a controlled female voice.

Stross reached over and thumbed the switch. "Stross—what is it?"

Ootherai frowned. "I wish he'd use his full title when dealing with subordinates," he muttered.

"Captain Picard is calling from the *Enterprise.* Shall I put him through?"

"Let me screen this, Excellency," Ootherai said. Stross responded with an affirmative gesture, and Ootherai moved to the two-way viewscreen in an alcove across the room. "Communications control, I'll take it." The receiver activated and Jean-Luc Picard's face appeared on the monitor. "Captain . . ."

"Minister Ootherai, is Protector Stross available?"

"I'm afraid not. He's involved in a critical consultation and cannot be disturbed. Perhaps I would suffice?"

"I'd appreciate your passing along the substance of our conversation to him."

"Certainly, Captain. I surmise from your tone of voice that the substance is quite serious."

"It is indeed. On an inspection visit to your storage facility, my first officer was apparently taken prisoner by a team of Sojourner guerrillas. I request your assistance in effecting his safe return."

The Thiopan's expression turned remote. "I'm sorry to hear about Commander Riker's misfortune. But I fear there is little we can do to help."

"Minister Ootherai," Picard said warningly, "even though Thiopa isn't bound by Federation laws, your government has a responsibility to—"

"Captain, before you finish that thought, I am constrained to point out that your officer would be safe aboard your ship had you simply beamed the emergency supplies down upon your arrival. There was no need for any of your personnel to set foot on Thiopa."

131

"We were not aware of any danger. Your government knew we were sending people down, yet you failed to warn us—"

"We didn't know circumstances would arise that would have required warning. In hindsight, of course we would have cautioned you to keep your people on your ship. But I'm afraid hindsight won't help Commander Riker."

"What can you do to help?"

"Nothing, really."

"Pardon me?"

"Do we have a faulty signal, Captain Picard? I shall repeat: there is little we can do to help you locate your missing man. Oh, certainly we can instruct our security forces to keep an eye out for him, and we can remain alert for intelligence we might glean from our agents watching the Sojourners. But we are fighting to retain order on this planet. We simply must devote all our resources to controlling the growing threat of civil unrest. I do regret that we cannot do more, but the simple fact is, we can't."

Picard's eyes grew steely, but his inflection became almost offhand. "Without more cooperation, I'm afraid we cannot even begin delivery of those supplies Thiopa evidently needs quite badly. I'll give you twelve hours to reconsider your current position. At that time, if your government isn't more forthcoming, the *Enterprise* will leave orbit."

"Without your kidnapped officer?"

"I've lost men before, Minister Ootherai. I value every member of my crew equally, but no single life takes precedence over the safety of this vessel or her mission."

"Captain, I can hardly believe—"

Picard cut him off. "Twelve hours. We shall look forward to a change of heart. Picard out."

"Captain," Troi said, "departing without giving them the relief supplies would be punishing innocent people on Thiopa—"

"Perhaps, Counselor. But everything we've seen so far casts severe doubts on the Thiopans' claims of widespread famine. They had enough resources to throw that anniversary feast."

"Which may have been staged for effect."

"Or it may have been an example of mismanagement of resources rather than outright shortages. The Federation is not obliged to sanction such mismanagement. If Thiopa's problems are self-made, so must the solutions be."

Data swiveled in his seat. "The ecological damage to Thiopa is verifiable, sir."

"I'm aware of that, Commander, and of the likelihood of food shortages in certain areas of the planet. But at present it appears quite unlikely that any of the food we've brought will reach those who are most in need, if they are allied with the Sojourner movement."

Wesley Crusher swallowed, then spoke up. "What about Commander Riker, sir? We aren't really going to leave without him in twelve hours, are we?"

"Not without doing everything possible to locate him and get him back to the *Enterprise* alive and well," Picard said, his tone softer, but still determined. "I have a strong hunch the status quo won't last the twelve hours. Meanwhile, let's utilize our own resources. Mr. Data, initiate a sensor search for Commander Riker."

Nothing could soothe Ruer Stross like the sweet aroma of sawdust tickling his nose. He knew it to be the first sensory impression he could recall, going back to infancy. More satisfying than mother's milk, food, sunlight, sex. His father had been a woodworker, and the memory of sleeping in the cradle next to his father's workbench still gave Stross a warm glow. Unlike some fathers who wanted their work to remain mysterious to their children, as if the withholding of that knowledge could help father retain power over son, W'rone Stross had initiated his young son before the child was old enough to use the tools himself. Ruer cherished the images that were still fresh and unblemished in his heart and mind—his father's massive hand guiding the son's tiny one, providing the muscle so the boy could learn the art. All the years he'd watched his father, Ruer knew that finding objects hidden in wood was more than W'rone's livelihood—it was his life. In all other things, the elder Stross was the mildest of men. He loved his wife quietly. He took pride in his son without boasting. He helped his neighbors without fanfare. Ruer could not recall his father ever raising his voice either in anger or in joy, and he had no memories of tears or broad grins. Except in his workshop. It was as if W'rone had stored his passions, saving them for the holy place where his hands joined with nature's invisible hands to make magic.

Wherever they'd lived while Ruer was growing up, Father had always set aside a shed or cellar or room, or just a corner, to consecrate as the place where his passion could take flight. It wasn't something Ruer ever quite understood, but he never questioned it. He'd somehow absorbed the feeling and made it part of himself. Which was why, all these years later, the most powerful man in the world could find true peace only at his own workbench.

"Is this the time for puttering?" Ootherai said to the Sovereign Protector's back, since that was all he could see with Stross bent over his woodworking tools. The sawdust made the policy minister's nose twitch with the beginnings of a sneeze.

Ayli was standing with her elbows propped on the workbench, watching with interest as her ruler carefully cut shapes out of wood. She had no idea what they might eventually become.

"Any time is the time for this," Stross said in a calm voice.

"We need those Federation supplies," Ootherai said. "They will be our insurance against future dislocations—not to mention a way of convincing the people in Endraya to forsake their loyalty to the Sojourners. Without the food from the Federation, we lose that tool. You know about tools, Lord Stross."

"That I do, my friend. You need the right one for the right job. And when you can't find the one you want, you have a choice: don't do the job, or find something else that works."

"Will anything else work?" asked Ayli.

"Maybe, maybe. If we have learned anything from the Nuarans, it is the value of having something somebody else wants. The *Enterprise* has what we want. The Sojourners have what Picard wants. Find Riker—and we will get our supplies."

"You make that sound so simple," Ootherai sneered.

"Who's in charge here, anyway?" Stross said without looking up. "We've got a good idea where they're taking Riker. Mount a force to get him back."

Ootherai snorted a derisive laugh. "Invade the Sa'drit? Impossible."

"We don't have to invade. All we have to do is punish them a little. We have weapons that can do that."

"And they have weapons that can stop us."

"Use that symbolic brain of yours," Stross prodded. "Find a way."

Captain Picard sat with his back to the huge ports in the bridge observation lounge. Across the conference table, Data was completing a report on his visit to Dr. Kael Keat and her lab earlier in the day. "Your foray seems to have raised as many questions as it answered."

Data nodded. "It is safe to assume there is much Dr. Keat has not told me."

"Did you get enough on this weather control plan to judge whether it's feasible?"

"No, sir. I was able to examine only the theoretical foundations of the project."

"And what's your opinion on that?"

"Theoretically their plan could provide the sort of weather modification they seek."

"But can they put these theories into practice?"

"Doubtful, Captain. Unless they possess technological capabilities we have not observed—which is possible."

"Speaking of possibilities, do you think Dr. Keat might reveal more information to you?"

"She did seem fascinated with me." From most anyone else, the statement would have smacked of conceit. From Data, it was a simple factual account.

"Well, you're a most fascinating fellow, Mr. Data. Depending on what happens with—"

The intercom tone interrupted, followed by the unwelcome imperious voice of Frid Undrun. "Captain Picard, I want an explanation."

"Of what, Mr. Ambassador?"

"Your unauthorized actions. We'll meet now."

"If you insist. Report to the bridge conference lounge. Picard out."

Data started to get up. "Shall I leave, sir?"

"No, no," Picard replied a bit too urgently, then flattened his lips into a mirthless smile. "I have no desire to be alone with Mr. Undrun. And you may be of some help."

Moments later the door slid aside and Undrun strutted in, not bothering to sit down. "You had no right to make a unilateral decision," he said.

"And which unilateral decision is this?"

"To threaten to leave Thiopa without delivering those relief supplies. You and your crew have bungled and interfered with my mercy mission almost from the minute we left Starbase."

"You are *not* on a personal crusade," Picard thundered, reaching the limit of his patience. He wondered for the tiniest instant if Riker had gone into hiding simply to avoid having to deal with this pint-sized tyrant. "*We* are on a Federation-Starfleet mission, and I take strong exception to your suggestion that my

137

crew has performed in anything less than exemplary fashion so far as their dealings with you are concerned. My decision, unilateral or not, is consistent with my powers as captain of this vessel."

Undrun hammered his fist on the table. "Powers I can override."

"Not when this mission imperils my crew and the *Enterprise*. I am becoming more and more convinced we should never have undertaken this mission, and I plan to say exactly that in my report to both Starfleet and your Aid and Assistance Ministry. And that, for the moment, is *all* I have to say on this matter." Picard rose to his feet and marched out of the room. He went directly to the aft turbolift without a word to his bridge crew, all of whom knew enough not to divert an angry captain from his chosen course.

Undrun slumped into one of the high-backed chairs in the conference lounge, carefully facing away from the observation windows. Data remained seated, but silent.

It was the Noxoran envoy who spoke first. "You seem to be the only person aboard this ship who hasn't condemned me as a useless slime toad, Commander Data."

"Perhaps if I knew what a slime toad was . . ." the android replied earnestly.

Undrun did a double take, then realized Data was not attempting to be glib or cruel. And *that* Undrun found funny enough to warrant a sad chuckle. "I meant you haven't judged me as a bad person, just because I'm trying to do my job the only way I know how."

"It is not part of my cognitive programming to

judge other beings—unless I am requested to perform that analytical function."

"Well, then, I'm requesting it. Judge me. Give me an android's objective appraisal."

Data thought for a few moments. "Your behavior patterns seem to have a common factor."

"Which is . . .?"

"You seem excessively bound by established guidelines and precedents."

Undrun's shoulders heaved in a helpless shrug. "I can't work any other way. I need those guidelines. They function almost like a funnel. I know that whatever I pour into that funnel will come out the other end in a narrow, compact stream."

"Such methods do have a directness to them. But I have noticed that humans—particularly members of the *Enterprise* crew—do not always approach problems in what I would determine to be the most direct way. Their capacity for unpredictability and irrationality is quite limitless. And yet, although I may find their strategies baffling, they achieve the desired results." A touch of wistfulness tinged Data's expression. "In spite of considerable study, I cannot quite grasp or replicate this whimsical human creativity."

"You've got an excuse," said Undrun, leaning across the table and resting his head on folded arms. "You're restricted by your programming. But I'm a flesh-and-blood humanoid. And creativity eludes me, too."

"Biological life forms can also be limited by programming. Perhaps something in your past . . ."

"You're right."

"Please elucidate."

"I'd rather not." The diplomat shook his head with regret. "It all seemed so simple. If this mission fails, my life is as good as over."

Data's yellow eyes crinkled in sudden concern. "Is there something Dr. Pulaski can do?"

"What?"

"You said your life is in danger."

"I meant my professional life, Commander Data. To me, that *is* my life. There's an expression: we are what we eat. Well, some of us *are* what we *do*. How could such a simple mission turn into such a disaster?"

"If I may differ, this mission was not quite so simple as it appeared. We knew about the Nuaran involvement, the Ferengi threat, a certain level of societal instability on Thiopa itself. Even excluding other factors that we did not know about until our arrival, how could you have considered the known complications and still judged this mission to be simple?"

"Fact is, I didn't consider all that. All I saw was a cargo convoy delivering emergency relief supplies for which the Thiopans had virtually begged. Bringing people what they want should not be a complicated mission."

"That is true—except that humanoid beings are often reticent about accurately expressing their wants and needs. This is another element of humanoid behavior I do not yet understand. Whether it is the result of dishonesty or fear, such reticence invariably causes complications."

"Fear . . . Can I tell you my fear?"

Data answered with an accommodating nod.

"My superiors will see how badly I managed this mission—they thought it was a simple assignment, too—and they'll decide I'm incompetent. I've alienated Captain Picard, caused Commander Riker to be kidnapped—"

Data was staring in wonder now. "Most intriguing. Is this what humans call self-pity?"

Undrun stopped abruptly. "Yes . . . I guess it is."

Jean-Luc Picard liked his crew to view him as a bit of an ascetic. Not that there was any pretense in it. He wasn't an especially demonstrative man, a characteristic that arose naturally from having spent most of his adult life as a commanding officer and the bulk of that time as captain of the deep-space explorer *Stargazer*. The two-decade duration of *Stargazer*'s voyage of discovery had encouraged camaraderie, but he hadn't viewed it as a captain's option to form any deeper relationships with those serving under him.

So far he'd applied that policy to the *Enterprise* as well. Employed judiciously, it imparted an aloof mystique that elicited an extra measure of respect—a commodity that tended to facilitate the exercise of authority.

Even his physical presence contributed to Picard's aura of leadership. Not a conventionally handsome man, he had an aristocratic profile and a stern jaw. A fringe of silvered hair served to highlight the clear, piercing eyes. He wasn't a big man, yet he could dominate without effort, thanks in part to regal bearing. But his voice—alternately tempered with unadorned compassion or ringing with the resonance of confidence and power—was the key attribute with which he commanded.

All of that aside, however, the few who knew this starship captain best were well aware of his Gallic appreciation for the proverbial pleasures of wine, women, and song. And, if anything, those tastes had been honed by the relative deprivation of his years aboard the *Stargazer*. Still, that vaguely hedonistic aspect of his personality was something he preferred to keep private, which meant he kept his visits to the *Enterprise*'s Ten-Forward lounge to a minimum. He went there only for an irresistible party in progress or when he had an undeniable need to unwind.

Without question, dealing with Envoy Frid Undrun fell into the latter category. Which explained Picard's unaccustomed appearance at the end of Guinan's pastel-lit bar. She greeted him with a friendly nod. "Captain."

"Guinan."

"What can I get you? A bit of Wesburri fizz might give you a lift."

"Just some sparkling spring water with a twist of lemon, please."

A moment later she placed a tapered glass before him. "There you are."

"Thank you." He sipped. She stood, patient as always, an almost-smile playing at the corners of her mouth. Picard had noted her knack for matching her mood to that of her clients, then elevating theirs by changing her own so subtly as to escape notice. For the moment, however, she was still measuring his.

"Sometimes, I just like to watch the bubbles rising," Guinan said.

He lowered his eyes to the glass. "Mmm. Buoyancy. Not always easy to attain for the uncarbonated human."

"You've had better days . . .?"

"Does it show?"

"You're not exactly one of my regulars."

His voice dropped to a conspiratorial whisper. "How would it look to have the captain on a constant synthehol high?"

"Not good at all, Captain. But sometimes you should stop by just to say hello. I wouldn't be here if it weren't for you."

He sipped his drink. "You're doing a fine job, Guinan."

"Thank you. You know, Ambassador Undrun came in yesterday." She saw Picard's expression turn sour, as if he'd bitten into his lemon twist. "Ah, sore point, is he?"

"Not my first choice as a dinner guest."

"Also not the only thing bothering you, I'd guess."

He frowned in mock anger. "You and Counselor Troi are starting to sound very much alike."

Guinan grinned. "Our jobs do have similarities."

"But you don't have her Betazoid empathic capabilities."

"I get by," she said lightly. She took his empty glass. "More?"

Picard shook his head. "I'd better get back to the bridge."

She let out a snort. "Good thing the rest of your crew isn't so tight-lipped, or I'd never feel as if I accomplished anything. You came in here to unwind, but you still look wound up to me, Captain."

"Let's just say I'm less tightly wound."

"Captains never really unwind, do they?"

"We get by." He smiled. "Thanks for the chat."

He did feel better as he left the lounge, aware that the eyes of crew members were watching him as he passed. Guinan was correct about captains never unwinding completely. *Too much tension and you'd snap. Too little, and you'd founder at the first sign of a storm. Just enough,* he thought, *and you're braced for action.* As he headed for the bridge, Picard felt braced for the next few hours, when the decisions he would have to make might save Thiopa and Commander Will Riker—or condemn them.

Chapter Nine

RIKER'S WORLD comprised a shade more than one cubic meter, and it was dark, except for pinpoint rays of light filtering through two breathing screens, each the size of his hand. It also shook to an irregular rhythm of bone-jarring bounces. Once he'd awakened, it hadn't taken long to figure out he was being transported by motor vehicle, like a trapped animal. And, as an animal might, he wondered if he was being taken to a place of safety or slaughter? He'd tried banging on the sides and shouting, without response.

The frequent bumps and noises from outside made it clear they weren't traveling at a very high rate of speed. But since he couldn't even guess how long he'd been boxed and unconscious, there was no way to estimate how far he'd been taken from the warehouse in Bareesh. His communicator was gone—that he knew. Nothing much to do but wait . . .

It must have been three hours later when the vehicle rolled to a stop. Riker could hear distant voices, as if they were near a bazaar or shopping district. Then he heard the unmistakable click-slide of latches unlocking. Riker crouched on bruised haunches, prepared to spring at whomever or whatever he saw first. The lid opened a crack—and a blaster muzzle poked in. He made a fatalistic grab for it, but the person on the outside held fast.

"Let go or you're dead," said a gruff voice.

Riker did as he was told. The lid fell open, forcing him to squint against blinding daylight. As he took a gulp of outside air, Riker prepared to fight back his cough reflex. Compared to the city, though, this air was fresh and pure. At least breathable. After a couple of seconds of adjustment, his eyes focused on the grizzled whiskers of the Thiopan with the blaster pointed at him. "Who the hell are you?"

"Durren." He thrust a bundle of dirty tan clothing at Riker. "Out of yours. Put these on."

"One size fits all?" The man didn't seem to get the joke. "Sojourner, I presume?"

The man continued to ignore him, and began humming a mournful folk melody. So Riker unzipped his uniform and stepped out of it. He felt a little foolish getting undressed under these circumstances. He could see that his packing crate was in fact on the bed of a small cargo vehicle with a bubble-shaped cab up front. And they were indeed parked just off a bustling marketplace. As he put on the gauzy leggings and shirt and tied a blue sash around his waist, he took in the surrounding area.

The marketplace and its alleys and stalls were filled

with people, but they looked more like refugees than shoppers or traders. Many appeared to have their meager belongings with them, some heaped on emaciated animals, a few in decaying motor vehicles overloaded with packs and people, but most of the Thiopans were stooped by the weight of duffels and sacks strapped to their backs and clutched in whatever arms were not already holding small children. Older children were themselves carrying backpacks.

"Put the hood on," Durren said. Riker did, but Durren tugged it farther forward, making it harder for anyone to see that he wasn't Thiopan.

"Where are we?"

"Get out."

Riker would have preferred to vault out of the crate and make a gymnastically perfect landing on the ground. But his head throbbed from whatever had been spritzed in his face back at the Bareeshan warehouse, he'd been knocked around inside the box for an indeterminate period of time, and he was wobbly from hunger. So discretion won out and he clambered over the side carefully. Still pointing his blaster barrel, Durren hopped off the truck bed after Riker, who found himself facing two more Thiopans, with rifles and knives hanging from their bright sashes.

The other two were younger than Durren. One had a baby face and burning eyes. He held his weapon with palpable affection. The third man was somewhat older, with a nervous blink and darting eyes.

"Tritt," Durren said to his nervous companion, "don't take your eyes off him. If he tries to get away, shoot him."

147

"Shouldn't we burn his uniform?" Tritt asked.

"You couldn't," said Riker. "It's flameproof. Besides, I'm kind of fond of it."

"Forget the damn uniform," the young Thiopan said. "I'm starving."

"Mikken, you're always starving," Durren complained.

"We haven't eaten since before daybreak. We have to eat something before we cross the Sa'drit."

Durren acquiesced. "But make it fast."

Durren fell back to Riker's side as Mikken led the way along one of the narrow streets, looking for a booth that sold food. Durren resumed his soulful humming, and Tritt trailed so close behind that Riker could almost feel the blaster muzzle in his ribs. Except for Durren's humming, they walked in silence. Riker noticed that there were precious few luxuries on sale here—utilitarian clothing similar to what he'd been given, baskets and sacks, harnesses and halters for livestock, well-used pans and pottery, and some tools and hand weapons. Mikken finally found a food stall to his liking, apparently by following the trail of the tangy aroma of sizzling meat. On an open grill, charred nuggets were interspersed on skewers with chunks of fruits and vegetables, the flames in the pit hissing and flaring as juices dripped down.

Riker's stomach rumbled. "How well do you treat your prisoners?"

Durren nodded to the stall keeper. "We'll take four."

Riker gratefully accepted the food-laden stick. He was so hungry, he didn't care much what was on it. He cared even less after his first bite—whatever it was, it tasted great. "Thanks."

Once more, Durren avoided addressing him directly. "You are not a prisoner."

"I'm obviously not free to go."

"Let's move on," Durren said, ignoring him again.

As they left the cooking stall, Riker's attention was snagged by a scene at the adjacent booth. A woman with an infant in her arms pleaded with a man seated on a wooden bench under a sagging canopy. The man on the bench was fat and self-important and his lips were thinned to a disdainful line.

"Can't you see my baby's *dying?*"

Riker stopped. His escorts made no immediate effort to move him. No one else seemed to be paying much attention to the desperate drama being played out between the woman and the unsympathetic man, as if a dying baby was totally unremarkable. Two other painfully skinny children clung to their mother's hips, fingers gripping her threadbare clothing like tiny claws, eyes hollow with fear.

"Yes, I can see that," the fat man replied. There was a border of kindness around his words, but the words themselves were neutral, as if he had to keep them untainted by any hint of compassion. "He's not alone."

Riker drew closer and saw the baby in her arms. It wasn't moving. Even the eyes were unblinking. It was wrapped in a tattered remnant of a blanket. Tiny feet stuck out, bones covered by sallow skin. The face had none of the roundness of a baby's face. Instead, it looked like the face of an old man, withered and wintry and worn, cheekbones and chin stretching shrunken skin. Its chest twitched shallowly as lungs did their minimal best to keep the match-stick body alive.

Alive—it never had a chance to live. Riker listened, drifting still closer.

"But you have the medicine he needs. *Please*—"

"Too many need it. There's not enough. We have to save the ones who are still alive."

"He is alive." The woman thrust the baby at the man on his bench.

But his arms remained folded as if any unfolding would unseal a judgment already delivered. "Even if I could help, could you pay?"

She drew the spindly baby back to her breast and her head bobbed. "Yes, yes, I can pay. Whatever it takes, you can have it."

"You don't have anything."

"I have my children."

Riker's mind reeled in horror. He knew what the woman was about to say.

"I'll give them to you if you'll save my baby."

"They're not worth anything. There's no more slave trade. And they're too young to work."

"They can work! Save my baby with your medicine —I'll buy my children back later. *Please!*"

"Forget the baby. Save the others."

"Please!" Her plea became a keening cry. It cut into Riker's heart, but Tritt and Mikken took hold of his arms and pulled him away.

"Why wouldn't he save that baby?"

Durren shook his head. "No time to be saving babies. Have to save the ones that can help now."

"How do you know that baby wouldn't have helped someday?"

Mikken stared at him. "That baby dies today or he dies next week. He'll never reach 'someday.' "

"If you can't guarantee life for infants, what future do you have?"

"If we don't save this planet from the destroyers and their new ways," Durren said, his jaw tight, "there won't be a future for *any* people on Thiopa—old, young or unborn."

"Don't you understand?" Riker said. "We've got enough medicine to save all the babies like that one. We brought it to help you."

"You brought it to give to the government." Mikken spat. "And they'll never give it to us."

"Not unless we deny everything we believe in," Durren said. "Would you give up all of your truths if that's what it took to buy survival?"

"Knowing the people on the other side of the bargain lied to you all the way before that?" Mikken added.

"No. Nobody should have to do that. But there's got to be another way."

"There is," Durren said. "Get rid of the oppressors."

"What if you can't?"

"Then we shall die trying," Mikken said with finality.

They continued walking and munching on their food. Tritt dropped a piece of meat in the dirt and Mikken whirled on him. "Hey! Be more careful, idiot."

"Calm down," Durren said.

Mikken's face reddened. "This stuff costs too much to waste it like that."

"I didn't mean to," Tritt stammered. "D-d-don't call me an idiot."

"What do you want him to do, Mikken—pick it up and wash it off?"

"Maybe."

"It hasn't come to that, not yet."

"Not yet," Tritt echoed, keeping Riker's bulk between him and his angry partner.

"Durren," said Riker, "where the hell are we? You said I'm not a prisoner, but Tritt's not about to let me get away. So you can at least tell me that much."

"Crossroads."

"This town's called Crossroads?"

"Yeah."

"Where is Crossroads located?"

"You're in the Endrayan Realm," Durren finally said.

"That's the desert quarter." Riker waved a hand to indicate their surroundings. "All this suffering. There's nothing like this in Bareesh."

"What do you think this war is all about, Riker?" said Mikken with a sneer. "All this is because the government wants to wipe out the Sojourners and everyone who might support us."

"Has Crossroads always been like this?"

Durren shook his head. "Never had too much rain in these parts. But before the weather changed, there used to be enough rain and snow in the mountains to water the fields."

"All these people—where did they come from?"

Durren chewed the last piece of fruit off his skewer and discarded the stick. "Farms and other towns. They left dried-out dirt behind, hoping to find a better patch somewhere else . . . or at least enough food to fill their hungry bellies."

Riker took a grim breath and shook his head. "Our cargo ships have everything you people need to end all this suffering. What about a cease-fire? Maybe that would be enough to get the government to distribute the relief supplies."

"You're dreaming, Riker," Mikken said, the set of his jaw hard and harsh.

"What about other places?" Riker wanted to know. "Are other areas like this?"

"No," Durren said.

"Surely other places are enduring the same drought."

"But they don't harbor Sojourners."

"Almost everyplace else," Mikken said, "the cowards caved into Stross's genocide plans."

"Genocide? They're killing people who disagree with the government?"

"Not killing people," Durren clarified. "Just their traditions, their identities. It's called Fusion."

"We heard about that. What is it, exactly?"

"Making everybody talk, think, eat, and act the same." Durren shrugged. "In some places it doesn't matter. In some places people don't believe in anything anyway. But we do, and the Sojourners' way is the right way, the only way to save Mother World."

"You were in Bareesh," Mikken said. "You tried to breathe that foul soup they call air. The old ways, from the Testaments . . . they can get us back to when the world was pure, when it was clean."

"T-t-tell him about the circle," Tritt said, as he carefully nibbled a chunk of fruit on his skewer.

"Circle?" Riker repeated.

"That's what we believe in," said Durren. "Circle of

life. The Hidden Hand leads us on the path . . . it's a circle. No beginning, no ending. Just goes on forever. But everything that's happened to the world since Stross tried to change it, all the new ways—well, the circle's broken." He opened his hands to present all that was around them as proof. He took Mikken's skewer and drew two figures in the dirt, one a full circle, the other incomplete, with its line veering off uncertainly. "That's where Stross is leading us. We go that way, we lose the circle, can't ever get back on, keep going that way and soon all the life on Thiopa will disappear."

"Let's go," Mikken said. "The sooner we get back, the sooner we can see what Riker's worth."

"What I'm worth?"

"How much your Captain will pay to get you back."

Riker knew the probable answer to that—nothing. If he was a hostage, Captain Picard's hands were tied by Starfleet regulations. While it was permissible for a starship commander to talk with hostage-takers, the line was drawn at ransom. Some discretionary leeway existed, allowing for the possibility that, under certain circumstance, beings driven to such extremes really did have legitimate grievances that had never been given appropriate attention. A captain who became tangled in such cases was prohibited from rewarding kidnappers by paying with goods or favors for the return of crew members or diplomats. However, upon unconditional release of any and all captives, a commanding officer would be free to offer a hearing, without prejudicial backlash resulting from the initial hostage situation.

That last part had always piqued Riker's curiosity.

How many ship's captains were capable of totally setting aside all rancor and chatting with hostage-takers as if nothing had happened? Picard could, he felt certain, as long as no blood had been shed or serious damage inflicted to persons or property. And if these Sojourners did indeed have legitimate grievances, they would never find anyone with a more open or fair mind to hear them out than Jean-Luc Picard. Riker decided to do what he could to encourage the Sojourners to take advantage of such an offer should Picard extend it to them.

For now, though, he would keep all that to himself. Durren, Mikken, and Tritt were obviously not the leaders of the Sojourner movement. "Where am I being taken?"

Durren grunted. "You'll know soon enough."

Captors and captive walked toward the outskirts of what appeared to have been a busy town in the past. There were signs that the marketplace which was now concentrated into a few narrow blocks had once filled every street. But the farther they got from the hamlet's heart, the more of the two- and three-story stone buildings were abandoned and boarded up. A few were nothing but collapsed rubble. According to Mikken, they were the result of bombs planted by government agents in the earlier days of the conflict over Stross's Fusion policy.

Such paramilitary forays had been only sporadically successful, and they were often costly, since government agents rarely made it out of Endraya alive. Once the drought hit the planet, ruining Endrayan agriculture, government policy toward the Sojourners changed radically to the current starvation campaign.

On the outskirts of the little town, they reached a rail line running past a loading platform a few hundred meters long. The line consisted of one wide rail mounted on a track bed raised about two meters above the ground. A single car, apparently built of cannibalized parts, sat waiting. The wheelless chassis, seven or eight meters long, hugged the guide track, but the passenger compartment was an amalgam of different shapes, heights, and colors. It had openings instead of actual doors and windows, and it was battered and rusting.

But it worked. The Thiopans and Riker climbed up a short ladder hanging over the side of the car, and Durren turned on a humming motor. Within seconds, the car levitated a few inches above its guide rail and moved away from the loading dock, floating smoothly on an electromagnetic cushion.

"A little more comfortable than the first leg of my trip," Riker quipped.

"For us, too," Durren agreed.

"Who built this system?"

"The government, about thirty years ago. The Nuarans, really."

"Seems like a big project to take you out to the middle of nowhere."

"They used it to bring minerals and ores back from the mines and quarries out in the desert," Durren said, his eyes sad. "That was one of the turning points. They ripped the heart out of Mother World . . . butchers. After about ten years, there was nothing left to take."

"What happened?"

"They left. Closed the mines. When the Sojourners

moved back out to the Sa'drit, we found this line abandoned. We put some pieces together and made it work." He shrugged. "They would bomb it sometimes. We rebuilt it."

Riker scanned the badlands around them, the rock and dirt and dust and sand. "Doesn't look as if it was ever the easiest place to live."

"It wasn't," Durren said. "Always hotter and drier than most of Thiopa. But the Endrayans managed, even before Evain started preaching about the old ways."

"How?"

"How did they live here? By working *with* the world and not against her. Simple." He pointed out to gray hills. "Look . . ."

Open pits scarred the ashen land like fatal wounds inflicted so long ago they were past bleeding. "That's what the Nuarans did?" Riker asked. He got no reply, but he didn't need one. The sorrow in Durren's voice, the anger in Mikken's eyes, told him what he needed to know.

"There's something I don't understand," Riker said. Durren looked at him. "If there's nothing out here that anybody wants, why has Stross declared war on Endraya?"

"Because of us. Because we won't give up our right to live the way we want."

"Durren," Tritt suddenly shouted. "Stop!"

"What?"

"Out th-there."

The track bed ran past a watering hole, which was nearly dry. But a handful of large animals were lying on their sides in the mud. Durren throttled the motor back to reduce speed. "They're dead, Tritt."

"N-n-no—I saw them move. I g-g-got better eyes than you."

With a sigh, Durren brought the rail car to a full stop. Tritt jumped down and trotted across the few hundred meters to the pond. The others watched but made no move to follow.

"Why are you letting him do this again?" Mikken complained.

"Means something to him."

"What's he doing?" asked Riker.

Mikken scowled in annoyance. "Putting the ealixes out of their misery."

"The water," said Durren. "The government and the Nuarans used it up, made the weather dry it up—or poisoned it."

"We found out about the poison when people drank the water and died," Mikken said. "Toxic dumping from the mining operations. But the animals can't test for toxic waste, so they drink it and die. Except sometimes, they're not quite dead and Tritt has to stop and kill them. He gets along better with animals than he does with people. So he feels he has to do this whenever he sees some that aren't dead yet."

"Not an easy way to die, drinking poisoned water," Durren said softly. "Eats your insides. I've seen it happen to people."

They could see Tritt shooting the dying animals, but the sound of his blaster was too faint to be heard over the drone of the wind and the hum of the motor. He walked back over the scrub weeds and low dunes and climbed up the ladder. Durren pushed the throttle to midspeed and the car leaped ahead.

* * *

The captain's seat was, for the moment, empty. In fact, so was the whole center well of the bridge. The three seats normally occupied by Picard, Riker, and either Counselor Troi or Chief Medical Officer Pulaski were all empty. As ranking officer, Lieutenant Commander Data was nominally in charge. But with no pressing crisis, he simply remained in his low-slung seat at the Ops console up near the viewscreen. He seemed preoccupied with running calculations on his computer terminal. Ensign Crusher glanced across from his adjacent station.

"What're you working on, Data?"

"A theory, Wesley. But I lack certain information. I shall try to get it from Dr. Keat when I return to Thiopa."

"When are you beaming down?"

"As soon as the captain returns to the bridge."

Wesley watched the planet that filled the main viewer. "I don't get it."

"Get what?"

"How anybody could let outsiders turn their planet into a toxic dump."

"Shortsightedness."

"I guess. In one of my history courses I learned about how we humans almost turned earth into a polluted mess, and we didn't even need any advanced aliens to help us."

Data's head bobbed owlishly. "Yes, humans have a long record of self-inflicted disasters. It is amazing your ancestors survived long enough to develop space-flight."

"Do you think the Thiopans will survive all their problems?"

"Unknown, Wesley."

"Is that what your theory's about?"

"Yes."

The forward turbolift opened and Captain Picard stepped onto the bridge. Data swiveled toward him as Picard sat in the command chair. "Captain, request permission to beam down to confer with Dr. Keat."

"Granted. Oh, and you may show her that weather control file from our memory banks. Do your best to get something in return."

"Yes, sir." The android left the bridge and a young female ensign took his place at the Ops station. Only a few years older than Wesley, she had honey-gold skin and Polynesian features framed by lustrous raven hair. Wesley greeted her with a shy smile. When she smiled back, he had trouble taking his eyes off her.

"Mr. Crusher," Picard said sharply, "mind your station."

Wesley's face turned crimson. "Yes, sir." After a few moments, when his blush subsided, he glanced over his shoulder. "Captain?"

"Hmm?"

"About Commander Riker . . . we're running out of time."

"Are we?"

"Your twelve-hour deadline . . ."

Picard got up and stood behind Wesley's seat. "I haven't heard any orders to leave orbit, have you?"

"No, sir."

"Then I'd concentrate on my duties if I were you, Ensign." The voice and expression were stern. But a reassuring hand rested on Wesley's shoulder for just a moment.

* * *

"Do androids eat and drink?"

Kael Keat leaned across her desk, golden whiskers twitching tentatively as her wide pale eyes gazed at Commander Data.

"It is not actually necessary for sustenance. But I was constructed to accommodate ingestion of solid and liquid food."

"To make you more compatible with the humans you were designed to live with?"

"Apparently so. Since humans have some of their most interesting conversations at mealtimes, I am glad that eating is one of my functions."

"Do you actually get hungry?"

"No."

"Do you taste things?"

"Oh, yes, and I do have definite preferences."

"You are just *the* most fascinating . . . well, I was going to say 'thing,' but biological or not, you are definitely a person."

Data flashed a thoroughly pleased smile. "Thank you, Dr. Keat."

"Don't be so formal. Call me Kael."

"Very well, Kael. Is there anything else you would like to know?"

"Are you joking?"

"Joking? No. As my shipmates so often observe, I could not tell a joke if my life depended on it, if it walked up and introduced itself to me, if I tripped over one, if it ran up and bit me on the—"

"I get the idea, Data," Kael chuckled. "Back to your question—I would love to know everything about you—how you were built, how you function, how you get along with a shipload of biological beings—" She stopped when she saw a faint cloud of disappointment

161

shadow his face. Or was she imagining it? "Oh, I'm sorry. I'm talking about you as if you're a behavioral science experiment."

"In a way, I am. My existence is, to some extent, an ongoing case study."

"Does that bother you?"

"No. Should it?"

"It would bother the hell out of me, knowing my every action and interaction was being watched and cataloged by somebody."

"But interaction with humans and with other life-forms is endlessly intriguing. Although I am being closely observed because of my unique origins, I am always observing my observers. They are my teachers, even when they are not aware of it. I believe it is possible to learn something of value from every life-form we encounter."

"What a wonderful attitude."

"The variety of behaviors exhibited by living beings is astonishing. I find this especially true of humans, since they are the species with which I have had the most extensive experience."

"Do you understand these people you live and work with?"

"Not entirely. The complexities of love, hate, greed, sacrifice . . ."

"So you learn from both the good and the bad?"

"Oh, most definitely. I *do* understand why human artists, poets, and writers make such frequent use of the most intense emotions, both positive and negative."

"We've certainly got plenty of those flying around here on Thiopa," Kael said ironically. "Think you've learned anything from us?"

"From you."

"Really? What?"

"I have learned more about love and dedication from your devotion to science and truth."

Kael blinked in embarrassment. "Well, it's very nice of you to say that. And speaking of science and truth, there are things you want to know about Thiopa, right?"

Data nodded. "If I may, I would like to see your planetary meteorology records."

"Meteorology records? Temperatures, rainfall—that sort of thing?"

"Exactly."

"How far back?"

"As many years as you have on record."

"Do you mind if I ask why?"

"I need additional information to test a theory."

"What kind of theory?"

The android's yellow eyes blinked in hesitation. "I am not quite ready to discuss it with anyone, Kael."

"Well, when you *are* ready, will you tell me about it?"

"Certainly."

"Then you're welcome to see whatever weather records you need."

"The overthrow of the government?" Riker's eyes darted quickly from Durren to Mikken, then back again. He couldn't believe what he'd just heard.

"It's the only way we can find our way back into the circle," Mikken said fiercely, his powerful hand curled around his blaster, as if caressing a lover. "We've been forced to it by Stross and his forty years of collaboration with the scum Nuarans."

"Is this Sojourner policy, Durren?"

"No. But plenty of our people want what Mikken wants."

"What about you?"

Durren squinted, scanning the desolate beauty of the mountains guarding the horizon before he replied. "Don't know, Riker. I'd rather have it another way."

"It's too late for any other way. Stross picked this path," said Mikken. "Then he dragged us down it. The Hidden Hand can't find us here."

"How do you expect your handful of believers to bring down an entire planetary government?"

"The simple d-d-days," said Tritt quietly. "We have to go back to them. We just have to."

Up ahead, less than a kilometer away, the track bed ended in an old crater formed by an explosion. Durren backed the throttle down, and the car coasted to a stop within a few meters of the damaged section. A young woman waited for them, with five of the same beasts to which Tritt had tended back at the watering hole. His face lit as he saw them nibbling on some prickly brush clinging to the hillock where they stood untethered.

"Mori!" he shouted. The young woman replied with a wave, and Tritt jumped down to the gray sand before the car had quite stopped moving and ran over to greet the animals. He gave each one a thump and a hug. Riker and his remaining captors followed Tritt over.

"Is he talking to them?" Riker asked.

Mikken's head quirked in disgust. "He's named them. Swears he recognizes each one on sight."

"Ealixes seem to know each other," Durren said.

"That's by scent. They all smell the same to me—bad."

Riker walked cautiously around the animals, looking them over. They, on the other hand, showed little interest in him, except for twitching their snouts as they caught his scent. They looked to him like an ungainly cross between camel, horse, and hippo. Barrel-shaped bodies with small humps just behind their withers, wide heads with dainty mouths that seemed frozen in a Mona Lisa smile, soulful eyes with long lashes, nostrils that opened and closed tightly, probably to prevent them from breathing in grit whipped up by the wind, wide flat feet with toes that splayed for better traction in the sandy terrain. Two of the ealixes also had double sets of horns sprouting from their brow ridges. Males, Riker guessed. The only noise the animals made was a rhythmic snorting as their nostrils sealed and snapped open with each breath.

Riker approached Tritt, who was vigorously scratching the nose of one of the horned animals. The ealix yawned in pure contentment. "So these are ealixes . . ."

"Best friend you could have out here." Tritt's stammer disappeared as he stroked the animal's neck, ruffling its fine pinkish fur.

The ealixes all had blankets thrown over their backs and bridles and reins over their heads. Since there weren't any bits in their mouths, Riker guessed them to be docile animals. He touched the one Tritt was petting and felt it actually purr. The notch on its back between shoulders and hump seemed amply padded with fat to provide a reasonably comfortable seat.

Riker watched the young woman adjust an additional harness around the neck and shoulders of one of the ealixes. Another animal had a similar rig, which held a dull brown metal tube as long as a man's armspan. "Weapons?"

Mori nodded. "Ground-to-air slasher launchers."

"What do you shoot at?"

"Government hoverjets. We were easy targets before we got these."

"And now?"

"Now we get the jets more often than they get us," she said in an all-business tone, as if she'd been shooting down attacking aircraft most of her life, which might have been the case, for all Riker knew.

"Are you a good shot?"

She fixed him with a flinty gaze. "I get my share." When she was satisfied she had the launchers hanging properly, she moved around the second ealix to face Riker. "Can you ride?"

"I've ridden a lot of different animals on a lot of different planets. These don't look like much trouble."

"They're not. Comfortable, too."

"Where are we going?"

Mori turned and pointed off to a distant pass between majestic cliffs. "Sanctuary Canyon."

"How did it get that name?"

"When our ancestors came out here to the Sa'drit, that's where they found water and fruit growing. And that's where our legends say Mother World handed down the Testaments—the writings that told us how to live in Fusion with the land and sky."

"Fusion. That's the same name Stross uses for his plan."

Mori's eyes flashed. "He stole the name, thought he could fool people. His Fusion mocks what the name stands for."

Mikken vaulted smoothly up onto one of the ealixes bearing a slasher. That didn't surprise Riker, considering this Thiopan's affinity for weapons. Mori climbed onto the shoulders of the other animal with the launcher rig. Riker, Durren, and Tritt mounted the remaining three. Although there were no stirrups and saddle horn, human hindquarters fit snugly into the crook of the ealix's back and Riker felt sufficiently secure.

"Out there, Riker, is the heart of the Sa'drit, the heart of the Sojourners," Mikken said with a grim smile. "The heart of the revolution that's going to save Thiopa from ruin at the hands of Ruer Stross."

They left the rail line behind and began to ride across the barren plain of the Sa'drit Void. From the slate-colored faces of far-off mountains to the pallid gray-blue of the sky, this land was as bleak as a moonscape. Riker wondered at the crazed courage it must have taken for the first Sojourners to venture out here centuries ago—and at the fanatical dedication to a Sojourner renaissance that was driving these people who'd had the audacity to snatch him from the middle of Bareesh.

Along the way, they passed mute evidence of past clashes—burned carcasses of hoverjets scattered grotesquely, like dead birds shot down by desert marksmen. Whether because of the destructive power of the slasher weapons, the impact of the crash, or both, little was left to give Riker an idea what the hoverjets would look like whole. But the charred and twisted bits told a story all their own.

The other side of the story was also told by the ashes of a small encampment, still retaining the two-dimensional layout of a place where people had lived. But the third dimension, height, had been burned to the ground. Somehow, a tent-pole here, a structural frame there, still stood, blackened and so fragile they would not stand long against a strong wind.

The caravan slowed as it passed the burned campsite. "What happened here?" Riker asked Mori, who rode flank to swaying flank with his ealix.

"This is what the hoverjets could do anytime they wanted before we got the launchers."

"When was that?"

"Six months ago."

"Where did you get the weapons?"

"From the Nuarans."

Riker was shocked. "The Nuarans! I thought you hated them."

"We do," Durren said from the animal behind Riker. "But they gave us what we needed to defend our land."

"Your archenemy gave you weapons?"

"They sold them to us," Durren said, "in return for the rights to future resource mining in our territory and any other places we might conquer."

"They were hedging their bets," Riker concluded. "Just in case. But I thought there wasn't anything left to mine out in Endraya."

"There's plenty," Mikken said from the lead ealix. "It's just that the mines had to be dug deeper and deeper, and out in areas that were open to our surprise attacks. The government decided it was too expensive and too dangerous. That's about when they broke off ties with the Nuarans. So the Nuarans came to us."

"I'm a little surprised the Sojourners would deal with the embodiment of evil," Riker said.

"The Nuarans are not honorable," Durren said. "And so we took their weapons, knowing we would never give them anything in return."

"What if they come back to take what they want? They can do a lot more damage than government hoverjets."

"We can handle it," Mikken boasted.

Without anyone else noticing, Tritt had reined his mount away from the others and was wandering through the ruined camp as if searching halfheartedly for something he knew wasn't really there.

"Damn him," Mikken said. "Does he have to do that every time we pass this place?"

Mori silenced Mikken's complaint with a warning glare. "You can hardly blame him."

"Why?" said Riker. "What happened?"

"Tritt lived here," Mori explained. "He lost his wife and child when the hoverjets attacked. Almost everyone in the camp died."

"When was this?"

"Almost a year ago," Mori said. "Back then we still had some people living outside of Sanctuary Canyon trying to farm, trying to lead a normal life. They were the brave ones—"

"Stupid ones," Mikken sneered. "You can't farm in a war zone."

"It wasn't supposed to be a war zone."

"Lessandra never should have let them live here," Mikken went on. "We warned them . . ."

"We are supposed to be fighting for the freedom to live anywhere and in any way we want." Mori's face reddened and her voice rose in anger. "We are not supposed to be telling people how to live."

"Dream all you want." Mikken swung his arm out toward the ashes of the settlement. "*This* is reality. The sooner we accept that, the sooner we'll take Thiopa and get back to the circle."

Riker had noticed that Durren was steering clear of the heated exchange, concentrating instead on humming to himself. Silently, Tritt and his ealix drifted back to the group and fell in at the rear, leaving a plume of ash and dust curling up into the breeze behind him. The bickering between Mikken and Mori faded, and Riker thought about the latest twists in what he knew of the Thiopan conflict.

The Nuarans giving weapons to the Sojourners— that was a shock. Did the Nuarans do it just to wreak vegeance on the Thiopan government, which had booted them off the planet? Or did they really believe they could turn the Sojourners away from their sacred quest? And how did the Sojourners justify their acceptance of help from the off-worlders who personified everything they were fighting against?

From a pragmatic standpoint, the Sojourners' actions made a certain amount of short-term sense. Accepting the weapons was the only way they could obtain the armaments they needed to keep Stross's protectorate from overrunning Sojourner positions out here in Endraya. But how many principles could the Sojourners overlook, and for how long, before they began to forget the beliefs that ignited the whole conflict?

It was a rare cause that reached its goals without some compromise, Riker knew. But the purer the underlying principles, the more brittle the crusade. And the Sojourners were obviously a zealous lot, guided by a righteous doctrine that did not appear to leave much room for transgressions. If his escorts were at all representative of the attitudes of their group as a whole, Riker wondered if they would defeat themselves from within before the government could do it from without.

Durren suddenly stopped humming and swiveled about, scanning the sky all around for—for what? Tritt, who'd claimed to have a sharper sense of sight, apparently had better hearing, too. He spun halfway around on his ealix, then pointed in the direction of the pollution-veiled sun.

"Out there."

An instant later, Riker picked up the sound, too—a throaty whine that came from flying dots too small to see in detail. But there was no doubting what was about to happen. Mori goaded her ealix into a trot. The others followed her toward a steep hill. Once they reached its protective shadow, the Thiopans and then Riker dismounted and took up defensive positions behind a pile of boulders. Mori and Mikken each hefted a slasher, balanced it on one shoulder, and sighted through scopes protruding from the launcher barrels.

"Do they know we're here?" Riker asked.

"Probably. They may be looking for you," Durren said.

Riker grunted. "Great to be wanted."

"But we want you alive. They might be just as happy to send you back dead."

"So they could tell Captain Picard the nasty Sojourners killed me?"

Durren nodded. "Stross can claim he did his best to get you back alive—but got there too late to save you from those fanatics in the desert."

The hoverjets were close enough to make out now—a random formation of four bullet-shaped craft, glinting white against the sky. They were moving slowly, drifting in a search pattern, their vertical-control engines kicking up clouds of dust as they combed the badlands for their quarry.

"Can you hit them from this distance?"

"Yes," Mikken said quickly.

"*Maybe,*" Mori said. "Once we fire, if we miss, they'll be locked onto our position—"

"And then it's a matter of who's got a faster trigger finger," Riker said.

Mori nodded. "Right. Also, if we can shoot when they're closer together, if we hit one, the explosion might take a second one out, too."

"The waiting game," Riker observed. "Tests your nerves."

"We may not be able to wait," Durren said. "It looks as if they've found us."

The four hovercraft slid into a stricter formation. They were indeed headed directly for the Sojourners' hiding place. Riker glanced at Mori and Mikken. Both seemed steady, their fingers poised on the trigger buttons.

Riker wished he had something to shoot, too. It

would be better than sitting like a clay pigeon waiting to get blown away. He licked his lips and peeked over the rocks. The hoverjets had slowed their advance. What the hell are they doing? he wondered. Somebody's going to take the first shot. If it's them, they could blast the mountain open and bury us. In this case, I'll be a lot happier if we shoot first and ask questions later.

As if reading Riker's mind, Mori centered a hoverjet in her cross-hairs and squeezed the trigger. A red ball of roiling energy pulsed out the front of her barrel and screamed across the desert. The hoverjets saw it coming and broke their grouping, spiraling as they tried to evade the slasher bolt. Mikken fired his weapon an instant after Mori, knowing her decision to fire first meant the enemy was on the defensive until Mori's shot either hit or missed. It hit—dead on—and the lead hoverjet exploded into a fireball. But the other three were far enough away to escape the black smoke from the fist of flame that was already crashing to the ground. Two hovercraft cannons opened fire, spraying a volley of pinpoint energy bursts. The top of the hill erupted in a shower of dirt and rock. Riker and the Thiopans ducked and covered their heads. The hill itself was too thick for the government aircraft to shoot through. They'd have to move around it, and that's what they did. Two came from one side, the third from the other.

Mori and Mikken crouched back to back. Virtually simultaneously, they fired—and two more hovercraft exploded. The last remaining hunter had become the prey in this deadly game, and the pilot knew he was outgunned. He rattled off a salvo of cannon bolts, then heeled over so hard his hoverjet was tipped almost on its side. With a rapid attitude correction, the pilot kicked his craft to full throttle and fled at top speed, leaving a streak of white exhaust smoke behind.

The Thiopans broke into cheers. Riker wiped beads of sweat off his face, silently relieved. He still wasn't free, but he'd survived the encounter without a scratch. And it was better to be a live hostage than a liberated corpse.

Chapter Ten

ONE THING ABOUT AIR POLLUTION: when it wasn't obscuring the sun, it made for gorgeous sunsets. Today was one such sunset, and Sovereign Protector Stross took a break from his woodworking to watch the sky set aflame, a palette overflowing with golds and umbers near the horizon, ribbons of streaked clouds, purple and finally black on the far side of the sky.

The door of the workroom swung open and Policy Minister Ootherai came in, heels clicking on the hardwood floor. He looked haggard, his face drained of color. He raked his fingers through his beard. "Lord Stross?"

"What?" Stross didn't bother to turn.

"The Endrayan mission—it, uh, the squadron didn't accomplish what it set out to do."

Now Stross faced his aide. "You mean it failed.

175

Come right out and say things, Hydrin. How bad is it?"

Ootherai swallowed, betraying uncharacteristic jitters. "We, uhh, we lost three hoverjets."

Stross's baggy eyes opened wide. "Three out of four?"

"Yes, my lord."

"Damn those Nuarans," Stross hissed, his jaw clenching. "That party in the desert must have Riker. There is no other reason for anybody to be going from here to the Sa'drit."

"Not likely."

"They were going in that direction, weren't they?"

"Yes, my lord, they were."

"Then we know where they'll be. It's about time we showed Lessandra and her terrorists they're not safe anywhere. When was the last time we attacked Sanctuary Canyon?"

"Five months ago. That's when we discovered the bastards had Nuaran slashers. We lost ten hoverjets."

"I remember. This time will be different. Get our best pilots together and plan an attack for dawn tomorrow."

"On the canyon?"

"That's what I said."

"What makes you think they won't shoot us down again?"

Before Stross could answer, his communication channel beeped for his attention. He reached for the wall intercom. "Stross."

"Captain Picard calling from the *Enterprise,* my lord," said the communications control voice. "Shall I tell him you're in a meeting?"

"No, I'll talk to him. Put visual through to this terminal."

"Yes, my lord."

A moment later, Picard's face appeared on the small wall viewer. "Protector Stross, thank you for taking my call," he said soberly. "I had hoped to have a response from you regarding my conversation with Minister Ootherai."

Stross nodded with a benign half-smile. "Hmm. You made some threats."

"They were not threats." Picard was calm. "I simply wanted your government to be aware of the consequences of a lack of cooperation."

"I'm sorry if Ootherai gave you the wrong idea. I believe in speaking plainly, Captain. I have a feeling you do, too."

"Then let's speak plainly, Protector Stross."

"Fine. We need the supplies you have brought us, and the Federation needs Thiopa. I'm personally very sorry that your first officer got caught up in our troubles. We *are* trying to get him back for you."

"That's a step in the right direction. Have you made any progress?"

"Can you give us till morning? By then I think we'll have something definite to tell you."

"Very well, until morning. But decisions will have to be made then."

"Understood, Captain. We appreciate your patience."

"Is it also understood that patience has its limits?"

Stross nodded. "It is. We shall talk again in the morning. Stross out."

* * *

The Thiopan leader's image blinked off the main viewscreen on the bridge and was replaced by the standard orbital view of the planet below. Picard crossed his legs and sat thoughtfully in his bridge seat.

"I don't trust him, sir," Worf rumbled from over Picard's shoulder.

The captain turned. "Why is that, Lieutenant?"

"I don't trust sudden course changes."

"Neither do I. Counselor?"

Deanna Troi regarded her commander with her usual directness. "I think Stross was hiding something. At the moment, I wouldn't classify him as trustworthy."

"Mmmm." Picard was silent another moment. "I think we'll see what the lord protector has to say in the morning, before we make our decision." He stood. "I'll be in the ready room if you need me. Mr. Data, you have the bridge."

The rest of the ride to Sanctuary Canyon was uneventful, and Riker's group had finally reached the towering ridges that stood like sentinels at the narrow mouth of the Sojourners' spiritual homeland. In single file, the animals picked their slow-footed way through the ravine until they reached the entrance to the canyon itself. Riker and the others dismounted, leaving the animals in Tritt's care. While he led them to join the herd grazing peacefully on the sparse canyon grass, Durren took the rest of the group up the side trail.

To Riker, the canyon had a forbidding majesty. And though he'd visited cliff dwellings before, he'd never seen anything quite like the elaborate city perched on the far ledge, nestled beneath its soaring rock overhang, a wall at least a half-mile high. A wall that had long ago been the inside of this mountain, before it was split by nature's most elemental forces, then carved and shaped and worn smooth by flowing water and blowing wind. By the Hidden Hand the Sojourners believed in, extended by Mother World to guide and protect them. The surrounding grandeur of Sanctuary Canyon almost made Riker a believer, too.

They rounded the canyon rim and entered the Stone City, where Riker was presented to Lessandra in her barren garden. The old woman hobbled up to him, then propped her weight on her walking crutch, the padded nob tucked under her arm. The crutch was adorned with intricate carvings, and polished ebony designs were inlaid along the shaft. In her white hair Lessandra wore a circlet of silver, finely wrought but tarnished by time in an environment that offered no protection for precious bangles.

Riker wondered about those elegant touches that seemed so out of place in the rugged world the Sojourners had chosen for themselves. As Lessandra sized him up, he did the same to her. A missing leg, one half-closed eye, weathered skin, missing teeth— life hadn't been easy for her.

"So you're Riker."

"And you're Lessandra. You lead these people?"

She snorted a mirthless laugh. "You could call it that."

"Then we've got important things to discuss."

"Oh, do we now? Let's do it over evenmeal. I've had food prepared. Little one," she said to Mori, "fetch some of the silberry wine." She turned to glare at a man and a woman standing beside her. The woman had a deeply lined face, though she was much younger than Lessandra. The man was also middle-aged, with a gray beard.

"We want to be part of this," said the woman.

Lessandra puckered her lips in annoyance. "I don't have to let you, Glin."

"Then Jaminaw and I will have to tell the people you're keeping secrets from them. That won't do wonders for your support."

"Come along, then, damn you."

She led the small group to her house. Even in twilight, Riker could see that the two-story building was constructed of sandstone bricks hand-hewn to exacting tolerances, their beveled edges so tightly aligned that a slip of paper would not fit between them. Inside, the walls were covered with large tapestries woven with abstract geometric designs, their colors amazingly vibrant, especially in contrast to the drabness of the desert terrain Riker had looked at all day. Candles in holders chipped from stone blocks were scattered liberally about the main room, bathing it in soft light that quivered with every breath and breeze. There was no furniture, except a few squat barrels serving as tables. Large pillows and heavy blankets littered the floor, and that was where they sat. Mori entered from a back chamber with a clay pitcher and mugs for Lessandra, Riker, Glin, Jaminaw, and Durren. A younger girl, in her mid-teens, scurried in with two platters of fowl roasted to a crunchy gold-brown over an open flame. They were still sizzling. The serving girl left the food on the barrel tables, then disappeared and hurried back with a meager salad of leaves and roots. Mori poured the drinks and then sat down.

Riker was glad for the hot food, since the temperature had started to drop with the approach of dusk, a common characteristic of most of the deserts he'd seen. "Tastes good."

"See? We're not starving," Lessandra said smugly.

"Of course this is the first time we've had meat in three weeks," Glin countered.

Lessandra flashed a dirty look at her, but Riker spoke first. "Look, let's get one thing straight. I'm not your enemy. My ship came here to help Thiopans who need help. We've got food, medicine, all sorts of supplies to help your world get back on its feet."

"Do you have weapons?" Lessandra said.

"Not for you—and not for Stross. This is a humanitarian relief mission."

"We're the ones who need what you've got. I'll trade you to your captain in return for all those supplies."

"We can't do that. We're empowered to deal only with the planet's authorized government."

"Come back soon and we will be the government."

"I might as well tell you now, Lessandra," Riker said in a firm voice, "that Captain Picard is not going to bargain for my release."

"I know one thing: he won't let you die in our hands. People who have come this far to help poor starving famine victims are too softhearted to leave one of their own in captivity."

"Nobody on the *Enterprise* is indispensable."

"Brave talk."

Riker nibbled on a leg of fowl. The meat was tough—these birds had not been raised on quality feed, that was certain—but however they were cooked, the flavor had a satisfying tang to it. "Not brave—just factual."

"So your captain thinks you're worthless."

"I didn't say that, Lessandra. But Starfleet has very clear guidelines for dealing with terrorists."

"We're not terrorists!" Lessandra sputtered.

"You may have perfectly valid grievances, but the second you kidnap hostages, you become terrorists. If you give me back unconditionally, I promise you'll get a fair hearing from Captain Picard."

The old woman grunted disdainfully. "And you'll overthrow Stross for us."

"We can mediate."

"Mediate what?"

"A settlement—not a surrender."

Jaminaw stabbed an enthusiastic finger into the air. "Listen to him!"

Riker frowned, trying to fathom this battered leader who, at the moment, held his fate in her hands. "What exactly do you want—and don't tell me the overthrow of the government."

"But that *is* what we want, Riker."

"Give me something realistic, and maybe the Federation can help you."

"Why would Stross listen to the Federation?" Lessandra asked.

"Because he wants Federation aid—and the Nuarans aren't the only alien race who would like a piece of your planet. Stross can accept aid from the Federation—or dominance from the Nuarans or the Ferengi. I know which one I'd pick if I were sitting in his chair."

Glin munched reflectively on a root. "So you're saying that in return for aid, Stross might be inclined to pay some mind to what the Federation says about our fight?"

"Don't misunderstand me. We have a very strict

rule called the noninterference directive. We can't meddle with the internal affairs of any world, nor can we change how any society is developing just because we think our way is better. But if we're asked to help settle a dispute, we *can* try to bring two warring parties together for their own common good."

"Tell him what we want," Mori piped up. The older council members looked at her, and when no one spoke right away, she told him herself. "We want the right to live our own way. We want a chance to convince other people that our way *might* be better, but if they don't choose to agree with us, then we won't force them—sort of our own noninterference directive."

Riker looked at the others. Lessandra's face furrowed in disapproval. But Glin and Jaminaw were nodding. "Is Mori right?" he asked.

"The essence is there," Glin said, her graying whiskers twitching.

"Ealix dung!" Lessandra exploded. "You're all ready to betray everything our ancestors stood for, everything Evain taught us and died for. You're ready to believe that Stross and his criminals will learn to love Mother World overnight and accept the Hidden Hand and live in true Fusion with the land. And if you believe that, you've all got sand for brains."

"Lessandra," Riker said, "governments sometimes do incredible turnarounds when the alternative is extinction. And in the case of Thiopa, your environmental disasters could mean the extinction not only of the government but of life itself."

"Besides," Glin added, "no agreement is forever. If they break a pact, we're free to start the battle again."

But Lessandra wasn't buying. She folded her arms

across her chest, her chin and whiskers jutting out pugnaciously. "Stross has led us halfway to hell, and the rest of the route's a downhill slide. He and the protectorate have to be swept from Thiopa. That's the only hope for our future, any future. I will do anything, even trade with the Nuarans, to rid Thiopa of Ruer Stross. We shall build an army strong enough to ride out of the Sa'drit and overwhelm Bareesh. We've sat out here in the sand long enough. It's time to take Thiopa back and restore the old ways before Stross destroys what's left of Mother World. Either we win or we weep."

The chill of the night made Riker's nose tingle, and the condensation of his breath collected on his mustache. A crescent moon rode high in the sky as he walked along the Stone City's front ledge with Mori. A few flickering torches moved along the canyon rim as sentries marched between the lookout posts on the outer ridges.

"Lessandra really hates Stross," he said.

"That is certain," Mori replied. She wrapped her collar scarf around her neck and chin and slipped her hands up under her arms.

"It sounds more than political. It sounds personal."

"It is."

"Tell me about it."

"Her leg—that's how she lost it."

"What do you mean?"

"Back twenty years ago, she was Evain's deputy. At that time the Sojourners were picking up more and more followers. Stross wanted us controlled, and he wanted Evain stopped. That's when my father went into hiding."

"Your father?"

"Evain was—is—my father." She saw Riker's eyebrows arch in surprise. "Stross told Lessandra the government was willing to negotiate. They agreed on a neutral place. I think Stross was hoping my father would show up."

"Did he?"

She shook her head and raked a hand through her spikey hair. "He wanted to go, but Lessandra wouldn't let him. She was right, too. They arrested her and took her to Kahdeen, the most notorious prison island on the planet."

"What did they do to her?"

"Tortured her . . . beat her," Mori whispered, a shiver in her voice. "For two weeks. Without medical treatment."

"What did they want to know—where your father was?"

Mori nodded. "But she wouldn't tell them anything. They executed friends of hers right in front of her. But she still wouldn't talk. They broke both her legs, and when they finally let her go, they dumped her in the desert. By the time the Sojourners found her, one leg was so badly infected that it had to be amputated."

"What happened to your father?"

"He sent me to live with his friends, and he stayed on the run for a few more months. But Stross's men eventually found him. They tried him for treason, and of course they convicted him."

Riker's eyes were gentle, his voice soft. "Did they . . ."

"Execute him?" She shook her head. "They didn't want to create a Sojourner martyr." She told Riker the rest of the story—how the government sentenced Evain to life in Kahdeen Prison, how they said he had died of natural causes two years later, and how many prisoners insisted that Evain was still alive, being shunted from island to island in the penal system so that his survival could never be confirmed. "I know he's alive," Mori said. "I *know* it."

"So you don't believe anything the government said after they imprisoned him."

"Why should I? Would you?"

"No, I guess not." He took a deep breath of the brisk night air. "And I can understand why Lessandra hates Stross and his government."

"The strangest part is that Stross blamed my father for starting the attacks on the Endrayan mining operations. But they didn't start until after he went into hiding. Evain hated violence. Anybody who reads what he wrote about the Testaments would know that. Lessandra's the one who ordered the attacks. But they blamed Evain anyway."

"Does anybody else think your father's still alive?"

Mori's shoulders flexed in a resigned shrug. "Very few believe it, and nobody will come out and say it. They're afraid it will encourage me, get my hopes up, make me do something crazy to try to get him freed. I think Lessandra believes he died sometime during the last twenty years, even if it wasn't when the government says he died. Maybe Durren thinks he might be alive."

"It sounds pretty tenuous."

"I really want to know the truth." She shook her head slowly. "And I thought we could use you to find out, but nobody thinks it's important enough to include as part of any deal with your ship."

"Remember, there won't be any deal. You people either let me go or you're going to have a houseguest for a long time."

Mori shoved her hands deep into her pockets. "It's time to go to sleep. I've been assigned to guard you."

Riker nodded toward the moonlit badlands stretching infinitely around Sanctuary Canyon. "Where could I possibly escape to?"

"Nowhere," Mori said grimly. "Don't forget it. You'd die out there before you got anywhere."

"Fine—you've convinced me."

"I'm still going to have to tie you up. Let's go." She led him toward the lodge where her rooms were.

"Tell me—where did the name 'Sojourners' come from?"

"Our people believe we're just passing through this place. Mother World lets us use her treasures, but we're just borrowing, not taking. The land doesn't belong to us; we belong to the land."

"Like caretakers?"

"Right. Mother World lets us use what she has while we're here. It's our responsibility to leave the land in as good or better condition than we found it."

"A little different from the government's attitude, eh?"

"Yes."

"Sojourners' beliefs," Riker mused as they walked, "are not all that different from what my people believe in."

Most of the lodges they passed were dark, but a few windows glowed with candlelight. Furnishings were similar to those in Lessandra's chambers, mostly blankets and pillows, with a few crude pieces made of wood or flat stones to serve as tables or seats. All the occupants he could see were adults, with occasional teens on the cusp of adulthood. It dawned on Riker that there didn't seem to be any younger children here. He asked Mori about it.

"Some wanted the little ones to live here, too, but Lessandra and some of the other leaders decided it was too dangerous and too rough for children who weren't old enough to take care of themselves."

"Where do they live?"

"They stay with families back in the villages and on the farms."

"From what I saw in Crossroads, that's not an easy life, either."

"There is no easy life in this realm—not as long as we refuse to surrender to Fusion."

Mori's quarters were two rooms on the ground floor of a sandstone dwelling considerably smaller than Lessandra's. Riker glanced up at the daunting rock overhang rising high into the darkness, and he couldn't shake the uneasy feeling it gave him. Not that it was about to tumble down, but the way it vaulted overhead made him feel that he was in the belly of some impossibly huge beast. *Primal dreads?* he wondered.

Mori pushed back the blanket draped over her entryway, then stopped short with a gasp.

"What's wrong?"

"Cave spider." She cringed, her voice a dry whisper.

Riker rolled his eyes in disbelief. "You shoot down hoverjets without so much as flinching and yet a little spider petrifies you?"

She crept back as gingerly as if afraid of awakening

some fetid, fanged monster slumbering inside. "It's not little."

"How big can it be?"

She stared at him peevishly. "You're so brave, see for yourself."

Riker pushed past her and swept open the drape. His feet froze in midstride. "Well, well, that *is* a sizable spider."

And it was, with a leg-span nearly the width of a man's forearm and a body the size of a melon coated with glistening brown fuzz. Three stalked eyes quivered as the creature clung to a thick web it had spun across the ceiling. "Uhh, do these things come to visit often?"

"Now and then. They think the buildings are caves because they're cool and dark. They don't like light. If you leave a candle burning, that's usually enough to keep them out."

"But you've got a candle burning," Riker noted.

"Yes, but you have to leave them near the doors and windows to keep the spiders from going inside."

"How do you get them out once they're in . . . or do you just move to another town?"

Mori giggled at Riker's quip, in spite of her fear. "You scare them away with a light."

"You've done this before?"

"Sure . . . lots of times. Do you want to try it?"

He sidestepped out of her way. "No, no . . . I always defer to experience."

He did hold the blanket open for her as she scuttled in and ducked low, staying as far away from the spider as she could. She reached for the cut-stone candle holder, which was sitting on a slab, then held it high in outstretched hands. "I'd stand back if I were you." As she edged the candle closer to the spider, it twitched nervously. Suddenly it dropped down on a sturdy strand of silk and launched itself toward the nearest escape route—right past Riker. It landed on its springy legs and scrabbled off into the darkness.

"You can come in now."

Riker remained skeptical. "How do you know that was the only one?"

"They're very territorial. If two tried to come into a space this size, they would have fought till one was dead . . . or maybe both. So if there *were* two in here, one would be just mangled pulp."

"That's . . . that's very comforting." Still, he entered while Mori set up two piles of pillows and blankets for sleeping. He watched her arrange things and then reach into an animal-hide pouch and take out a wooden box. She opened it carefully and pushed aside a soft cloth covering, revealing an exquisitely crafted doll. It was about the size of Mori's hand, made of ceramic with daintily painted Thiopan features and a colorful costume. Mori set the doll on the stone slab next to her. She seemed almost unaware that Riker was in the room.

"It's very pretty," he said.

She looked up with a start. "Oh . . . thank you." Then she shrugged as if embarrassed. "I don't know why I even keep it."

"It must be important to you."

"I guess."

"It looks old."

"It is." She cradled it in her palms and handed it to him.

Riker held it gently. "How long have you had it?"

"As long as I can remember. My father gave it to me. It's supposed to bring luck. I used to have a whole collection of them back when we lived in a town in a regular house."

"Is this the only one you have left?"

She nodded. "Most of us had to give up most of what we had." She didn't sound happy about that sacrifice, as if she'd done it without question, but always wondered why. "I felt that I had to keep one, though."

"I know the feeling. I took some of my favorite things from home when I joined Starfleet."

She brightened with interest. "What kind of things?"

He smiled sheepishly. "You don't really want to know."

"I do."

"Well, I was born in a place called Alaska, one of the few places on Earth where we managed to preserve lots of original wilderness."

"What's it like, this Alaska?"

Riker sat down on the pillows. "Cold, and bigger than life—everything, the mountains, the valleys, icebergs and glaciers, plenty of wide-open spaces."

"Those favorite things of yours—they're from Alaska?"

"Yes. We've got these great animals that roam the oceans. They're called whales. Lots of different kinds. Many of them were hunted to extinction, but some kinds were saved and over the years, they repopulated the seas. When I was growing up, there were as many of those whales as there had been hundreds of years before. You could stand on a cliff and watch them swim by for hours." Riker paused in fond reflection, thinking how he would love to stand on that cliff again. "I had a favorite kind—called an orca. A beautiful animal. When I was a boy, I collected little sculptures of orcas. Some of them were really old."

"Do they remind you of home?"

"Yes." He handed the doll back to her and watched as she balanced it on the stone again, gazing at it as if it could somehow restore all the innocence stolen away by time and circumstance.

"This is the oldest doll I had. My father said it was my mother's when she was a girl. She died soon after I was born."

"I'm sorry."

"It's okay. I never knew her, so when I miss her, I'm not really missing *her* . . . I'm missing the idea of having one mother."

"Who took care of you when you were a child?"

"My father's friends. Glin, Durren . . . I never felt unloved. It's as if I had lots of mothers and fathers. Just sometimes . . ." She sighed. "Sometimes I wanted just one of each." Mori stroked the doll's cheek with her fingertip. "She's been through a lot. Sometimes I think it would be easier to give her away, or leave her somewhere . . . or just break her."

"Keep her," Riker said softly.

The moonlight was bright enough to cast shadows, including a shadow of two figures embracing on a breezy bluff, high over the cleft in which the Stone City was cradled. Though more of comfort than passion, it was still an embrace of lovers, as Jaminaw tenderly stroked Glin's cheek and whiskers. But his voice was apprehensive. "What should we do?"

They sat on a flat rock, their heads together. "This

could be the best chance we'll ever have to come to reasonable terms with the government."

"But reason is not enough for Lessandra."

Glin scowled. "Lessandra is only one person—"

"She still leads the biggest faction. Say by some miracle—by the Hidden Hand—we actually reached a compromise and then we couldn't all agree . . . it could split the Sojourners. It could destroy us."

"Lessandra's path is going to destroy us sooner or later anyway. Only her way will also kill us."

Jaminaw sighed. "Why can't she and the others see that we don't live in a world where absolutes apply anymore. They want to go back to the old times, but these aren't the old times, and they can't ever be that way—that innocent—again."

"Are you writing all this in your journal?"

"Of course. You know I write everything in there. Maybe someday I'll publish the story of the Sojourners."

Glin sat up straight and placed her hands on her hips. She frowned harshly at her companion. "Why is everything 'maybe someday' with you, Jaminaw?"

Her sudden anger shocked him. "What do you mean?"

"You know."

"I don't."

"You *talk*—you don't *do.*"

Jaminaw spread his hands plaintively. "How many publishers do you see up here?"

"You always twist what I say. I don't mean this second on this mountain. For once in your life, commit yourself to something and work toward it."

"And set myself up for disappointment when I can't make the impossible happen? You know what Mother

World told us—it's not the destination that counts, it's the journey."

"I don't know if I believe that anymore," she stated. "If you don't steer during the journey, you might never reach *any* destination. The destination *does* count for something. It *must.*"

"What are you saying?"

"I'm saying if we want to even *have* a someday, we might have to do something about it *today.*"

"What should we do?" he repeated. The pliancy in his voice made it clear he would do whatever she decided.

Chapter Eleven

"WESLEY, what should I *do?*" The petite fourteen-year-old girl with shaggy dark hair whispered through clenched teeth to Ensign Crusher, who stood three heads taller and three feet behind her. A brigade of Lilliputian Starfleet officers stood between them, complete with phasers, tricorders, and miniature uniforms. Including Wes and the girl fronting the group, there were eight youngsters ranging in age from ten to Wesley's sixteen. Seven were human, one a Vulcan.

"Wessssleeeeeee," she hissed again.

"Gina, you're the captain," he whispered back, trying his best to master Captain Picard's trick of sounding both stern and reassuring at the same time. "You have to figure this out yourself—and you can *do* it."

Gina shifted her attention back to the slavering pack of canines blocking the forest path. Standing in dappled patches of sunlight on moist, moss-covered ground, the dozen animals looked almost cute. They were barely a foot tall at the shoulder, with stocky bodies, short legs, large triangular ears, and button-nosed snouts. Adorable—except for saber-teeth, eyes like green fire, and horns covered with blood as if the pack had just gored some poor beast to death. Add to that the deep snarls rumbling up from their throats, and they weren't so cute after all.

The Vulcan girl tapped Gina on the shoulder. "Would it be logical to offer them food?"

Gina blinked as she tried to make some sense of the situation. "Food, food, food . . . Do we *have* any food? And what do these things like? What if we start a feeding frenzy? What if they want more and we don't have more? Oh, why doesn't my chief engineer get that damn transporter fixed?" She hammered her fist onto the emblem communicator pinned to her chest. "Enterprise? Enterprise! Come in or you're all fired!"

"Captain," Wesley reminded her, "our communications system hasn't worked for two days."

She turned her head slowly and glared at him. "Let's feed Crusher to the dogs."

T'Jai, the Vulcan, bit her lip and pointed. "Captain, look out!"

Gina faced front again just in time to see three vicious blurs of fur and fangs hurling themselves through the air directly at her throat. In a panic, she flung her arms up to protect her face and fell back, knocking everyone else down like a row of dominoes. At the same moment, the forest and the dog pack winked out of existence, and the children were left piled on the floor of the bare holodeck, with Wesley at the bottom.

"Poetic justice," Gina sneered at him as they untangled themselves and got to their feet. Then she felt something paw at her ankle. She glanced down, saw one of the little animals there, and let out a shriek that sent the dog skittering across the deck. It dropped down into play position, wriggled in glee, woofed twice, and then disappeared like the rest of its computer-generated pack mates and their forest home.

The holodeck entrance slid open and the exercise programmer marched in, chortling to himself. Commander Data and Ambassador Undrun were right behind him. "That's all for today," he said. "Did you enjoy being the captain, Gina?"

The girl pulled her hair in front of her face. "It wasn't fair, Lieutenant Berga."

"Why not, Captain?"

"Because Wesley didn't provide me with the advice I needed on what to do about those awful little beasts."

"I couldn't," Wes protested. "I helped program the simulation."

"Then you were *perfect* for telling me what to do."

"That wasn't the point of the simulation," Wesley said defensively.

"Ensign Crusher is right," Berga said.

"What *was* the point?" Gina wanted to know.

"Perhaps I shall ask Commander Data to answer," said Berga, "since he is an experienced away team member."

The children looked at the android for enlightenment. "The purpose of the simulation is to train you to assimilate what you observe with what you know, as quickly as possible. I believe the expression is to 'think with your feet.'" He looked dismayed when the human children burst into giggles.

"You mean 'think *on* your feet,' Commander," Wesley offered.

Data smiled. "Of course. For instance, Gina, you wasted valuable time asking an ineligible participant to share his classified knowledge with you."

"You mean Wesley," Gina said.

"Correct. And you forgot that Science Officer Kolker had visited this planet before and knew about the behavior patterns of the canines."

"Darn it," Gina moaned, then glared accusingly at her science officer, a burly thirteen-year-old. "Why didn't you tell me what you knew? I'm not supposed to have to ask *all* the time."

"I forgot I knew," the boy said sheepishly.

Lieutenant Berga clapped his hands. "That is all for today. When we meet tomorrow, be ready to analyze today's exercise. Off you go." The children hurried out of the holodeck.

"Lieutenant Berga," Wesley said, "what *were* those things, anyway? Were they real?"

Berga chuckled. "No, no—I made them up." Obviously pleased with the results, he couldn't help laughing a bit more. "By the way, Wesley, you did quite well as my assistant."

"Thank you, sir."

"But tomorrow, it is back to being a student, my friend."

Wes grinned. "I figured this was too good to last. I didn't even escape a day's homework."

"Ensign." Ambassador Undrun, who had observed the exercise with Berga, stepped forward. "Didn't I see you assigned to the bridge, too?"

"Yes, sir."

"Officer, student, teacher-in-training, all wrapped into one?"

"Why not? A lot of the older kids on the ship—if they're interested in being starship crew members later on—get to combine practical experience with classroom learning."

Undrun shook his head in genuine wonder. "So much freedom and flexibility. Not at all like our education system on Noxor when I was a boy. Consider yourself lucky."

"What's Noxoran school like?" Wesley asked.

"We had masters who guided us very strictly—lots of learning by rote, spitting back facts, replicating results produced by generations of students before us on the same tests and exercises." He exhaled a sad sigh. "We learned quickly that the best way to advance and win the favor of the masters was to do exactly what was expected."

Wesley regarded the ambassador with sympathy. "What if you didn't?"

"We would be punished," Undrun said, mouth pursed with unpleasant memories.

Berga shivered at the thought of running *Enterprise* classes along Noxoran lines. "Discipline is needed, yes, but so is creative challenge."

"The only time we were permitted to exercise individuality was in self-defense contests." Undrun glanced up at the faces around him, taking note of eyebrows raised at the concept of bantam beings like Noxorans, known more for intellect than brawn, engaging in formal martial arts competition. He took their nonverbal response in stride. "Don't let our stature deceive you, gentlemen. Noxoran defense techniques can be quite effective even against opponents of considerably greater size and strength."

"Well, Mr. Ambassador," Berga said, "feel free to visit any of our classes while you're aboard."

"Thank you, Lieutenant. If time permits. At any rate, thank you, and you"—he nodded toward Data —"for showing me this holodeck simulation. Most interesting."

The soft beep of the intercom interrupted the conversation. "Picard here. Lieutenant Commander Data, to the bridge conference lounge."

Data tapped his communicator badge. "Data here, sir."

"I have some free time now, and I would like to hear about your second meeting with Dr. Keat—as well as that theory of yours, if it is ready for presentation."

"It is, sir. I am on my way."

"Captain Picard, this is Ambassador Undrun. If this is about Thiopa, I'm entitled to hear it, too." Then the confidence drained from his voice. "If you don't mind, that is."

There was a moment of hesitation from Picard's end. Undrun's unaccustomed meekness had caught him by surprise. "Of course. Mr. Data, bring Ambassador Undrun with you. I'll be waiting. Picard out."

Fingers interlaced, Picard rested his hands patiently on the long table. "So she didn't hesitate at all in giving you access to their weather records?"

"No, sir."

"What exactly were you looking for?"

"Patterns."

"What kind of patterns, Commander?" Undrun asked.

"Anything that would indicate the true state of Thiopa's overall ecology. How much of their current crisis is natural and how much is the result of their abuse of resources and natural corrective capacities."

Picard looked at his android officer. "Presumably you found such a pattern?"

"I did, Captain. And the news is not good. Thiopa appears to be reaching the most critical stage of a cyclical drought phase. Most planets go through such cycles. On some planets they cause considerable dislocation of plant and animal life, but other planets have sufficient reserve capacities of vital resources—water, for instance—to withstand the drought cycle with little permanent effect on existing life forms and topography."

"Topography—meaning the shrinking of forests, deserts, the expansion of that sort of thing?" Picard asked.

Data nodded. "Exactly. On Thiopa, the past forty years of rapid development proceeded with a total disregard for conservation."

Picard's mouth quirked uneasily. "Meaning . . .?"

"For example, sir, a change in rainfall patterns or an overall reduction in precipitation need not be critical if reservoirs and subsurface aquifers have been maintained at high capacity. But the Thiopans used up much of their freshwater reserve, and they have allowed toxic substances to leach into and poison the underground water supplies."

Undrun waved a dissenting hand. "They've got seawater. Desalination should solve whatever—"

"There is much more, Ambassador," Data said gravely. "I combined all available information on Thiopa's weather and the rate of environmental degradation caused by pollution, resource exploitation, and other negative inputs to create a model depicting Thiopa's condition fifty years from now."

Picard exhaled slowly. "Let's have it, Data."

"Computer," said Data, "please display appropriate charts."

The graphics appeared, suspended above the table, as Data continued. "The current trend in weather patterns shows a further dehydration of northern fertile zones, with additional rainfall in deserts."

"Won't that convert the deserts into arable land?" asked Picard.

"No, sir. In most places it will simply cause flooding and accelerate erosion. The soil is not of sufficient quality to permit large-scale agriculture. In addition, all rainfall on Thiopa now is highly acidic, due to industrial pollutants. Acidic precipitation kills plant life, and when it collects in smaller bodies of water, such as lakes and rivers, it kills aquatic flora and fauna. That same industrial pollution, coupled with combustion of fossil fuels in energy production and transport vehicles, will result in a fifty percent increase in carbon dioxide levels. This will, in sequence, lead to a greenhouse effect, which will force the planet's mean temperature to rise by four degrees centigrade—a greater increase in only half a century than in all the twenty-two thousand years since Thiopa's last ice age ended. Polar ice caps will melt, resulting in an eight-foot rise in sea level and inundating coastal zones and islands. Since storm intensity is linked directly to oceanic surface temperatures, there will be a fifty percent increase in severity of storms."

"Translating," Picard said, "that means it won't be uncommon for tidal waves to wash over coastal communities not already flooded by higher sea level?"

"Correct, sir. And there are interesting paradoxes. Higher air temperatures will cause more evaporation of seawater, which must then condense into precipitation. But none of Thiopa's major land masses are situated so as to benefit from the extra rain. As a result, areas that are now populated will become increasingly more arid, and rivers, lakes, and aquifers will dry up. There will be a total disruption of life cycles and fragile ecosystem balances."

Picard's forehead creased anxiously. "That's quite a catalog of environmental horrors."

"Oh, there's more, sir."

"I've heard enough. What will all of it mean to intelligent life on Thiopa fifty years from now?"

"If these trends are not arrested by massive corrective action now, almost all Thiopan land masses will be uninhabitable by anything more than a small population. Millions of Thiopans will starve to death, and their civilization will crumble."

"Do the Thiopans have the technology to reverse all this?" asked Picard, his tone grim.

"No, sir—but we do. I have created a comprehensive analysis, with long-term corrective measures, including the desalination of seawater as Ambassador Undrun suggested, pollution controls, alternatives to fossil-fuel usage, changing land-mass structure to rearrange rainfall patterns and rebuild water reserves, revival of degraded farmland . . . Shall I continue, sir?"

"No, I think we've got the picture, Data," Picard said, reflecting on the enormity of Thiopa's dilemma. "Do you think Dr. Keat is aware of this looming disaster?"

"No, sir. She is an influential member of Thiopa's government hierarchy. If she were aware of the situation I have described, it is likely she would have been able to convince Protector Stross to initiate emergency corrective measures."

"Yes, one would think so. A potential disaster of this magnitude should certainly transcend political bickering."

Undrun fidgeted in his seat, as if capping an incipient eruption. "This is it," he blurted, "the confluence of circumstances we need!"

"For what?" Picard said.

"Once the Thiopans know about all this, they'll have to let us help them!"

"They don't *have* to let us do anything, Mr. Undrun."

"What choice do they have, Captain? If they don't listen to reason, they're condemning their whole world to another dark age. We can put them back on the road to self-sufficiency."

Picard sighed, speaking softly to counterbalance Undrun's excitement. "Conclusions that seem apparent to us may not match Thiopan conclusions based on the same set of facts. I don't think their situation could have reached this crisis point without a highly developed ability for self-delusion."

"Then we'll just have to make them see these facts the same way we do."

Data slipped back into the conversation. "Captain, I was also able to pinpoint the area most affected by the drought. I memorized Dr. Keat's charts and maps and have already entered them into our computer."

Picard stood. "Then let's put them on the main viewer. I want Mr. Worf and Counselor Troi to see this, too." Undrun and Data followed him through the lounge door and out to the bridge. Worf, as usual, was at his aft security console, and Deanna Troi sat with Dr. Pulaski in the lower command center. Picard acknowledged Pulaski's presence with a perfunctory nod. "Doctor, you might as well see this, too. Your medical services may be needed. Mr. Data, proceed."

"Computer," Data ordered, "display Thiopan surface map on main screen."

The computer replaced the orbital view of Thiopa with a sectional map of the entire planet.

"The Endrayan Realm is the area suffering most seriously from the drought. It had the lowest annual precipitation level of any of Thiopa's densely populated realms even under normal weather conditions. So its agricultural output was at best precariously balanced."

"And most easily upset," Picard said.

Wesley swiveled away from his console. "Captain?"

"Something to add, Mr. Crusher?"

"The Endrayan Realm—that's where the Sojourners' Sanctuary Canyon is located."

"And where they are probably holding Commander Riker," Picard said, completing Ensign Crusher's thought.

"We could mount a rescue party," Worf suggested.

"We could also beam into a totally unknown situation and lose Commander Riker as well as the away team," Picard said evenly.

But Worf's bullheaded determination had already kicked in. "Then what about sending a recon team down first to survey the area and evaluate the chances for a successful rescue."

"A better idea, Lieutenant. Mr. Data, prepare a detailed chart of the Sanctuary Canyon area for Mr. Worf."

"Already done, sir," Data said, handing a computer disk to Worf. "It includes orbital views from the *Enterprise,* scaled to show objects as small as six inches across."

"Mr. Worf," said Picard, "study the terrain and come up with a suitable recon plan for my approval. Be prepared to lead a scout team down at planet dawn."

Frid Undrun had circled the back of the bridge and taken up an unobtrusive position near the alcove housing the door to Picard's ready room and the forward turbolift. Unnoticed, he was studying the maps of Thiopa as they flashed on the viewscreen and, using his schoolday skills, committing coordinates to memory. Moments later, still unnoticed, he sidled into the turbolift and left the busy bridge. After the doors slid shut, he stood without saying a word.

"Destination, please," the computer voice prompted.

"Umm—destination? Uh, the Ten-Forward lounge, please."

When he arrived, the lounge was nearly empty. He moved first toward the interior corner where he'd sat on his previous visit. Then he stopped and looked toward the expansive observation windows, slanting out and offering a wide vista of space. The mist-edged face of the planet below, the stark, star-dusted infinity of blackness beyond—this time they drew him close, and he eased into a booth within arm's reach of a window, facing out.

"Glad to see you've reconsidered." Guinan's tranquil voice came from behind him. "It has a certain magnetism."

He answered without turning away from the panorama. "Yes, it does. Mesmerizing . . . as if you could see tomorrow if you looked hard enough."

"I don't know about tomorrow, but you can see yesterday."

"Hmmm?" He still couldn't, or wouldn't, look away from the view.

"Starlight. We're seeing stars that are hundreds and thousands of light-years away, so we're seeing light that's hundreds and thousands of years old."

"That's *easy* to see, Guinan. Seeing tomorrow takes a bit more effort."

"Can I get you something, Mr. Ambassador?"

"A glass of that Kinjinn wine, if you don't mind."

Guinan brought him his glass and he thanked her. Then she turned away. "I think you and the stars need to be alone together," she said.

She was right, Undrun thought. How did she know? He wondered what else she knew about him. Could these starship people just look at him and know how much he envied young Wesley Crusher for the kaleidoscope of opportunities that were his to choose from, and for the encouragement given by his teachers who invited him to explore whatever struck his fancy?

They gave Wesley and the other children on the *Enterprise* the most precious gift of all: the chance to fail, and to learn from failure without fear of reprisal.

Could they know how much he admired Captain Picard and William Riker for their unerring sense of when to adhere strictly to the rules and when to bend them? Or how sorry he was, and how responsible he felt, for Riker's capture?

Did they have the slightest inkling of how much Frid Undrun, Federation Aid and Assistance envoy, youngest person to achieve this rank in the A and A Ministry, felt like a disaster waiting to happen? And the Thiopan mission, he feared, would reveal his true nature—an ineffectual, utter humbug. Did anyone know that he *dreamed* of being a maverick swash-buckler winning the day with wayward brilliance? Ha! Not a likely transformation . . .

Why not? he argued with himself. *I'll tell you why not—you let them beat every shred of original thinking out of you when you were a boy . . . let them lock your feet to a track that had to lead to success of a sort—just not the right sort. "By the book," Data had said. A machine has more self-awareness than I do! If the Thiopans were going by the book, they'd have accepted this damned aid and you'd be done with it—and you'd be able to keep going through life under the delusion that that was enough. This is the first time you've ever had to consider that it's* not *enough. Talk about rude awakenings!*

Did any of the officers here understand how desperately he wanted to help the people of Thiopa solve their problems and feed their hungry and repair all the heedless damage they'd done to their world?

Beneath his shell of mediocre, self-important con-
formity, Undrun knew he had one noble impulse—he
really and truly wanted to help where help was needed
and he could provide it. Which left just one monu-
mental question: *Do I have the nerve to do what I
should do instead of what's expected of me?*

"Did you and the stars find the answers you
needed?" Guinan was behind him again, and yet he
knew she hadn't been there a moment ago. Again she
had somehow sensed when he was ready to talk.

He slid out of the booth. "Yes . . . yes, we did." He
paused for a flicker of doubt. "I think so. Thank you
again, Guinan."

She tilted her head in a farewell nod and he hurried
from Ten-Forward with a purposeful spring to his
step.

The initial twinkling of a transporter beam took
shape in Kael Keat's lab office. In a few seconds the
shimmering shaft of energy became Lieutenant Commander Data. She sat perched on the edge of her desk,
wearing a beige lab coat over shorts and a loose-knit
blouse. Her eyes glittered with guarded curiosity.

"I didn't expect to see you again quite so soon,
Data."

"I did not expect to be back so soon."

"What's so urgent? Is it about that theory you were
working on?"

"Yes. I did say I would discuss it with you once it
was properly researched. I was somewhat surprised to
find you in your lab this late in the evening."

"Night, Data. When it's this late, it's night," she
said with a laugh. "But I don't need much sleep, and I

like it here when there's nobody else around. It's nice and quiet, and I do my best thinking here alone. Have a seat and tell me what you've come up with."

He repeated the presentation he'd given to Captain Picard, weaving in an even more detailed roster of statistical evidence to support his premise. Kael listened without revealing the slightest chink in her composure, despite the mounting testimony to impending planetary doom. When he finished his recitation, he looked at her, cocking his head in perplexity.

Kael's dark eyes widened, incising arched creases across her forehead. "You look confused."

"I am."

"About what?"

"Your reaction," he said.

"What did you expect?"

"Anxiety, astonishment, shock—"

"Why?"

"Because my findings do not augur a bright future for Thiopa."

"No, that's certainly apparent."

"Query: is it common for Thiopans to react in this dispassionate way to news of the near certain collapse of their civilization?"

"No—but it's not news."

It was Data's turn to be surprised, and he was. "It is not?"

"Not to me."

The android gaped at her. Silently.

"I didn't know androids could be struck speechless," Kael said.

"Neither did I," he finally replied. "I do not understand."

"Specifically, what don't you understand?"

With great care, Data tried to make some sense of what seemed to make no sense. "You are a scientist who has demonstrated a thorough grasp of the problems facing Thiopa. You have begun to restructure your world's scientific establishment so it may pursue empirical truth and be less susceptible to political manipulations."

"Accurate so far."

"Yet you respond to my report of the critical nature of the environmental changes Thiopa is undergoing—and the critical need for corrective strategies—by telling me this is not new information."

"Right."

"Which means you already knew all this."

"Right again."

"Yet your government has not implemented measures to counteract these detrimental conditions. What I do not understand is how they could ignore such overwhelming evidence when you presented it to them."

"Simple."

"It is?"

"I didn't tell them."

Despite his vast positronic memory, his total familiarity with dozens of languages, and a computational capacity that rivaled that of any computer in the Federation, Data found himself—for the second time in short order—at a loss for words.

Kael Keat seemed amused. "You're finding me quite a source of consternation tonight, aren't you?"

"Indubitably." He hesitated. "Would it surprise you to hear that I have also concluded that your proposed weather control satellite network is far beyond Thiopa's level of technology—for that matter, beyond the technological reach of the most advanced civilizations in the Federation?"

"No."

"You knew that, too?"

"Yes, I did."

Although his yellow eyes reflected all of his puzzlement, Data was by now past being dumbfounded. His pace of inquisition quickened. "Then why did you make the proposal to begin with? Did you know all along it would not accomplish its specified goal, or did you discover this as you followed through on your research?"

"Second question first. I always knew it couldn't possibly work. So why did I convince Stross and the government that it would?"

"I do not know—that is why I asked you."

"After I studied off-world and came back here, I saw what a muddle our scientists had made of things. Here we had a leader—"

"Stross?"

She nodded. "He practically worshiped science and technology, as if they were the saviors of Thiopa. But the man is barely literate and doesn't understand science at all. To him, it might as well be magic. Our Science Council could have built an empire. Instead, they were happy to be servants—and poorly funded ones at that."

Data gestured around the room. "This is your empire?"

"The beginning of one. I'm young, Data. I plan to be around a long time. And I knew right away that I wouldn't get unlimited money for research by telling leaders things they don't want to hear."

"Even if you are telling the truth?"

"Truth has nothing to do with it," she said dismissively. "Even Stross had to admit we had big problems, thanks to letting the Nuarans teach us how to ruin a planet in a couple of decades. But nobody could tell him, 'Hey, this is all your fault.' So Stross blames the Nuarans and tells them to get lost. Then I give him the means to become a planet-saving hero."

"The weather-control proposal? But you just admitted it will not work."

"You're being too logical." Kael took a deep breath. "Look, I could've told Stross we needed to eliminate acidic rain and industrial pollution, needed to clean up our fresh water, stop dumping toxic wastes in the oceans, stop cutting down forests, start using self-renewing sources of energy—"

"But you did not. Why?"

"Because those things aren't *magic*, Data," she said, thumping her fist on her computer console. "I needed to roll all those realistic, mundane objectives into something that would get people excited. I did that, and now I've got all the money I need to do all that boring but necessary research . . . *pure* research that really *could* lead to breakthroughs that'll save this planet. As long as they think I'm working on that impossible weather control network, I'll get all the money I want, and I'll get to spend it any way I want, and nobody will ask any questions."

"So your work is based on an elaborate deception."

She looked mildly offended. "I can't say I like that word, but I guess you could call it that."

"Have you thought about the consequences of failure? What if your research never does reach any important breakthroughs?"

"Then we're no worse off than we were before. If I

didn't cook up this deception, as you call it, Thiopan science would've limped along with a fraction of the support we've got now. And while lots of money doesn't guarantee success, lack of money *does* guarantee failure."

"But science is based on a search for truth."

"Maybe so. But I'd rather see our money wasted on science—where there's always a chance for that miracle this world needs—than spent on other things, like buying new weapons from immoral opportunists like the Nuarans."

"How can you hope to find truth through deceptive means?"

"Data, sometimes that's the only way."

With a blink of wonder, Data tried to reconcile all the contradictions he'd encountered in this one brief conversation. It only took a moment for him to realize he couldn't do it. Not now. *Probably not ever,* he told himself.

Chapter Twelve

THE STONE CITY SLEPT. The only Sojourners normally awake in the hours past midnight and before dawn were the night watch lookouts on the cliffs guarding the only entry into the canyon fortress.

Tonight, though, two others were up, sneaking between buildings, then hiding behind rocks near the lodge housing Mori and the hostage, Riker.

"This will never work," said Jaminaw in a worried whisper.

"It's two against one." Glin tried to sound confident.

"What about Riker?"

"He'll be tied up. He won't be able to do anything. We both go after Mori. When she's out, then we get Riker."

"What if he yells for help?"

"If we're fast enough and quiet enough, he won't

215

have time." Glin took a small spray gun from her pocket. "This solution is maximum concentration. Even if Mori wakes up, she'll be down again before she can do anything."

"What if Riker's *not* tied up?"

Glin rolled her eyes. "Mori is very thorough when it comes to security procedures. He'll *be* tied up."

"Look," Jaminaw whispered, pointing through a notch in the top boulder.

They saw Mori come out of her lodge and walk away from it, heading down the trail along the canyon rim.

"Where's she going?" he muttered.

"How should I know? Let's do it now, while she's gone. We can have Riker out before she gets back."

Glin started forward. Jaminaw hesitated, so she reached back and pulled him along. Moving quickly and quietly, they reached the lodge and ducked inside, their sandals barely whispering as they hurried across the tile floor. They found Riker sleeping on a nest of blankets in the main room. Glin leaned over him and squeezed her sprayer in his face. He shivered momentarily, and his eyelids struggled to open. But after a few ragged breaths, the paralyzing agent won out and he fell back into a calm, artificially enforced sleep— one from which he would not awaken for at least two hours. Jaminaw visibly relaxed. He unfolded a blanket from his backpack and threaded two support poles through hemmed loops, converting the blanket into a sling. They rolled Riker into it, lifted him up and left as quickly and quietly as they'd come in.

They carried Riker through one of the natural chutes worn through the canyon wall by aeons of rushing water. The rock tunnel took them up to a plateau above and behind the Stone City, a place seldom visited, and certainly not at this hour. From here, they picked up a narrow, roundabout trail that flirted dangerously with a steep drop. This was a longer route, but it met with the main trail farther around the canyon rim, and it was the best way to avoid running into Mori, wherever she might have gone.

They reached the bottom of the bowl, where the ealixes spent their leisure time. Most of the animals were asleep on their sides, nestled close to one another, but a half-dozen adults were contentedly munching the bark off thorny-bush branches. Glin and Jaminaw put Riker down on the ground, then grabbed the reins of three ealixes and pulled them away from their nocturnal snack. The animals responded with mild snorts of protest, but followed placidly.

The two Sojourners draped Riker's limp body across one animal. Glin secured him with ropes wound around the ealix's neck and belly. Then she and Jaminaw climbed astride the other two animals and spurred them into the arroyo leading out of the canyon.

To Glin, the rock walls rising high on either side looked like the dark flanks of sleeping mythical beasts as she and Jaminaw slipped past like thieves with a treasure in hand. Even if Mori returned to her rooms, they had enough of a head start to make it unlikely she could catch up with them. Once out of the Sojourners' Abraian Mountain stronghold, they would goad their ealixes across the Sa'drit at best speed. Their destination: an abandoned communications station near the depleted ore mines to the west, in the Sternian Foothills. The relay station had been used to contact Nuaran spacecraft in planet orbit when they came to pick up shipments of raw materials from that area. Now Glin and Jaminaw planned to use it to contact Captain Picard on the *Enterprise,* bypassing Lessandra and starting the process of making a deal that might finally give the Sojourners what Lessandra's opponents wanted most—to be left alone in peace. If Riker was right, and Picard could help by providing Federation mediation, then Glin knew she and Jaminaw would be hailed as heroes. She thought Evain would have approved.

But if Picard could do nothing, if the Federation was powerless to help, if Stross and his ruling protectorate refused to retreat from his quest for a monolithic world united by forcible Fusion, then Glin still believed she and Jaminaw would not be condemned for this action. She hoped the rest would accept what she knew in her heart—that this was something which had to be tried because of the promise it held.

The ealixes moved carefully over and around loose rocks scattered along the trail by occasional slides from the walls of the dry gulch. Jaminaw fought the urge to turn back. Glin had challenged him to act rather than talk, and here he was, doing something bordering on madness. The Sojourners were a fractious group, prone to heated arguments about tactics and strategies. But they were bound together by a solid core of faith in the teachings of their Mother World, faith in Evain's modern evangelizing, faith in the circle of life.

For all her autocratic tendencies, Lessandra believed in those basic principles as strongly as Glin or Jaminaw or anyone did. And the Testaments had always provided enough common ground for at least a modicum of agreement and compromise among all of the Sojourners. There had never been any discord so serious that it couldn't be dealt with. Sometimes quiet words were enough; sometimes it took the violent hammer of authority. But the Sojourners' internal divisions had never driven groups of members to splinter from the whole. Until now. If they failed, would he and Glin be accepted back into the Sa'drit circle? Or had they embarked on a trail that led in only one direction? He couldn't help wondering if he and his companion had committed the same sin of which they accused Stross—breaking the circle and galloping down a route that could lead only to oblivion.

The ealixes knew where they were going. They needed no prodding or steering. Their reliable steps rarely faltered. So Glin and Jaminaw rode toward the final exit from the canyon with their attention turned inward, sorting through private fears and wishes.

Neither one noticed the figure peeking around a boulder just off the path worn by uncounted footsteps. In its dark cloak, with a hood over its head and a scarf covering most of its face, the figure would have been hard to spot even by someone looking directly at it. To people whose concentration lay elsewhere, it was as invisible as a still breeze.

When the first animal in line, with Glin riding on it, reached the boulder, the figure stepped out quickly, blocking the way. It was aiming two blaster rifles, one in either hand. "Stop."

Glin tugged on her reins and squinted at the cloaked figure. "Mori . . .?"

"Dismount, both of you," Mori said in a flat voice that told Glin she meant business.

"Mori, what are you doing?" Glin pressed.

"Dismount—now!"

Both did as she ordered. She approached them warily, her steps precise.

Glin watched her with a probing eye. "Mori, you don't have any idea—"

"Down on your knees, both of you. Hands on your heads. Do it."

They did, and she backpedaled over to Riker's inert form on the third ealix. Then she came back to Glin and Jaminaw.

"What are you going to do to us?" Jaminaw asked timidly.

"What you did to him." Mori let one blaster hang by its shoulder strap and took a spray pistol from her pocket. "Someone will find you in the morning."

Glin's hands twitched on top of her head, as if she was contemplating a preemptive grab for Mori's paralyzer spray. But the quick upturn of a blaster muzzle quashed the idea. "Mori, just so you know, we were trying to take the chance for peace before Lessandra let it slip away."

"Me, too. But if you don't mind, I'm going to do this my way."

Before Glin could say anything else, Mori triggered the sprayer. It enveloped Glin and Jaminaw in a fine mist, and they both fell over. Mori shoved each one with her foot to make sure they were unconscious. Then she tied their hands and feet behind them with practiced efficiency. She knew that if they struggled, they could probably free themselves before anyone found them. But the time before they would wake up, added to the time it would take them to wriggle out of the ropes, meant that Mori would be too far from the canyon for anyone to catch her, even though they would know her destination—the same communications relay station to which Glin and Jaminaw had been heading.

She snatched the loose reins of the ealix hauling Riker and led it the rest of the way through the narrow ravine. At the mouth of the pass, she reached two other ealixes she'd left tethered to a bush. She no longer needed both, so she turned one around with a slap on its broad rump. Eventually it would shamble back to the herd. Mori tied a long lead between Riker's ealix and her own, then climbed on and rode out.

She stayed close to the foot of the cliffs. She'd been assigned to the lookout posts on top of this ridge often enough to know the sentinels couldn't see her tiny caravan if she hugged the contours of the steep rock wall. Besides, lookouts were more concerned about what might be approaching from a distance than they were about who might be leaving through the pass.

Mori knew her landmarks, and she knew her route. She continued around the outside of the Abraian formation. There had once been five separate peaks in this small range. But they'd been whittled by windblown sand and coursing water, driven by seismic jolts, and shaped by the slow shifting of tectonic plates until it was hard to tell where one ended and another began. The Sojourners' canyon was actually encircled by what remained of a mountain, now remolded into an artful jumble of forbidding walls and ridges, tapered arroyos, hunched hills, and of course the canyon itself. The other Abraian Mountains stood above and behind the Stone City.

At the base of the second mountain, to the west, a natural arch jutted out like a sculpted buttress. When she reached it, Mori knew she was out of sight of the lookout perches above the canyon. She grasped her reins and slapped her ealix's shoulders. With a snort of displeasure, the beast broke into a trot. The second one followed, and they headed out into the barren stillness of the Sa'drit.

It could have been the sharp jab into his gut. Or the pungent odor of animal sweat right under his nose. Or the chill in his bones. But something made Will Riker awaken. And he found himself apparently hanging upside down, his cheek resting on the fuzzy hide of an ealix. Which explained the odor flaring his nostrils. His awkward riding position—slung like a rolled rug over the ealix's back, belly down and not on the animal's cushioned part—accounted for the jabbing of ealix backbone into his abdomen. He managed to lift his head enough to see the dark desert night around him, and understood why his teeth were chattering with cold.

But what the hell am I doing here?

He turned the other way, toward the animal's head, and saw the rider in the lead, cloaked and hooded. Riker's first effort at a shout came out a breathless bleat or, more accurately, didn't really come out at all. He shifted his position—not an easy feat, since his hands were tied behind his back—and the maneuver allowed his diaphragm to resume its natural shape, free of intrusion by ealix vertebrae.

"Hey—" He coughed.

The rider turned her hooded head—it was Mori. "Are you all right?" she asked.

222

"I've been better." His voice was still a wheeze. "Do you think you could let me down?"

Mori stopped and jumped off her mount. She untied the ropes holding Riker atop the ealix in uneasy balance. Unfortunately for him, before she could pull him down feet first, he toppled off the other way, his short cry of distress muffled by his face hitting the dirt.

"Ohh, Riker, I'm sorry!" She scrambled around and rolled him onto his back. But he didn't move. She fell back on her haunches, intending to cradle his head on her thighs. In her haste, she wrenched his neck.

"Oww!"

"You're alive! I was afraid you'd broken your neck."

"With or without your help?"

A flash of anger lit her eyes, then faded in an instant. "I'm sorry. I didn't mean to hurt you."

"Mori, since yesterday, or two days ago—or whenever it was—I've been gassed, kidnapped, bounced around the inside of a box, kidnapped again, carted around like a sack of potatoes, dropped on my head—"

"I get the idea. What do you want me to do?"

"Well, you could call my ship and have them beam me up, but I'm not counting on that. For starters, how about untying me and letting me warm up."

"Don't you try to escape."

Without a free limb, he gestured with his bearded chin. "To where?"

She looked at him for a moment, then rolled him over again, face back in the dirt, and freed his hands and feet. With the stiffness of a wooden soldier, he got to his knees.

"Would you mind telling me what happened?" he

said. "Last thing I remember is sleeping in your lodge . . . and I think somebody gassed me again."

"You said you were cold."

"I'm freezing."

She pulled a blanket from the saddlebags draped over her animal and covered his shoulders with it. "Better?"

"Thanks."

"Hungry? Thirsty?"

"Both."

Turning to the saddlebags again, she came up with a small container of dried fruit and a canteen of water, which she shared with Riker. "So you want to know what happened."

Riker nodded. "What am I—what are *we* doing out here?"

"I decided you were my best chance to find out if my father is still alive."

"You plan to use me as leverage to get Captain Picard to put pressure on Stross?"

"Yes. But I wasn't the only one who thought you'd be worth something on the open market."

He squinted in puzzlement.

"While you were sleeping, I went out to move two ealixes out of the grazing area to the pass. I was going to come back and take you away. But Glin and Jaminaw must have been watching when I left the lodge. They're the ones who gassed you tonight."

"What were they planning to do with me?"

"Same thing I was—use you to get your captain to exercise his influence over Stross and the protectorate."

"So how did I wind up with you?"

"On my way back up to the Stone City, I saw them coming down with you, so I just waited and ambushed them." She dismissed Riker's alarmed expression. "Don't worry—I just sprayed them and tied them up. They'll be fine as soon as somebody finds them."

"Where were they taking me?"

"That request you made—"

"What request?"

"To call your ship and have them beam you up. That's what I'm going to do. Glin and Jaminaw were taking you to the same place I'm taking you."

"Which is . . .?"

"An old communications module out near some abandoned mines."

"Nuarans built it?"

She nodded.

He chewed a shriveled morsel of fruit. "If you people can't start agreeing among yourselves, you don't have a prayer against the government."

"I know that."

"But you're still running off with me to strike a private deal with Captain Picard?"

Her expression grew as frosty as the desert night. "Sometimes you've got to look out for yourself."

"What if everybody did that? Where would you Sojourners be?"

She pondered for a long moment. "I don't know, Riker. And I'm not sure I care anymore. It's not easy being part of a movement that's trying to show the whole world the way back to the circle, on one hand, and trying to keep from being exterminated by the government, on the other."

"The government's wrong. All Thiopans should

225

have the right to live their own way as long as they're not harming anybody else."

"Are you on our side?" From someone as young as Mori, that question might have been filled with naive hope at finding an ally. Instead, it came armored in skepticism.

"I'm not on anyone's side. No matter what my personal beliefs may be, I'm a Starfleet officer. The Federation has rules—"

"I know—your noninterference directive."

"But there is something I'd like to do . . . for you."

"For me?" For a moment, all wide-eyed, she seemed like a young girl instead of a guerrilla fighter.

"This might border on violating that Prime Directive, but I'm willing to consider it strictly personal."

"What?"

"If you get me back to my ship, I promise I *will* do whatever I can to find out if your father's alive."

Her excitement flagged. "I don't know, Riker. If I understand this noninterference thing, not changing the natural course of civilization on other planets . . . well, finding out Evain is alive is bound to affect Thiopa."

"I'd be willing to risk it."

Mori shrugged. "It probably doesn't matter. There's probably no way you can find out anyway."

"That's not what you thought when you decided to steal me from Sanctuary Canyon."

Another shrug, more sullen. "Maybe it was a stupid idea."

"Your way, maybe. My way, maybe not."

"Your way?"

"I told you—Captain Picard won't make a deal for my release."

"Then your way means that I let you go and you promise to find out about my father."

"I said I would try."

She let out a cynical snort. "I don't trust promises, Riker. Nobody keeps them. As you said, having you gives me leverage."

"As *I* said, there will be no deals."

"We'll see." She pointed her blaster rifle at him. "Let's go."

"Do I get to ride sitting up this time? Unboxed and untied?"

"Sure, as long as you—"

"—don't try to escape. I know. If I do try—"

"I'll shoot you." She meant it. "Oh, not to kill. But stupid or not, I've come too far to lose this chance now."

The ealixes stood placidly as they mounted. Mori scanned the sky canopy, detecting the first glimmerings of a distant dawn. "Let's go. I want to be there by first light."

There was no such thing as first light aboard a starship. But if there had been, it would have been before dawn as Frid Undrun left his VIP cabin, padded quietly along a curving corridor, and made his way to one of the starship's large cargo transporter rooms. Down on Thiopa, he knew, it would soon be sunrise in the Sa'drit.

The doors opened and Undrun entered. A fresh-faced young woman stood over the transporter console, engrossed in a standard maintenance check on the unit. She looked up and greeted him with a friendly smile. "Good morning, sir. Is there something I can do for you?"

"Yes. I'm Ambassador Undrun—"

"I know, sir. Ensign Trottier." She brushed a strand of dark hair away back from her cheek.

"Well, then, Ensign Trottier—you are a transporter technician?"

"Yes, sir."

Undrun circled the console until he was standing at her shoulder. "A question came to mind while I was falling asleep last night, and I wanted to ask someone first thing this morning. In view of the Nuaran attacks on our cargo drones, if one or more of the freight vessels were to be damaged, would the *Enterprise* transporters be able to transfer all that cargo either to this ship or down to the planet in short order?"

"Generally, that should be possible. I could give you a more specific answer, if you'd like."

"Yes, if it isn't a problem for you."

"Not at all, Mr. Ambassador. Let me just check on how much those cargo ships are carrying." Ensign Trottier activated her computer link and started to call up the information she needed. She didn't see Frid Undrun sidle behind her and quickly squeeze the back of her skull with one hand and her neck with the other. With the slightest backward jerk of her head, she folded like a marionette with its strings cut.

Gently, he lowered her to the floor. "Apologies, Ensign," he muttered. "Time for you to take a nap."

He stepped over Trottier and tapped location coordinates into the control keyboard. Then he activated the unit and sprang up the steps to the transporter chamber just in time to be enveloped by the familiar hum and sparkle. A few seconds later Undrun was gone.

* * *

Jean-Luc Picard's first sustained rest since the *Enterprise* had entered orbit around Thiopa was rudely interrupted by the soft summoning tone of his cabin intercom, and then by a hesitant female voice.

"Captain Picard—Lieutenant White on the bridge, sir."

With startling immediacy, Picard sat up, fully conscious and aware. Years of command had brought with them the skill to emerge from deep sleep almost instantaneously—a habit he found useful, to say the least. "Picard here. What is it, Lieutenant?"

"Sorry to wake you, sir. But we just got a signal— cargo transporter number two has been activated."

"Who is on duty there?"

"Ensign Trottier was doing a maintenance check. I thought she might have activated it as part of her work. But when I called, there was no response."

Picard rolled the bedcovers back. "Send a security team down there. I'll be on the bridge presently."

"Aye, sir. White out."

Chapter Thirteen

UNDRUN STOOD on a sloping dune facing the cliffs that guarded the Sojourners' canyon, where hulking sentries loomed against a charcoal sky. The rising sun had barely begun its day's work, and Undrun was thankful he still had the cover of darkness to conceal his approach.

It didn't take long for him to reach the gap between the cliffs. Undrun was surprised at how exhilarated he felt out here on his own, traversing an alien wilderness, taking a bold step toward solving problems for which there were no approved ministry procedures. His belly grumbled, displeased about an overdue breakfast, but this was no time to stop for food. He moved through the pass, crossing the invisible threshold into the ravine. In his single-minded determination, he saw nothing but the dusty trail that would lead him to the Sojourners.

Just then, without warning, a loop of sturdy rope tossed from above flopped over his head and slipped down around his chest where it was suddenly pulled taut, jerking him off his feet. His upper arms were pinned to his sides, but his hands were loose and he tried to squirm free. Before he could do so, two Sojourners were on top of him, trussing his hands and feet and throwing him into a blanket sling. His hard fall had knocked the wind out of him and he gasped for enough breath to talk.

"I'm—I'm Frid Undrun," he wheezed. He sucked down a few labored breaths before he could go on. "With the Federation—the *Enterprise*—have to see Lessandra—"

"That's where you're going," said Durren from Undrun's right side.

Mikken was holding the other side of the blanket. "One leaves—another drops in."

"What do you mean?"

"You'll find out."

"I came to trade for Riker."

Mikken and Durren looked at each other and burst out laughing. Undrun frowned in confused frustration.

"Why is that funny? I—I've got food, supplies, everything you need." When he realized he was being ignored, Undrun lapsed into silence.

"At least this one is light," Mikken said as they lifted him off the ground and started up toward the canyon rim.

* * *

The turbolift doors snapped open and Captain Picard came onto his bridge. He strode directly to Lieutenant White's station on the upper level. "Report, Lieutenant."

"Ensign Trottier was found unconscious in transporter room two."

Picard's mouth tightened into a grim line. This day was not starting off well. But he remained silent, allowing White to continue.

"She's been taken to sickbay, so we don't know what happened yet. We got the beam-down coordinates from the unit memory. Somebody beamed down into the Sa'drit Void, sir. Specifically, within a half-kilometer of Sanctuary Canyon."

Mikken and Durren hauled Undrun up to the Stone City, where they found Lessandra in her withered garden. She was in the middle of a bitter shouting match with Glin. Jaminaw stood meekly behind Glin, providing meager support whenever he could muster the courage to speak up. Both women fell silent when Durren and Mikken approached and stood the ambassador up like a statue between them, his feet still bound together.

Lessandra leaned on her crutch and turned a frosty eye on the little Noxoran, who straightened to his full height—though that still left him a head shorter than the diminutive Sojourner leader. "Who the hell is this?" she demanded.

Durren poked Undrun, then had to steady him when the diplomat wobbled from the push. "Talk."

Undrun cleared his parched throat. He wanted his voice to boom at full volume—he needed to impress these people, and fast. "I am Frid Undrun, ambassador from the Federation Aid and Assistance Ministry. I understand that you are Lessandra."

"You understand right. What do you want?"

"I want to help you."

The old woman's only reply to that was a derisive snort.

Hostile hearing or not, Undrun pressed on. "I really am here to help you."

Lessandra made no verbal response. But skeptical wrinkles creased her forehead and her good eye focused all her suspicion on this short alien.

"Tell her what you're here for," Mikken said with a snicker.

Undrun gave him a scorching look, then turned back to Lessandra. "I'm here to trade for Commander Riker. I've got access—"

Before he could continue, Lessandra broke into a short, loud laugh.

Undrun wanted to stamp his foot for angry emphasis but obviously couldn't. "Why does everyone here think that's so funny?"

Even Glin and Jaminaw were smiling now.

"Just what are you willing to give us in trade for him?" Lessandra said through a grin.

"Food, medical supplies, tools to help you become self-sufficient, to allow you to grow what you need to survive."

"Well, that's certainly an attractive offer. There is just one little technical problem."

"What?"

"We don't have your Commander Riker."

"*What . . . ?* But you Sojourners kidnapped him."

"I'm not saying we did or didn't."

"If you don't have him, who does?"

"A very stupid young girl." She pursed her lips in thought. "Thanks to you, though, Mr. Ambassador, we do have another hostage."

"Oh, no, you can't—"

"You may be even more important than a lowly starship officer."

Undrun shook his head. "Not to Captain Picard I'm not. I doubt very much he'll be willing to make any deals for my ransom."

Picard eased into his command seat. "Picard to Ambassador Undrun." No reply. "Picard to Ambassador Undrun!" Impatiently, he drummed his fingers on the armrest of his chair. When he spoke, that impatience darkened his tone. "Computer, is Ambassador Undrun in his quarters?"

"Negative."

"Location check. Where is he?"

"Ambassador Undrun is not presently aboard the *Enterprise.*"

The facts were fitting together, much to Picard's displeasure. "Sickbay, this is the captain. Has Ensign Trottier regained consciousness yet?"

"Dr. Pulaski here, Captain. She has. I'm with her, and she appears to be fine."

"I'm glad to hear you are undamaged, Ensign," Picard said. "What happened to you down there?"

"Ambassador Undrun came in to ask me some questions about cargo transport. The next thing I knew, I was waking up in sickbay, sir."

"He *attacked* you?"

"'Attacked' isn't exactly the word I'd use, sir. He must have crept up behind me. The last thing I remember is feeling his hands on my neck and head."

"Thank you, Ensign. Return to duty whenever Dr. Pulaski releases you. Picard out." The captain shook his head. "Our Mr. Undrun appears to have hidden talents."

"Captain," said Data, "the ambassador did mention undergoing martial arts training as a child."

"It would seem he remembered those lessons well. Lieutenant White, check Mission Ops monitors. What is Undrun's current status?"

She nodded and leaned over her console, her fingers hopscotching the keypad. "Locating . . ."

Picard waited, arms folded.

"He's down on Thiopa, sir. He's got his communicator. It's functioning normally, and he's alive."

"I may alter that condition personally," Picard muttered to himself. Undrun was once again doing what he seemed to do best—causing complications. Why in blazes would he have knocked out a transporter tech and beamed himself down without even the slightest nod toward the niceties of procedure or protocol? the captain wondered. Such actions seemed totally out of character, but then again, how much did they really know about him? *Damn, damn, damn . . . Not only is Will Riker missing down there but so is this infuriating little popinjay for whose safety I am responsible!*

Picard rose and paced the bridge's front perimeter. "Data, do a full sensor scan of Sanctuary Canyon. Apparently that was Undrun's destination. Use his communicator signal as a focal point. Pinpoint where he is, who is with him, and how many Thiopans are there."

With his accustomed efficiency, Data quickly completed the task. At Picard's request, he displayed his results on the main viewer, overlaid on a map of the canyon.

Thiopa's haze-bordered face was replaced by a green-lined cartography grid. The computer put up a two-dimensional aerial image of the canyon, clearly showing the narrow gulch that was the only route in, the central bowl of the canyon itself, the ledge on which the Stone City perched, and all of the surrounding ridges and peaks. Data tapped a command into his terminal and a few hundred tiny blue dots appeared in and around the canyon, with so many concentrated in the Stone City that they joined together to form a splotch. Then a single red dot flashed in the heart of the blue patch.

"Explanation, Mr. Data?" said Picard mildly, standing just to the side of the viewer.

"The blue dots represent individual Thiopans, based on sensor readings of their life signs. There are three hundred seventy-nine Thiopans in the vicinity of the canyon."

"How many in this area?" Picard asked, pointing to the concentration of blue.

"Three hundred three, sir. That is the residential section the Sojourners call the Stone City."

"And the red spot?"

"Ambassador Undrun."

"Any sign of Commander Riker in that immediate area?"

Data shook his head. "No, sir."

"Captain," said Worf, "I believe it's feasible to beam in there with a security team."

"Need I remind you," Picard said sternly, "that

these people evidently have advanced weapons? And that they appear to be quite capable of using them, in view of the fact they've managed to hold off opponents who greatly outnumber them?"

"I'm aware of that, sir, but we would have the element of surprise on our side. With phasers on stun, we would be able to initiate preemptive action if necessary."

"Beam in with phasers blazing, Mr. Worf?" asked Picard. "What would be the purpose of such a strategy?"

"To secure the position, rescue the ambassador, and use the area as a base camp from which to continue the search for Commander Riker."

"Opinions?" said Picard, glancing at Data and inviting comment with an arch of his eyebrows.

"To rescue Ambassador Undrun," Data said, "we merely have to lock onto his communicator monitor signal and beam him up. It is doubtful whether we could in fact secure the position because of the nature of the terrain. It is likely that many hiding places are available to natives who are familiar with the location. Our weapons will be on non-lethal settings, but theirs probably will not. The Sojourners would consider us invaders, and the risk of serious casualties to our away team appears to be unacceptable when compared to what might be gained."

The captain turned back to Worf. "Wouldn't you say the sudden arrival of a large armed force verges on the confrontational, Mr. Worf?"

"Yes, sir," came the reluctant answer. "Shall I beam the ambassador up?"

Picard returned to his seat. "Not just yet. It was his

idea, however foolish, to beam himself down. The fact that he's still alive indicates he has at least piqued the Sojourners' curiosity. Open a channel."

"Channel open, sir," Worf said.

"Let's give them a call. *Enterprise* to Ambassador Undrun . . ."

Lessandra and the others stared at the fettered diplomat. The voice again issued from inside his clothing. "*Enterprise* to Ambassador Undrun."

"Answer," Lessandra ordered.

"I can't. I have to activate the communicator. It's pinned to my shirt."

"Durren, get it out."

Durren tugged the jacket open and found the emblem on Undrun's chest. He took it out and held it up. "Well . . .?"

"Tap the front," Undrun said.

Lieutenant White looked across the bridge at Captain Picard. "The communicator's not on Undrun anymore. I'm getting unfamiliar readings."

Data's long fingers danced across his computer keypad. "Thiopan, Captain."

"Undrun here, Captain Picard," said the voice from the bridge speaker.

"Mr. Ambassador," Picard said in a frigid tone, "I was quite surprised to find out you were not on my ship this morning. Would you care to explain?"

"I have valid authorization to pursue all avenues available to me to complete my assignment."

"And did this particular avenue bear fruit?" Picard bristled at the return of Undrun's imperious attitude.

"Uh, no, not exactly." The arrogance was gone. "Fact is, I could use some help, Captain."

"Are you in any danger?"

There was a moment's hesitation. "No, not really."

"Then you don't want us to beam you up? We can do that. We have your location pinpointed."

"No . . ."

"Very well. Are the leaders of the Sojourners there with you?"

"Yes, Captain."

"What exactly is your status, Mr. Undrun?"

"I—uh—I'm a guest of the Sojourners."

"You're in no danger?"

"I'd say not, Captain." Undrun looked down at his shackled feet. "But I'm not exactly free to go."

"Who is in charge down there?" Picard asked.

"That would be Lessandra."

"I would like to speak to her, if that's possible."

Undrun looked her directly in the eye. "Is that possible?"

"What do I do?" she asked.

"Just talk."

"Captain Picard," she called, "this is Lessandra."

"I've gathered from Ambassador Undrun's diplomatic language that he is in fact a prisoner in your custody. I would like to point out that—as foolhardy as he may have been to beam down alone, without telling me or anyone on this ship—he has just displayed considerable courage. You are aware he could have asked us to transport him out of there just now and we could have done so before you could have harmed him in any way."

"I figured that, Captain."

"But he didn't. I hope you'll take that as a signal of his serious intent. He truly does want to help you."

"I'll consider that possibility."

"We know that your part of the planet has been most seriously affected by this drought. That means you're the people who would benefit most from the emergency supplies the *Enterprise* has brought."

"Captain Picard," said Lessandra, "I think you're already well aware of the political situation down here."

"We've been getting a rapid education."

"Then you know Stross will do whatever he can to prevent any of your aid from reaching our people. His goal is to absorb us through Fusion—or to eliminate us through murder or starvation. We don't plan to let him do either one. We know this land. If Stross sends a military force to defeat us, we will scatter like sand to the winds, then regroup and strike like a savage storm when the time is right. They may try to starve us, but we know the whole world is suffering from the same climate changes. And no one on Thiopa is better suited to survive such a disaster than we Sojourners."

"But, Lessandra, there are other choices besides apocalypse."

"Are there? This mediation your Commander Riker talked about . . .?"

"Yes. Riker told you the truth. We can't force your government to change, but we *can* try to bring the two sides together to negotiate for your mutual survival."

"What's in it for you?"

"Nothing. Such mediation is part of the mission of this vessel."

"Riker said you wouldn't bargain for his release. Is that true?"

"Yes, it is."

"If we give Riker back, why would you bother to help us?"

"Because the Federation believes very deeply in the right of all life-forms to choose the way they wish to live, free from domination by anyone else. *Can* you return Commander Riker to us?"

"We don't have him."

"But you know who does?"

"Maybe—maybe not."

"What would we have to do in order for you to help us get Riker back safely?"

"I thought you said you wouldn't bargain."

"Maybe what you ask is something I can provide."

Lessandra considered her choices. "Come down here and talk to us."

Picard raised one eyebrow. "For what purpose?"

"To prove you mean what you say. I guarantee your safety. As you pointed out, your ship can transport you away in a second. But I don't think you care enough about us to—"

"I'll be down in a few minutes," Picard said in an unruffled tone.

"With an armed party, I'll wager," Lessandra goaded.

"Alone and unarmed."

"I'll believe it when I see it."

"Then you'll believe it very shortly. Please stay where you are. We'll use these coordinates. Picard out."

Picard saw all his bridge crew staring at him, including Counselor Troi, who had entered quietly during his conversation with Lessandra. Worf was the first one to voice his dissent.

"Sir, as your security chief, I urge you to reconsider. If they're lying, they could injure or kill you before we could beam you out of trouble."

"Mr. Worf, I evidently have greater confidence in your reflexes than you do."

"Commander Riker would not permit you to beam down into a situation with so many unknowns, sir," Data pointed out.

"And as my senior tactical officer in his absence, you are required to state your opinion as he would if he were here."

"That is correct, sir."

"But the fact is, he's not here," Picard pointed out. "I believe the Sojourners have a damned good idea where he is. And, as captain, the final decision is mine. Counselor Troi, it's your turn to suggest I reconsider."

"There is risk involved, but your position as captain entails some risk. I sensed that Lessandra is wary of our presence. She doubts that we can really do anything to mediate the Thiopan conflict . . . but she seems to be sincere about guaranteeing your safety."

Picard nodded. "Thank you all for your thoughts. I've got a promise to keep." He headed for the aft turbolift, pausing at the open doors. "Keep your eye on my monitor channel, Lieutenant Worf. Should anything go awry, my fate is in your hands." With a confident smile, he left the bridge.

"What are you going to say to him?" Glin demanded of Lessandra.

The older woman remained enigmatic. "I'm going to see what he has to say to me—if he comes."

"He will come," Undrun said. He was now sitting on a stone bench. "If he said he would beam down, he will do so."

Any further debate ended with the hum and shimmer of a transporter beam taking shape a few yards away. Once materialized, Picard strode directly to Lessandra, greeting her by name. "I hope our dealings will be fruitful," he said.

"I doubt that's possible, Captain."

"Would you cut Ambassador Undrun loose?"

Lessandra nodded toward Mikken, who used his knife blade to slit the ropes around Undrun's wrists and ankles. The little envoy thankfully rubbed the places where the bonds had been, trying to restore normal circulation.

"Thank you, Lessandra," Picard said, his voice resonating with an arresting combination of calmness and authority. "I take that as a sign of good faith, and would like to offer you a similar sign in return."

Lessandra limped closer. "And what would that be?"

"A small shipment of food and medicine."

"Mm-hmm." Her tone was skeptical. "And I suppose you'll expect another gesture in kind?"

Picard's gaze held steady, eye to eye with this small woman who wielded outsized influence over the future of her planet. "I expect nothing. I don't believe in quid pro quos."

He knew the only way to establish any level of trust at all was to proceed one tiny step at a time, each one building on the one before. There were currents in such encounters, and the *Enterprise* captain obviously had the sensitivity to discern them, to know when to remain anchored and when to follow the tide. It was a skill of which Undrun believed himself totally devoid, an instinct he simply didn't have.

"Well, then, let's see your good faith, Captain," Lessandra said.

Picard touched his Starfleet emblem. "Commander Data . . ."

"Data, sir."

"I would like you to beam down one ton of grain, one ton of seeds, and one hundred kilograms of medical supplies—to these coordinates."

"Yes, sir."

Picard, Undrun, and perhaps two dozen Sojourners waited. Undrun had observed the entire exchange without a word, admiring Picard's adroit application of the most fundamental principles of diplomacy. *I think I misjudged this man, and if we get out of this, if I have one honorable bone in my body, I should tell him that.* Thirty seconds later, the crates materialized nearby.

"Thank you, Data. Stand by for further instructions." Picard watched as several Sojourners approached the containers, wonder on their faces. "If you'd like to check the contents, Lessandra . . ."

"That won't be necessary, Captain," she said from behind a mask of detachment. Then she fell silent.

Glin and Jaminaw scuttled up behind her, one on either side. "Tell him where to find his first officer," Glin hissed.

"Tell him," Jaminaw echoed. "You have to . . ."

But the old woman's expression didn't waver. Neither did Picard's. They were as stolid as two poker players with unknowable hands, playing for the highest of stakes. When the interval of silence had stretched long enough for the next move to seem like her idea and hers alone, Lessandra spoke.

"No guarantee on this, mind you, but we know who took Riker, and we have a pretty fair notion of where they're headed."

"Can you take us there?"

She shook her head. "We can't catch them on foot or by ealix. But you could beam over there in a wink." She crooked a finger at Durren. "Map . . ."

Durren obediently unfolded a well-worn map and spread it on the stone bench next to Undrun. Lessandra's gnarled hand hovered over the paper. Then a fingertip landed on a spot near foothills to the west of the canyon. "That's their likely destination. By now they may even have reached it."

"What is there?"

"A communications installation," Glin said, "capable of reaching ships in planet orbit. The government used to use it to contact Nuaran ships making pickups at the mines out there."

"The people holding Riker—who were they going to call?" asked Picard.

"You," Glin said. "And it's just one person who's got him—a girl with a lot of determination to get some answers."

"Answers to what questions?"

Glin sighed. "Better if you ask her when you find her, Captain. I don't think any of us can speak for her."

"Picard to *Enterprise*," he said activating his communicator again.

Data answered. "Standing by for your orders, sir."

The captain had a tricorder slung over his shoulder. He opened it and held it over the map. "Are you receiving my visual signal, Data?"

"Affirmative, sir. It correlates closely with our orbital charts."

"Good. Calculate the coordinates of the cross near the Sternian Foothills, as it appears on this map."

"Calculated, sir."

"We need an immediate sensor sweep of that area."

"What are we looking for?"

"Commander Riker, and one Thiopan life-form."

"That should not be hard to find," Data said.

"Good. Make it so, Mr. Data. Inform me when you've found something. Picard out." He turned to Lessandra. "I'm willing to beam down more food and supplies, but I want it to go to the people who need it the most."

"That would be the population center of the Endrayan Realm, Captain. The town of Crossroads. That's where most of the refugees from the dried-up farmlands are going."

"Is there a workable government structure there?"

"Durren," Lessandra said, "you were there last. What's going on in Crossroads?"

He shook his head sadly. "The local government is crumbling."

"Do you have people there who could see that these supplies get fairly distributed?" Picard asked.

"Yes," said Lessandra. "We can do that."

"Fine. As soon as my first officer is safe and sound, I shall transport twenty percent of our total cargo to whatever location you designate."

Undrun rose and hobbled over. "Captain Picard, what you're doing is highly irregular and . . ."

"Yes?" Picard's piercing eyes gave Undrun a probing look.

"And it seems like the best thing to do for now." The ambassador smiled. "I concur wholeheartedly with your decision."

"I would like you to beam up to the *Enterprise*, Mr. Ambassador," Picard said. "I am responsible for your safety, and I believe you could use some nourishment and medical attention. I won't take no for an answer."

Undrun responded with a weak nod.

"Picard to *Enterprise* . . . Lock onto Ambassador Undrun's position and prepare to beam him up."

"Enterprise," said Worf's voice. "Locked on, Captain."

"Mr. Ambassador," Picard said, holding out his hand, "give me your communicator." But Undrun didn't have it. Durren did, and he flipped it to Picard, who caught it neatly in his palm, then handed it to Lessandra. "I want you to hold on to this for the time being, in case there's a need for us to renew this contact. Mr. Worf, ready to transport . . . Energize." Undrun's form dissolved into a glittering pillar, then faded out entirely.

"Captain," said Lessandra, clutching the metallic insignia Picard had given her, "you should know Undrun's main reason for sneaking down here himself."

"I imagine he meant to figure out a way to get that emergency aid to the people who needed it."

She shook her head. "His first priority was to free your Commander Riker."

Picard's eyebrows twitched in surprise. "Really," he murmured.

"Data to Captain Picard," said the voice from Picard's communicator.

"Report, Data."

"We have located a pair of life-forms in the general vicinity you suggested."

"Is one of them Commander Riker?"

"Uncertain, sir. There is some interference with our sensors due to the magnetic properties of various ores and minerals present in fairly large quantities at or near the surface. That, added to the similarities between human and Thiopan physiological readings, makes specificity difficult. I could program sensors to compensate."

"Do we have time for that?"

"Not if we consider one additional factor."

"What additional factor?"

"Whoever they are, they appear to be under attack by Thiopan government aircraft."

"Hoverjets," Lessandra said sharply. "If that's true, they're in great danger."

Picard whirled toward her. "Do you know of any other people—your people—who might be out there?"

"It's possible, Captain."

"I've got to know for certain. Data, transport me to that position."

"But, sir, the risks—"

"Don't argue with me, Commander. Beam me directly there on my order. Then stand by to beam all of us up to the *Enterprise.*" Picard stepped away from the rest of the group. "Lessandra, we'll talk again."

"Good luck out there, Captain Picard."

"Data, energize!"

Chapter Fourteen

THE QUARRY HAD BEEN gouged carelessly out of the hillside, then left like a gaping wound when the mine was abandoned, mute evidence of the pillaging of Thiopa. A permanent scar, cut so deep that it revealed millions of years' worth of sedimentary rock built up by heedless forces of nature—and torn apart by the heedless hand of man.

All that might have interested Will Riker at any other time. At the moment, however, his only concerns were the seven military hoverjets regrouping for another strafing run at the spot from which three other hoverjets had already been shot down in flame and smoke.

Riker and Mori hunkered down near the lower edge of the old quarry, concealed by two piles of rock that intersected to form a sort of protective angle. Protective, but far from invulnerable. Mori's aim had been nothing short of miraculous so far, but Riker knew the odds were against her continued success. If he could have offered a viable alternative to attempting to blast seven more aircraft out of the sky, he would gladly have done so. But there was no other escape from here. It was fight or run. Riker feared the final results of either choice would be the same—the charred remains of bodies smoldering where he and his sharp-shooting companion had been crouching.

Mori shifted the balance of the missile launcher on her shoulder, then took aim on an incoming hoverjet. "If I can get two more, the rest will run."

Before she could fire, the hoverjet shot a burst of energy bolts their way, blowing pebbles and dirt into the air, forcing them to cower with heads covered until the rain of rocks ended.

"Number One!"

At the inconceivable sound of a familiar and very welcome voice, Riker's head jerked up. "Captain!"

Another salvo of hostile fire set off a small mushroom cloud of dust and stones. Riker lunged for Picard's arm and pulled him down to the ground. "What the hell are you *doing* here, sir?"

"Getting you out of here." Picard slapped his chest insignia. "*Enterprise,* three to beam out—*now!*"

"No," Mori shouted, popping out of her crouch, tracking a swooping hoverjet in her scope. "Let me shoot—"

"Are you crazy?" Riker shouted. He clamped both hands on her launcher and wrenched it away from her—as the three of them sparkled back into existence in the *Enterprise* transporter room. Mori was still scuffling to get her weapon back, when the sudden realization of her abrupt change of venue hit her. She froze—but only for a beat. Then she straightened with dignity far beyond her years.

"I could have shot all of them down."

Riker shook his head, a combination of relief and amusement glinting in his eyes. "Not in my transporter room. Captain Picard, meet Mori."

Picard nodded stiffly. "How was she doing?"

"Three out of ten when you interrupted me," Mori stated.

"Commendable. Number One, you're out of uniform."

"Long story, Captain."

"I'll look forward to hearing it—later." He faced Mori squarely. "I'm told you are a young lady of uncommon determination."

She opened her mouth, but Riker silenced her with a sharp look. "I'll explain, sir." He reminded Picard about Evain, the latter-day prophet who had revived the Sojourner movement with his writings and preaching.

"What does all that have to do with this young lady?" the captain asked.

"Mori is Evain's daughter."

Mori explained the rest. "And I believe all the reports I have heard of prisoners seeing my father alive long after the government said he died."

"Ahh, I see."

"Captain," Riker said, "I made her a personal promise that I would try to find out whether Evain is alive or dead."

"Hmmm. What would prompt you to make such a promise, Number One?"

251

"I'm not sure, sir. I guess I was impressed with her guts, if not her judgment. I'd like to keep that promise, with your permission."

"You realize we're treading a very fine line," Picard warned.

"The Prime Directive. I'm aware of that, sir. The knowledge that Evain is alive could conceivably change the balance of power on Thiopa, and if we're responsible for that . . ." His voice trailed off.

Picard exhaled slowly, mulling over the implications. "I take it you have something in mind . . .?"

"I do, sir."

Arms folded across his chest, Picard gave Mori a stern look. "Commander Riker does not make such promises lightly. Nor is he impulsive. I will allow him to keep his word to you."

Mori met his gaze without flinching. "Thank you, Captain."

"Let's go to sickbay," said Riker.

"Sickbay?" said Picard.

"I'm going to need Dr. Pulaski's help to carry out my idea."

"It sounds like grave-robbing," Kate Pulaski said as she faced the dusty trio in her office.

"Not robbing—just peeking, sort of," said Riker defensively.

Pulaski looked up at the two officers who outranked her on the *Enterprise* and pursed her lips skeptically. "Let me see if I understand this. You want me to take a genetic scan of this young woman, then beam down to a graveyard and scan the inside of a tomb to see if anyone's home, as you so quaintly put it, Will."

"If there is a body in the tomb, you can do a genetic

scan of it, too, to see if it matches Mori's gene pattern," Riker said.

"To see if they're related." The doctor shook her reddish gold curls.

"Is this technically feasible?" Picard asked somewhat impatiently.

"Well, of course the genetic scans would tell us whether there is a familial link. But depending on what this tomb is made of, my tricorder might not be able to penetrate."

"But if it can," Riker prodded, "would we find out what we need to know?"

Pulaski looked at Mori. "We would be able to tell if that's your father buried inside that tomb, yes."

"Then we'll give it a try," said Picard. "Where is this tomb?"

"In a war memorial park in Bareesh," Riker said. "Do you know exactly where, Mori?"

"I've never been there myself, but other people have told me where it is. I think I can find it."

"What makes you think you're transporting down?" Riker said.

Mori lowered her eyes, one of the few times Riker had seen her show any vulnerability at all. "Please let me. I could never go before, and I may never be able to go there again. If my father really *is* buried there . . ." She paused. "It would mean a lot to me . . . to say good-bye."

"You won't do anything dangerous?" Riker said.

"I promise."

"Very well," Picard said. "Give the coordinates to the transporter chief, Number One. I want you to beam down in Thiopan clothing. The less suspicion you arouse, the better."

"Agreed, sir. Let's make a stop at ship's stores and get this over with."

"Oh, Number One," Picard called, stopping them at the door. "My compliments on skirting the Prime Directive. If you are able to come to a definite conclusion one way or the other, only we and Mori will know for certain. And she won't be able to prove it to anyone on Thiopa, not from what we find out today."

"That was my thinking exactly, sir."

"Wait," Mori protested. "What do you mean I won't be able to prove it?"

Riker's expression was not unkind, but it was firm. "I told you I made a personal promise—between you and me. There will be no permanent record of our findings, if any, and we can't offer any testimony to back you up."

The young Sojourner's expression darkened, as if she felt cheated. "Then what good does this do me?"

Picard approached her. "You'll know—for sure, we hope—whether Evain is alive or dead. This will be your own personal knowledge. It may give you some peace—or it may not. But it will guide you in whatever you decide to do next. If it turns out your father is dead, you'll be able to get on with your life."

"And if he's not buried there, then what?"

Picard spread his hands uncertainly. "Then you'll know the government lied about his death twenty years ago. And you'll have a solid reason to continue your quest for the truth about his fate."

"That's the best we can do, Mori," Riker said. "I hope it's enough."

"It's better than anyone ever offered me before,"

she said with an acquiescent shrug. "I guess it'll have to do."

Three figures dressed in billowy robes, with loose hoods shading their heads, shimmered into being on a cobblestone walk in Bareesh's memorial park. The path on which they had materialized was one of a dozen fanning out like a sunburst from a central plaza with a building that looked like an administrative office. Each ray was connected to the others by short paths in between, subdividing each segment of the whole. Riker realized they were in a gently sloped valley, with the walkways going up over the surrounding hills and out of sight. He didn't want to spend any more time here than they had to. "Mori, which way?"

For a moment, she looked lost. "Umm—wait a minute. Okay—up this way. Had to get my bearings —I'm not used to beaming into places. Takes a second to figure out directions." She led them along a connecting path and halfway up the hill, which was matted with the brittle remains of grass too long deprived of water. Riker took a quick look around at the grave markers and mausoleums. There were no representational statues, no literal images. Instead, Thiopans favored geometrical headstones and obelisks.

Mori's steps slowed as she caught sight of a white pyramid, rising tall and stately above the graves around it. It was made of a marbled stone, with an epitaph and dates chiseled into one side at eye level.

"What does it say?" Dr. Pulaski asked.

Mori stood in bitter silence. When she spoke, her

voice was edged with disbelief. "Evain—The Truth of Thiopa Saved His Soul."

Riker motioned to Pulaski and she snapped open her tricorder. He tried to put a reassuring arm around Mori, but she shook it off and stared at the graven words as if trying to burn them into oblivion. The words of those who had imprisoned her father because of the things he'd said and written. Words that mocked his life and his memory.

Pulaski turned off her tricorder. "There's someone in there, all right."

Mori didn't hear. She'd left Riker and circled to a blank side of the tomb, reaching out to touch it.

"Hey!" A voice called from down the hillside. Riker turned to see a guard laboring up the slope toward them. "Hey!" he shouted again. "This place is closed. How did you get in here?"

Riker grabbed Mori by the wrist, reached under his cloak and touched his communicator. "*Enterprise,* this is Riker. Energize, *now.*"

They materialized in the secure confines of the starship's transporter chamber. Mori nearly stumbled as she came down the steps. "He's in there," she whispered in a numb voice.

Kate Pulaski gripped her by the shoulders, gently but firmly. "Mori, listen to me. All we know is that *someone* is inside that tomb. But we don't know if it's your father."

"Who else would it be?"

"It could be anybody," Riker said. He found himself annoyed that she was so ready to let go of her faint hope, so ready to forget how much she distrusted the government that had imprisoned her father all those years ago. Then he chastised himself for having seen Mori only the way she'd wanted to be seen—as a tough desert fighter capable of shooting down an entire air squadron and more than willing to die in the attempt. Right now she was a trembling young woman overwhelmed by the possible reality of the death of a father she could barely remember. His expression softened. "They could have buried any dead prisoner and said it was your father."

"Do you want to know?" Pulaski asked.

Mori managed a nod. "I have to."

"Then we have to go back to sickbay so I can take a genetic I.D. on you and compare it to the readings I got from the remains inside the tomb. Are you ready?"

"Yes, Doctor."

Picard sat in the ready room just off the *Enterprise* bridge, elbows propped on his desk, fingers steepled, eyes focused in far-off thought. With Riker's safe return and Undrun's retrieval, he would be able to leave all this bad business on Thiopa behind, knowing at least that his ship's complement was intact. For all the brave ship-captain talk about no single person being more important than any other, and about every life aboard being secondary to the survival of the ship and the majority of her crew, no commander could accept the loss of a crew member or passenger without losing a piece of himself in the bargain, without feeling that he'd failed. *I'm responsible for every life on this vessel—and every life is sacred.* For one more day, at least, that was one internal conflict he wouldn't have to fight.

He was also pleased that he'd established a dialogue, however tenuous it might be, with Lessandra and the Sojourners. The people most in need would get at least some measure of relief from the two shipments of food and supplies he'd beamed down to drought-stricken Endraya. But the most difficult loose end remained loose: what, if anything, was he to do about Thiopa's long-term difficulties?

Data had given assurances that his projections of Thiopa's bleak environmental future carried with them a 97.8876 percent probability, if none of the worst-case variables were affected for the better by positive steps. And Picard had shared Data's astonished reaction at Dr. Kael Keat's ready admissions. Data still couldn't grasp the notion of overlooking the truth to enhance one's personal power. Picard could understand it, but that didn't make it any easier for him to accept it. And the revelation that Thiopa's chief scientist didn't think indisputable conclusions of ever-darkening disaster were reason enough to alter her empire-building strategies—well, that certainly was a bad omen.

Starfleet and Federation regulations and laws were clear: it was not the Federation's place to tell the rest of creation how to live . . . but sometimes some creatures were so damned stupid—Picard caught that thought before it could fully emerge. The legal code he'd sworn to uphold by accepting his Starfleet commission limited his actions. But it didn't relieve him of his conscience.

Captain's Personal Log, Supplemental.
I face a decision that is both difficult and simple. In spite of the paradox there, such decisions are all too common in this line of work. The simple part is

this: I feel morally bound to present Thiopa's leaders —both government and Sojourner—with the facts as we know them to be. And to offer our help, if they ask for it. After that, it's up to them. *That* is the hard part.

All eyes turned toward Jean-Luc Picard as he came out of his ready room onto the bridge. He took his seat between Riker, now cleaned up and back in uniform, and Counselor Troi. "You look as if you've made up your mind," she said.

He nodded. "We will not turn our backs on people in need," he said with quiet fortitude. "Not unless they force us to."

"What about the Federation, sir?" Riker said. "It's not likely they're going to want to prop up a poor leader with a shaky grip on power."

"True enough, Number One. But that's for the Federation Council to decide, not one starship captain and his first officer. Lieutenant Worf, open two channels to Thiopa, please."

"Aye, sir. Channels open."

"*Enterprise* to Thiopan Communications Network . . ."

A brisk male voice replied. "Thiopa responding, *Enterprise*."

"This is Captain Picard. I would like to speak to Sovereign Protector Stross."

"Please stand by, Captain Picard." A moment later, the voice returned. "Putting you through to Protector Stross's office—visual signal."

The main bridge viewer switched from orbital image of the planet to the inside of Stross's office, where the Thiopan leader sat at his desk. Next to him stood Policy Minister Ootherai. "Captain Picard . . . Sorry we haven't been able to find out anything about your missing officer."

"We have obtained his release from the Sojourners."

Stross seemed unperturbed. "So you had direct contact with them, then?" he noted mildly. "They're considered criminal terrorists here, Captain. Your talking to them isn't going to sit well with—"

"The details and consequences of that contact are not the purpose of this communication." Picard's tone was direct and controlled.

"Oh? What is?"

"The consequences of Thiopa's lack of regard for its own future. I have a decision to make—whether or not to give your government the rest of the emergency supplies. Would you stand by, please?" He didn't give Stross a chance to dissent. "Mute audio." He paused for a moment as Worf cut the sound portion of their signal. "Captain Picard to Lessandra. Come in, please."

After a moment, they heard her crusty voice over the speaker. "Is that how I get this thing to work?"

"Yes, it is. We hear you, Lessandra," Picard said.

"Captain, did you get Riker back alive?"

"Alive and unharmed. We also brought Mori aboard temporarily—some unfinished business. We'll transport her down shortly."

"We got word from Crossroads that you sent down the supplies you promised. You're an honorable man, Captain—thank you. We'll see that the people who need help get it."

"That was only a fraction of what we've brought to

help Thiopa. What we do with the remaining aid depends on how you respond to my next proposal."

"Try it."

"I propose a conference between you and Protector Stross—"

"Never," Lessandra spat. "I trusted him once—"

"You don't have to trust an enemy in order to talk to him," Picard said forcefully. "This will be an electronic conference—right now. Lieutenant Worf, resume second-channel audio. Lord Stross, Lessandra —you may now speak directly to each other."

Stross's eyes were stormy. "Picard, if you think you can bully—"

"I apologize for any rudeness, Lord Stross. I have a proposal, which I urge you to accept. It involves no risk on your part."

"What kind of proposal?"

"Talks between you and Lessandra."

"Stross doesn't want to talk any more than I do," Lessandra said.

"We don't deal with criminals," Stross shot back.

"I'm not asking you to do that," Picard said. "In order to decide how to distribute the Federation relief supplies, I need to present some vital information to both of you first. In the interest of fairness— and our best effort to remain neutral in your dispute—I wanted you both to hear this presentation at exactly the same moment. When I'm done, if either or both of you have nothing further to say, we'll cut off both signals."

He paused as the bridge doors opened, and Ambassador Undrun emerged.

"The future of your world is at stake," Picard went

on. "Is it too much to ask that you both listen to what I have to say?"

Stross's shoulders rose into a hostile hunch. "I'll listen."

"So will I." Lessandra's voice was equally antagonistic.

Picard thanked them, took a deep breath, then cited the litany of facts and projections Data had listed in his report. The greenhouse effect, its causes and consequences, the abuses inflicted on water and air, the savage exploitation of nonrenewable resources, the destruction of forests and other natural hedges against environmental ruin—all of it, leading to one inescapable conclusion: if Thiopans didn't change their ways and learn to cooperate—or at least co-exist—their civilization faced certain collapse. The Federation could help avert it, if such help was requested.

When he was finished, Picard felt drained. He'd been blunt, but believed there was no other way to convey to them the gravity of the crisis, and to circumvent the political posturing he expected from both sides.

During his lecture, Dr. Kael Keat had joined Ootherai at her leader's side in Stross's office. She was first to respond. "We don't dispute your facts, Captain Picard. And, as I told Commander Data, we're aware of the mistakes of the past and the problems they've caused for our world."

Picard leaned back in his seat. "But you do dispute our findings?"

"Yes, I do. They're based on limited knowledge of the work we've been doing. Long before the environmental catastrophe you're predicting, we will have mended our ways. We'll also have mastered nature's mysteries. We will be in control."

Data started to say, "Dr. Keat—"

But Picard cut him off. "Mr. Data, mind your post. It is—"

Data turned, confusion in his eyes. "But, Captain, that is not—"

"It is not our place to contradict Dr. Keat." He addressed the Thiopans again. "What if your scientists can't produce this weather control miracle, Protector Stross?"

"We didn't get where we are by doubting science, Captain Picard."

"We trusted outsiders before," said Keat, "and that brought us to the brink of catastrophe, Captain. We're never again going to let outsiders tell us what to do."

"What about you, Lessandra?" Picard asked. "Do you also believe Thiopa is in no danger?"

"What if it is? The collapse of their civilization is what we want. If we can't bring it about, we'll wait for Mother World to punish them herself. Meanwhile, we can defend ourselves . . . and when she takes her vengeance for the ravages of others, we'll still be here." The old woman's voice was untroubled, almost stunning in its tranquillity. "We are caretakers—not conquerors."

Stross couldn't contain his fury. He rose from his chair. "I heard that, Lessandra!"

"I know you did."

"You can't stop Fusion—you can't stand in our way. You can't stop us from building a future where your Mother World can't threaten us," Stross raged.

The angrier Stross became, the more placid

Lessandra's voice grew. "We have the power because we have the sense to keep the circle intact."

"You and your circle!"

"We've heard enough," Captain Picard thundered. When the bickering on the comm channels subsided, he continued in a voice hushed by hopelessness. "You've given us little choice but to leave you to your own fate."

"What about the rest of the relief supplies, the food?" Lessandra wanted to know.

"Since it is apparent that your two sides are incapable of compromise or cooperation on even a small scale, I will transport half the remaining supplies to your people, Lessandra, and half to your government, Protector Stross."

"Captain," Stross protested, "I am the leader of this world's government."

Lessandra ignored her opponent's tirade. "I knew you were an honorable man, Captain."

"This has nothing to do with honor. There seems to be all too little of that on Thiopa," Picard said sadly. "We're just completing our assignment in the only feasible way."

"I'll register an official complaint with your Federation," Stross went on.

Frid Undrun suddenly spoke up, stepping to the center of the bridge to stand near Picard. "Feel free, Protector Stross. But I am the Aid Ministry's authorized emissary in this matter, and I concur completely with Captain Picard's judgment."

"Use what we give wisely," Picard said wearily. "I doubt there will be more."

Stross scoffed. "The Federation won't let us starve. You need us."

"Perhaps. But I wouldn't stake my future on it, if I were you. We'll beam the emergency supplies down within the hour. After that, we shall leave orbit. Picard out."

With communications ended, the viewscreen resumed displaying the hazy face of Thiopa. Riker stretched his long legs and sat back. "There's a view I won't miss."

"Nor I, Number One."

Riker turned slightly. "Worf, see to the transfer of our cargo to Thiopa."

"Right away, Commander."

Picard stood before Ambassador Undrun. "Thank you for your support."

"Thank you for your patience," Undrun answered warmly.

"Number One," said Picard, "I believe we have one more item to see to."

The first officer rose to his feet. "To sickbay, sir?"

Picard responded with a nod and they strode up the side ramp. "Mr. Data, you have the bridge."

As the turbolift doors shut out the hum of bridge activity, Picard said, "What would you recommend to the Federation about Thiopa?"

"I think the Federation should look somewhere else for a reliable ally."

"Agreed," Picard said. "The real tragedy, though, is the future of this world."

"Bareesh isn't really feeling the pain yet. Maybe they'll change their tune when things get worse."

"Maybe. But will anything ever make the Sojourners change theirs?"

They arrived at Dr. Pulaski's office to find Mori pacing nervously, alone. "Where's the doctor?" Riker asked.

Before Mori could reply, Pulaski entered from her lab. "Right here."

Mori's whole body stiffened with pent-up anticipation. "Do you know—"

Pulaski's mouth softened into a reassuring smile. "It's *not* your father's body in that tomb."

The young Sojourner exhaled the breath she'd been holding and sank down into the nearest chair. The three starship officers surrounded her, concern lining their faces.

"I thought you'd be happy to hear it." Pulaski began.

"I am, in a way," Mori said in a small voice. "He's not dead inside that pyramid . . . but he might still be dead." She stopped, her eyes revealing confusion and something unexpected: *shame.*

Riker saw it clearly. "There's something else bothering you . . . Whatever it is, it's okay."

She shook her head vigorously. "No, it's *not.*" She groped for the right words, or any words. When she found them, they were whispered. "Part of me was hoping it *was* Evain buried there. Then at least I would have known." Her shoulders began to tremble, but she asserted control over the whirlwind of emotions swirling inside her. "So I don't know. Not for sure. But I *will* find out."

"I believe you will," Picard said, helping her up with a fatherly hand. "We'll be leaving orbit soon. Time to send you home."

With the *Enterprise*'s two commanding officers

flanking her, Mori paused at the sickbay door. "Dr. Pulaski—thank you."

"You're welcome. And good luck."

On their way to the transporter room, they saw lanky Wesley Crusher and tiny Frid Undrun coming toward them around the curving corridor. "Ambassador Undrun," said Riker, "I didn't get a chance to thank you."

"For what?"

"Captain Picard told me how you tried to get the Sojourners to turn me loose. That took a lot of guts, going down there alone. Not a lot of brains—but a lot of guts." He smiled.

Mori tugged on Riker's sleeve. "Hey, that's the same thing you said about me."

"Well, you two have a lot in common—bullheadedness."

"A good quality to have," Undrun boomed. Then he smiled and added: "When tempered with some clear-headed common sense. In any case, you're welcome . . . *Commander* Riker."

"I think I misjudged you, Mr. Ambassador."

"No, you didn't," Undrun said with a shake of his head. "But I've realized something I should have known before: not every obstacle can be hurdled with a computer analysis and a five-year plan."

Riker grinned. "Do you think you can nurture this newfound wisdom?"

"I plan to try. I have to get used to the concept that experiences are to be learned from, not just filed away in mission-briefing reports."

"C'mon, Ambassador," Wesley urged. "We'll be late."

"Late?" Picard's eyebrow rose. "For what?"

"Wesley has invited me to address his class in Problems in Cross-Cultural Contacts. Maybe they can learn from my mistakes."

Wes pulled the diminutive diplomat along, saying, "Guest speakers don't get demerits for being late . . . but I do!"

Once they reached the transporter room, Mori bounded up to the beaming chamber, propelled by a clear sense of purpose. "I can't wait to get back. I've got a lot of work to do."

Riker admonished, "Remember what the ambassador just said."

"About learning from experiences? I will."

"You're going back to a dangerous world."

"I know."

"Your own people may not give you the support you want, to do what you want to do."

"Then I'll find it someplace else." She smiled. "And maybe I'll find my father, too."

Riker nodded. "Be careful down there."

"I will," she said. "And thank you, both of you."

Transporter Chief O'Brien tapped in the beam-down coordinates. "Ready, sir," he told Picard.

"Energize," the captain said.

O'Brien touched the control pad again, and Riker watched Mori's silhouette fade away until she was gone. Her life hadn't been an easy one, and the odds against finding her father and winning his freedom were too high to calculate.

Still, whatever tests she had yet to face, Riker had a feeling Mori would hold her ground.

Epilogue

WITH NO IMMEDIATE NEED to return to the bridge, Picard and Riker took the opportunity to do something they both enjoyed—take a stroll through the *Enterprise*. As they passed a small recreation lounge, a strident braying crashed into their ears at pain-inducing volume. To Picard it sounded like a herd of bellowing beasts undergoing unspeakable torture.

Riker, of course, knew what it was instantly.

A second blast of noise virtually paralyzed them in the corridor. The moment it ended, Picard lunged for the rec-room door, with Riker just behind. The door slid aside, revealing no beasts being butchered—just Worf, Geordi LaForge, and Data sitting on stools around a computer screen displaying what appeared to be musical notation. Each player cradled his own Klingon *chuS'ugh*.

Riker went pale. A whole orchestra?

As always, Picard retained his composure. "So this is a Klingon, uh—"

"*ChuS'ugh,*" Worf said, his tone defensive.

Picard reached out with one finger to pluck a single string on Geordi's instrument. The engineer positively beamed at the reverberating noise. "Isn't that the most amazing sound?"

"Amazing," Picard said with a wan smile.

"Geordi liked it so much," Data said, "that he had the computer manufacture two more, identical to Worf's."

"I thought Data should learn more about music," the chief engineer added, as if explaining the android's presence.

"Music," Riker muttered with a shake of his head.

But Geordi continued without skipping a beat. "And *then* I thought, since you didn't seem too excited about having a *chuS'ugh* in the ship's jazz combo, well, why do we have only *one* combo?"

"You mean . . . a *chuS'ugh* combo?" Riker asked numbly.

"Hey, why not? Once we get good enough, we can have an old-time battle of the bands."

"I surrender," Riker said quickly, already backing out of the room.

He and Picard escaped before the next sonic disruption from the rec lounge. They headed for the nearest turbolift back to the bridge.

"I'm afraid you've released an elemental force," Picard commented, with a thumbed reference back toward the raucous rehearsal.

Riker chuckled. "Two in one day, sir."

"You mean Mori?"

"Yes, sir. You know, she *really* wanted a shot at the rest of those hoverjets."

"Determined young lady."

"Stubborn is more like it."

"That characteristic could serve her well," Picard allowed, "if properly directed."

"Or it could get her into trouble she can't get out of someday."

"Like her planet?"

Riker nodded wistfully as they entered the turbolift. "Bridge." The doors slid shut and the pod rose through the ship. "People can get so damned self-righteous—their answers are the *only* answers. Just butting heads at cross-purposes—can't they see they're destroying their own future?"

Picard's expression turned philosophical. "Seems to be part of the maturation process for most civilizations, ours included. Takes a bit of luck to survive it."

"The Sojourners seem so certain they'll come out on top, no matter what the sacrifice," Riker observed.

"Sometimes the only way to win a battle is to avoid fighting it."

"That doesn't seem to have occurred to either side on Thiopa."

With imperceptible deceleration, the lift came to a stop and opened onto the *Enterprise* bridge. Picard and Riker joined Counselor Troi, who was seated on the lower level. Wesley Crusher was at his console, enjoying a whispered chat with Ensign Lanni Sakata, the raven-haired young woman he'd found so distracting on other occasions.

"I think I see a developing crush," Riker murmured to Captain Picard.

"Mmmm. That's your department, Number One."

271

"Captain," said Lieutenant White from behind the command seats, "we've completed off-loading of all relief supplies."

"It'll be a *relief* to get away from Thiopa," Riker quipped, prompting a trace of a smile from Picard.

"Amen to that, Number One."

"Mr. Crusher," said Riker, drawing Wesley's attention. "I believe the *Enterprise* was meant for better things than playing nursemaid to freight drones. Do you concur?"

"Yes, *sir,* I do," Wesley replied with crisp assurance.

"Then set course for Starbase Seventy-seven. Let's get rid of those empty cargo carriers and get back to work."

Wesley's slender fingers danced across his panel in a flurry of electronic tones. "Course plotted, Commander."

"Thank you, Ensign. Captain . . . ?"

"Engage," said Picard. He settled back into the firm padding of the command chair, watching Thiopa's murky image recede as the great starship made a graceful roll and left orbit. He wanted to feel that relief Riker had joked about a moment before, feel the tension recede much as the planet itself was being left behind. But he couldn't, not just yet. "Let's look ahead," he said. *To the missing detail . . .*

Riker discerned the double meaning. "Forward view," he ordered.

Ensign Sakata touched her keypad. "Forward, sir."

The main viewscreen switched from the troubled world behind to the mystical cleansing clarity of star-strewn space. Picard had noticed Wesley sneak a look at Lanni Sakata. *Can't blame him—she's lovely* . . . But now both Captain Picard and Ensign Crusher had eyes only for the stars spread before them.

"Better, Captain?" Riker asked.

"Much better, Number One." Picard's stern features glowed with the satisfaction of a man who knew where he belonged. "Ensign Sakata, ahead, warp factor four." At tempo allegro, the *Enterprise* swept toward the stars.

About the Author

HOWARD WEINSTEIN's name may already be familiar to *Star Trek* fans who buy books and read credits. His first *Star Trek* novel, *The Covenant of the Crown,* was published in 1981 and became the first original *Star Trek* novel to be reprinted in a special Science Fiction Book Club hardcover edition. His 1987 Trek novel, *Deep Domain,* climbed high on a number of bestseller lists, including those of the *New York Times,* the *Washington Post, Newsday, Publishers Weekly,* and the B. Dalton and Waldenbooks bookstore chains.

In 1974, at age nineteen, Howard Weinstein became the youngest person to write professionally for *Star Trek,* selling "The Pirates of Orion" episode for the Emmy-winning animated revival of the show, which aired on NBC-TV from 1973 to 1975.

He also received a screen credit for some story-development tidbits he contributed to the making of *Star Trek IV: The Voyage Home.*

His other writing credits include a trio of original novels based on the NBC-TV science fiction series, *V;* articles and reviews in *Starlog* magazine; columns in the *New York Times* and *Newsday;* and award-winning radio public service announcements. He has also written numerous slide shows presented at science fiction and *Star Trek* conventions around the country.

Since 1976, Howard has made more than one hundred appearances at conventions, universities, schools, and libraries. He lives in suburban New York with Mail Order Annie, his short but faithful Welsh Corgi (that's a dog). Annie occasionally tastes books by other authors, and she often joins Howard for convention appearances. She will kiss fans and shake hands, but she rarely signs autographs. When Annie starts getting invited to conventions without him, Howard will know it's time to change careers.